The
Secret
of Sam
Marlow

The
Secret
of Sam
Marlow

The Further Adventures of the Man with Bogart's Face

By Andrew J. Fenady

Contemporary Books, Inc.
Chicago

Library of Congress Cataloging in Publication Data

Fenady, Andrew J
    The secret of Sam Marlow.

    I. Title.
PZ4.F332Se   1980   [PS3556.E477]   813'.54   80-19031
ISBN 0-8092-5989-3

Published by Contemporary Books, Inc.
180 North Michigan Avenue, Chicago, Illinois 60601
Manufactured in the United States of America
Library of Congress Catalog Card Number: 80-19031
International Standard Book Number: 0-8092-5989-3

Published simultaneously in Canada by
Beaverbooks
953 Dillingham Road
Pickering, Ontario L1W 1Z7
Canada

for My mother and father
together again
and
of course
Mary Frances
always together

CHAPTER
1

HE lit a cigarette and took another hit from the office bottle. Sam Marlow was celebrating his first birthday.

It was a year ago today that the plastic surgeon removed the bandages. The operation proved successful. Very successful. Dr. Inman's patient looked exactly like Humphrey Bogart. But it wasn't just the face that was changed. From now on it would be a new name and a new life. With danger, dames, and dough. Like Bogart. Yeah, Bogart. He knew how to live and love. There'd never been anyone quite like him. Until now.

That's how Sam Marlow, private investigator, was born. And during the last year, Sam had come close to dying more times than he could keep track of. He'd dodged bullets and bombs. He'd been slugged and sapped. Shot at and wounded. He'd been the target of hit men—and women. Cheap hoods. Ex-Nazis and high-priced professionals. Dangerous blondes and deadly brunettes. But Sam Marlow had survived. Of course, it took some killing on his part.

Sam looked at his watch. Six o'clock. The sun would be up

1

soon. And he'd be driving due east right into it. Sam was on a case, but first he wanted to stop by his office on the corner of Larchmont and Beverly and have a birthday drink.

He rose from the rolltop, crossed under the ceiling fan, walked into Duchess's office, wrote a note saying that he'd be in late and put it on her desk.

Yeah, the delectable Duchess—honey blonde hair, big blue-green eyes and luscious wet pink lips, with a body better than a Greek Goddess but soft and sexy as lace pants—which she didn't wear.

Her combined measurements probably exceeded her I.Q. but she was a sweet, loyal kid in the mean, cynical world of a private eye. And she'd been with Sam Marlow almost from the day he was born. Her office was scented by her perfume and bananas. Duchess loved bananas. Sam spied a limp peel poised on the edge of the wastebasket. He reached down and flipped the peel into the basket, which already contained plenty of other banana peels.

He adjusted the brim of his grey felt hat and left through the door with the inscription painted on its frosted glass:

SAM MARLOW
Private Investigator
"I don't sleep"

Sam glanced across the hallway at the sign on the opposite door:

MOTHER'S GYM

Mother owned the gymnasium and the building. She was bigger than a linebacker, had a face like a basilisk and a boyfriend named Nicky. Sizewise, Nicky fell somewhere between Mother and her pet Pekinese. Closer to the Pekinese.

Sam walked down the dark stairway and out to Larchmont Boulevard. In the last year Larchmont Village had changed, too. The donut shop had moved out and Coldwall Banker, a swanky real estate outfit, had moved in right below Sam's office. Across the street on the corner where the empty gas station used to be there was a Wells Fargo Bank. The smaller shops were moving out and the high rollers were moving in. Iranians had bought up everything that was for sale. They were squeezing in and taking over. Sam thought to himself that he'd like to see some Iranian try to put the squeeze on Mother.

Sam pulled the keys out of his trench coat pocket, got into the '39 Plymouth coupe and headed down Beverly Boulevard. He took a right onto the freeway and went through the interchange, picked up Highway 10 and drove east toward Palm Springs. By then the sun was shining directly into his eyes.

But that didn't bother Sam. Nothing bothered him. He was doing what he wanted to do. The way he wanted to do it. How many people could say that—and mean it?

Two hours later he had driven through Palm Springs. In the early thirties, Ralph Bellamy and Charlie Farrell picked up fifty-three acres on Indian Avenue for thirty-five hundred bucks and started the Racquet Club. Bogart was a good tennis player and golfer. He came down to Palm Springs quite often and played at the Racquet Club. But now Palm Springs was Dixie. The elite had moved farther east toward Rancho Mirage, Palm Desert, Indian Wells, and La Quinta.

Sam drove past Cathedral City and Palm Desert. In the old days the streets had Indian and Spanish names. Now they were called Frank Sinatra Drive and Bob Hope Drive. Sam liked the old days better, even if he couldn't pronounce the names. He took a right on a street that still had a name he couldn't pronounce and headed toward the high-rent district. The road snaked up a hill and the houses became fewer and more expensive.

It was a swell hideaway spot. Right at the brim of the tree-topped hill. The house was a combination of Spanish and modern. Sam parked the Plymouth next to the Porsche in the porte cochere.

He flipped down the sun visor, took the Derringer from its custom holster, and put it in his trench coat pocket. Sam walked toward the entrance, listening to the soft echolalia of the warm wind through the trees and to his footsteps crunching the gravel. He tried the doorknob. Locked. The door was part wood, part glass.

Sam kicked in the glass part, reached through and turned the knob. The door opened and Sam walked in. From another room came the sound of pulsating music. Sam looked around. The room was well appointed but disheveled. A woman's room. Sam walked on past an open door that framed a bedroom—a woman's bedroom, all done in mirrors and pink and all messed up like the huge round bed that dominated the chamber.

Sam walked toward the music and a door that was half open. He pushed it all the way open and walked through.

She was dancing. Her legs and arms were spread, holding out the fluent, gossamer nightgown. The material was a sort of skin pink and pellucid, revealing everything about her. Everything. And she had plenty. A natural blonde. With all the right curves in all the right places. Only more so.

There were three other men in the room, besides Sam. One, a good-looking blonde fellow in a bathing suit and open sport shirt danced opposite but close to the girl.

The second, a mountainous fellow in a more abbreviated bathing suit, a male bikini, was a moving monument to muscles. An obvious weight lifter, he was looking into a large wall mirror while rippling his biceps, triceps, and trapeziuses to the music from the stereo.

The third, a small sinewy fellow with a straight smile and crooked teeth, Oriental or maybe Polynesian, sat like a snake charmer, oscillating arms and shoulders to the music.

Everybody in the place except Sam was high on some kind of stuff. Sam looked at the charade for a couple of moments, concentrating on the girl. She was a darb. Beautiful, if a little worse for the orgy.

Finally the quartet noticed him. The girl moved even more sensually and trilled her tongue toward Sam. The male dancer looked insouciantly at Sam, then turned away. The weight lifter smiled at Sam and went on rippling. The snake charmer nodded at Sam and still oscillated. Then Dancer reached into the pocket of his sport shirt, pulled out a couple of pills and tossed them into his mouth. He took another look at Sam but kept on dancing as he moved toward Weight Lifter.

"Hey, Reggie, these soapers are dynamite. They make this guy look just like Bogart. Don't he look just like Bogart, Reggie?"

"I think he's taller," Weight Lifter responded. "But who cares?"

Sam walked over to three thousand dollars worth of Fisher stereo equipment, lifted the arm, took off the record and broke it into pieces.

"All right, Sandra," Sam said, "let's shove."

Sandra licked her lips just as suggestively as she knew how—and she knew how.

"I don't think my friends want me to shove with you. Do you, friends?"

Dancer danced toward Sam, picked up another record and started to put it on. "We're freakin'," Dancer said. "You got anything against freakin'?"

For answer Sam took the record from Dancer and broke it. Dancer studied the situation and Sam.

"Maybe you care to join us? Huh, Bogey? Always room for one more."

Sam didn't speak. Dancer reached for another record and smiled his California beach boy smile. "We only been freakin' for three days."

Sam took the third record and broke that, too. "It's a wrap."

Dancer's smile took a downward turn. "Gonna get tough, huh, Bogey?"

Even as he said it, Sam gut-hit Dancer with a left, grabbed him by the loose sport shirt and propelled him smack into the mirror, shattering it and Dancer, who rumpled into a free-form heap on the carpet as Snake Charmer screamed a shrill scream and sprang to his feet in an attack stance.

"Fair warning!" he shrilled. "KARATE!! HA-HA!!!"

Charmer thrust forward, Sam sidestepped and shot a left hook hard into Charmer's jaw. Charmer bounced back, stiff as a plank.

Sam twitched and looked toward Weight Lifter. Weight

Lifter smiled and shook his head negatively. "I'm a lover, Bogey, not a fighter."

Sam thumbed toward the door. "All right, lover, stop by the locker, pick up your jock strap and blow."

Weight Lifter smiled, nodded and rippled out of the room.

Sam moved closer to Sandra. He drew the nightgown so it covered her nakedness. She pulled it apart, revealing herself to him, and he pulled it together again.

"Get into something a little less comfortable, angel; they're waiting."

"How much is he paying you this time?"

"Three grand."

"Cheap. I'm worth a lot more on today's market."

"You keep popping pills and the market's gonna drop . . . dead."

"I'll go out with a bang, not a whimper."

"Get dressed."

"Sam, we're in the middle of the desert. Why don't you take off that trench coat?"

"You've taken off enough for the both of us. Get dressed."

"You know, Sam, you're cute."

"Yeah, I'm cute and you're cute. Get dressed."

She smiled, stuck her tongue out at him and glided toward the bedroom. She slid the flimsy nightgown down her long willowy body and was naked as she went through the door.

Sam tugged at his ear, shook his head, lit a Lucky and walked to the telephone. It was off the cradle. He picked up the receiver, got a tone and dialed long distance. He glanced at Dancer. Still a heap. Then at Charmer. Still stiff as a plank.

"Hello, operator. Person to person. Adam Mellon. Pantheon Pictures. Hollywood . . . *yes*, California. Sam Marlow calling."

Charmer stirred, made a humming noise and looked toward Sam. Sam adopted a modified karate stance. "AH-HA!" Charmer decided to roll over and rest some more.

The voice on the phone had an eager but gruff edge and didn't waste time with hellos.

"Marlow. Did you find her? Have you got her?"

"Yeah, Major, I got her. Have Orlando ready. She'll need steam, massage—the works."

"How soon can you get her here?"

"Three, four hours. And have the money ready, too."

"Marlow, where'd you find her? Is she . . . ?"

"See you in the movies, Major." Sam hung up and looked toward the bedroom. "Angel, are you ready?"

"Sure, Sam, I'm ready."

"Good. You've kept Major Mellon and Pantheon Pictures waiting long enough." Sam walked into the bedroom. "You know, Sandra, one of these days . . ." Sam stopped in his tracks and twitched.

She lay on the center of the rumpled bed naked as a newborn babe, but looking like anything but. She looked like what she was—the current reigning Sex Goddess of Cinema. Everyman's fantasy lover. And Sam could see why. He couldn't help looking a little longer than he wanted to let himself. She knew it and smiled as her big eyes turned from silver to cobalt blue.

There were bodies and then there were bodies—and *then* there was Sandra Kent. It wasn't just the shape and size, the curves and arches, the sweeps and bends. There was something radiant about her coloring and complexion that gave her body motion even when she was standing—or lying still.

"Help yourself, Sam."

"No, you help *yourself*." Sam went to the wardrobe closet, pulled out a dress and tossed it at her. "Here, put this on."

She rose slowly and breathed deeply so her bountiful breasts shimmered just the way she wanted them to. "Sam."

"What?"

"Can I help it if I can't help it?"

This time he gave her the double O. Took his sweet ol' time while he looked her up and down and around.

"You don't make it easy."

"What's the matter, Sam? Haven't you ever seen a naked woman?"

"Not like you."

CHAPTER
2

Sᴀᴍ drove for ten minutes before Sandra, with an unlit cigarette between her lips, leaned her head on his shoulder.

"Sam."

"Yeah."

"Know what I've been thinking about?"

"For the last ten years."

"Fifteen," she smiled with the cigarette still dangling, "but I mean just now. I've been thinking let's drive to Vegas."

"Now you feel like gambling?"

She relaxed back into her seat and an entirely female glint came into her big blue eyes. "Sort of. I feel like marrying you."

"Sweetheart," Sam said sibilantly, "I hate to say this to somebody who's nuts. But you're nuts."

"I mean it."

"*Today* you mean it."

"Sam, I need a man like you."

"Angel, you need a battalion of men like me."

"Maybe you're right."

"I'm always right. Except when I'm wrong."

Sam looked around at the beige desert rimmed by the saw-toothed Santa Rosa Mountains.

"You know it wasn't too far from here that they shot *Gunga Din* back in '38. Ol' Ben Hecht and Charlie MacArthur wrote the story from that poem by Kipling. Course, except for the title, those boys didn't bother using much of the poem. Matter of fact, what they did was take the plot from their play, *The Front Page*, move the action from Chicago to India and toss in an elephant. But those two buckos knew how to spin a yarn—and ol' Charlie, he had the sweetest left hook that . . . well, I'll be damned."

She was asleep. No, not asleep. Passed out. The uppers and downers and dancing and prancing—all that "freakin' "—had wound up and landed a haymaker right on her beautiful chin. Sam reached over, lifted the unlit cigarette from between her beautiful lips and let her take the count.

He was coming toward an isolated intersection near a date orchard when he spotted it. The sleek black customized Cadillac looked about thirty feet long and probably cruised at a hundred miles an hour. But right now that black beauty wasn't cruising. She was just off the road and canting to the left because the left rear tire was platter flat.

Sam could make out a cast and crew consisting of four characters—all four on the dusky side. The leading man in the piece was just stepping out of the right rear door. He wore a custom-tailored, frost white, double-breasted suit and looked like Omar Sharif's taller brother. The door was held open by a burly, brownish gent who looked like he was born mad at the world and glad of it. Then there was a liveried chauffeur and a fourth countryman who held an Armalite automatic rifle like he knew what he was doing.

Sam slowed down to take a passing hinge at the proceedings. He had no intention of stopping and maybe having a conversation with the Armalite M-18.

It seemed like it happened in slow motion. But it couldn't

have taken more than two seconds. As the liveried chauffeur opened the trunk lid of the Cadillac, his world went to pieces—and so did he.

The explosion blew apart the back ten feet of the limousine and shattered the chauffeur into skeltered sections. There wasn't enough left of him to pack into a bowling bag. Omar Sharif's taller brother hit the dirt involuntarily and the burly gent landed on top of him as two cars—one green and one blue—screamed out of the date orchard, spitting lead from the open windows. The Armalite man spit back at them—until you could see through his ventilated midsection. He hit the sand dead as a beaver hat.

Down the road a piece, both the Green and the Blue screeched a perfect one-eighty and roared back for another pass.

It wasn't Sam's fight. All he wanted to do was live through it. But the boys in the Green and Blue were shooting at everything in sight, so Sam figured he better do something about it—fast. He hit the brakes, then shoved Sandra onto the floorboard. She went down peacefully—without coming to. Never even let out a peep. Then he pulled the sawed-off ten-gauge from under the front seat of the Plymouth. This was no job for a Derringer—or a Luger. He dove to the ground, aimed at the blazing Blue's windshield and let go both barrels. The blast probably took the driver's head off. The Blue careened crazily off the road, scudded against a large rock, rolled over twice, bounced around like a lead Frisbee and landed on its flattened topside.

Sam dropped the shotgun, beat Jesse Owens's record to where the Armalite lay and emptied everything it held at the Green.

Lucky for Sam—unlucky for the guys in Green. The gas tank must have been full. It went off like a barrel of nitro—with every color in the rainbow and then some. After the fireball there was nothing left but a scorched and twisted frame.

Sam dusted off his trench coat and meandered toward the two survivors of what was left of the limousine.

Omar's taller brother was staggering to his feet and talking to the burly gent in some foreign lingo. Sam couldn't understand the lingo, but he got the drift. The boss man wasn't talking about a bonus.

Both men stared at Sam as he handed the burly gent the Armalite.

"Thanks for the use of the piece." Sam twitched.

"Who are you?" Omar's taller brother asked in awed and slightly imperfect English. "A ghost? An apparition?"

"No. Just flesh and blood and trying to stay that way."

"But," he stammered, "you look like the actor, Bogart Humphrey."

"Yeah, a lot of people see the resemblance."

"*Are* you an actor?"

"No. I'm a private detective in Los Angeles. Name's Sam Marlow."

"How did it happen you were here, Mr. Marlow?"

"It just happened. Passing through. Working on a case."

"Very fortunate for me." Omar's taller brother gave the burly gent one of those scimitar looks, then back at Sam, "and for you. Your reward will be commensurate."

"If you don't mind, I'll take it in cash—American. Say, what's your handle?"

"My what?"

"Your moniker. Your name."

His eyes narrowed as he looked from the burly gent back to Sam. "You honestly do not know who I am?"

"Cross my heart and hope to die."

"And still you came to my rescue?"

"Could be if I knew who you were," Sam shrugged, "I might've had third thoughts."

"Don't you read the newspapers or watch the news on television?"

"No," Sam shook his head. "All I know is what I see in old movies."

"Tabriz," Omar's taller brother said.

"Say again?" Sam twitched.

The burly gent still holding the empty rifle stepped forward half a step, half bowed and half whispered. "Tabriz," he said. It came out like a prayer. "Shah Tabriz."

"Oh, yeah," Sam acknowledged. "You're one of those Arab kings without a kingdom anymore. Had to make a fast getaway."

"You might say that," the shah reflected.

"And you got away with plenty," Sam added.

"Enough to live lavishly." the shah smiled.

Sam looked around at the debris.

"You almost died lavishly."

"My enemies are everywhere," said Shah Tabriz.

Sam looked around again. "Yeah, well there's a few fewer enemies around here. Oh, oh!" Sam pulled the Luger out of his coat pocket as he spotted a car turning the corner toward them at about eighty miles an hour.

"It is not to worry. They are part of my security force. Abu Lobi called them."

"Who's Hobby Lobby?" Sam asked.

The shah motioned toward the uncomfortable burly gent. "He is the chief of my security force. He phoned them from the limousine when we became distressed."

"Must'a been a toll call."

Even before the car slammed to a stop, three doors sprang open and three swarthies leaped out with enough artillery to take Khartoum. Hobby Lobby made a slight motion with his left hand and the swarthies froze in the desert.

Sam picked up the sawed-off, stump-butted ten-gauge, broke open both barrels, tossed out the empty shells and closed up the piece.

"That is a unique, if ancient, weapon," Shah Tabriz observed with wonder. "I've never seen one quite like it. I am an admirer of firearms."

"Yeah, so am I. Picked it up at Stembridge's. They used to be on the Paramount lot. They're in Glendale now. Provide artillery for all the movies and TV series. Nick Adams used this in a series called *The Rebel*. Say there, Shah, about the cops . . ."

"Cops?"

"Yeah, you know—fuzz, gendarmes, police."

"Oh, police. I will handle them."

"Yeah, I bet you will. Well, boys, I hate to shoot and run, but . . ." Sam was already walking toward the Plymouth.

"Where can I reach you, Mr. Marlow?" Shah Tabriz called out.

"I'm in the book," Sam Marlow replied. "Corner of Larchmont and Beverly. It's a toll call."

As Sam approached the Plymouth, he noticed there was a bullet hole through the right front windshield just about where Sandra's head would've been if she weren't crumpled and dozing on the floorboard.

CHAPTER
3

Iᴛ happened between Beaumont and Banning, where the cops always meet and beat their quota of moving violations. They'd damn well better.

When Sam saw the black-and-white flashing behind him, he reached back and threw the comforter over Sandra Kent, who was still crumpled and dozing on the floorboard.

Sam pulled over to the shoulder of the highway and braked the Plymouth to a stop.

The officious officer, with a face red as a brick, strolled alongside as Sam rolled down the window, pulled out his driver's license and pushed it toward the cop.

"Howdy, Officer. Good day to be alive."

"Yeah, can I see your—thanks." The officer took a look at Sam's picture on the license and then at Sam himself. Then he pulled off his sunglasses.

"God Almighty!"

"Yes, He is," Sam smiled.

"You're the spitting image—"

"What can I do for you?" Sam twitched.

The cop rubbed his chin and got down to business.

"You realize what you were doing?"

"Fifty-five," Sam responded. "She won't do much more."

"Ever hear of the ecology?" the cop queried.

"Yeah, right between the *Decology* and the *Fecology*," Sam responded.

"What happened to your windshield?"

"Ran into a bird."

"Hmmmmph. What's that under the blanket?"

"Just a dead body."

"Yeah, sure. Do you realize you're polluting the atmosphere?"

"Gee, Officer," Sam said, "I brush my teeth three times a day."

"I'm talking about your *exhaust*."

"Oh, *that*."

"Yeah, *that*." The cop was already writing out a ticket. "Polluting the atmosphere," he repeated, "screwing up the ecology."

Sam put a Lucky to his mouth. "Say, Officer, you got a light?"

"No. I don't smoke and neither should you."

"Good advice."

"Damn well told." The cop handed Sam the ticket. "Get your exhaust taken care of."

"Will do. Straightaway."

The cop strolled back to his black-and-white, got in and drove off in pursuit of his quota. Sam pulled a kitchen match out of his trench coat pocket, set fire to the cigarette and then the ticket.

He tossed the flaming paper out the window and drove west on Highway 10.

CHAPTER
4

THEY had passed the interchange in downtown L.A. and were heading toward the Rampart exit when Sam de-blanketed Sandra. She came to in the process.

"What the hell am I doing down here?"

"Maybe searching for worms so we can go fishing?"

She started to get up off the floor.

"Damn, Sam, have I got a headache."

Sam glanced at the bullet hole but said nothing. She settled back into the front seat.

"Sam, you got any dexies or meth maybe?"

"No, nor aspirin or Bromo Seltzer."

Then she noticed the windshield.

"Did I miss some excitement?"

"Yeah, a cop near Banning gave me a traffic ticket."

"Sam, I never know how to take you."

"And vice versa."

Sam took the Silverlake cutoff and headed west toward Hollywood.

Most people all over the world think all the movie studios are bunched together in a province called Hollywood. Actually there are just a few studios left in Hollywood proper. And there weren't all that many to begin with. They were spread out from downtown L.A. all the way to the Pacific Palisades, plus the San Fernando Valley. Those still standing within the boundaries of Hollywood include Paramount over on Melrose. And since taking over the RKO lot, Paramount extends all the way to Gower. What used to be Columbia still stands near the corner of Sunset and Gower. It's a rental lot now called Sunset-Gower Studios. Columbia moved onto the Warner Brothers lot in Burbank.

It's easy to imagine the ghost of Harry Cohn cursing a red, white, and blue streak. He wanted to be buried at Hollywood Memorial Park on Santa Monica Boulevard so he could look out at Columbia just a couple of blocks north. Then they moved the damned thing over the pass all the way to Burbank. But it's not the same studio anyhow. Not with computers, committees, and the Begelman business. Maybe ol' Harry's better off being far away from all that. At least that's what Sam thought to himself as they drove by Hollywood Memorial Park and headed toward Pantheon Studio.

In the salad days of cinema—the thirties and forties—every studio had a personality. An aura, almost an aroma. MGM was the biggest, most star-splattered. 'And it knew how to show its stars to best advantage. Huge, glowing close-ups that were practically portraits. Under Louis B. Mayer it was the most American of studios. Mom's apple pie. Upbeat. Gable, Garbo, Garson, Tracy, Hepburn, and Turner. With a couple of Taylors—Robert and Elizabeth. Glamour. As a character named Harry Pebble said in *The Bad and the Beautiful,* "Give me a picture that ends with a kiss and black ink on the books." It might have been said by Mayer himself.

Warner Brothers was the tabloid of the studios. Stories right out of the headlines, the streets and alleys. Fast-paced gangster pictures with machine-gun dialogue and editing. Social dramas and, later, historical biographies with people like George Arliss, Paul Muni, Eddie Robinson, and Johnny Garfield. And, of course, Bogart.

Paramount's roots could be traced back to U.F.A. in the fatherland except, of course, for DeMille who came to specialize in biblical and historical spectacles. And Paramount was big with the social comedies. Pretty sophisticated stuff under the tutelage of Lubitsch, Von Sternberg, and then Sturges and Wilder.

Twentieth Century-Fox was the private printing and picture press of Darryl F. Zanuck. Universal—the Horror Factory and Comedy Shop—offered attractions ranging from *Dracula, Frankenstein,* and *The Wolf Man* to Abbott and Costello, *Ma and Pa Kettle,* and *Francis,* the talking mule.

The joke around the industry was that Pantheon couldn't make up its mind what it was. Not the biggest, not the smallest, not the best, not the worst. Mishmash movies. Some of this and some of that.

But the joke was on the industry. Aaron Mellon, Pantheon's founder in the late twenties, knew exactly what he was doing. He was an immigrant who came out of the garment business a millionaire. A rope-thin fellow with a beak of a nose. He resembled character actor Everett Sloane before Sloane had some of his beak chopped away. Aaron Mellon was fond of saying, "In the garment business I made clothes for all kinds of people. It's the same in the movie business. I make all kinds of pictures for all kinds of people. His theory worked—for a long time.

Some years back Aaron Mellon went public with a profit of twelve million dollars and started taking golf lessons. During the third lesson he dropped dead of a cerebral hemorrhage. His son Adam took over and still controlled Pantheon, but only one hand was on the controls. The other hand was fighting off the wolves of Wall Street.

Sam drove up to the main gate of Pantheon Pictures where a large banner stretched across the entrance.

The Don Sampson Company
presents a
PUBLIC AUCTION

of the many treasures
from
PANTHEON PICTURES

Sam pulled the Plymouth alongside the cops' cubicle near the gate. Ken, the studio's senior cop, leaned in.

"Hello, Sandra. Glad to see you. Oh, Mr. Marlow, Mr. Mellon asked that you go directly to his private elevator."

"Swell," said Sam.

As he said it, a face appeared near the window on Sandra's side of the car. It was a youngish face—coffee-with-cream colored and smiling. Not just smiling, adoring. The face spoke with a trace of accent. It was atop a body that measured about five feet in toto. But he was a pretty well-built lad, well dressed in dark trousers, a candy-stripe button-down shirt and red tie.

"Miss Kent," the face almost implored, "is there anything I can do for you? Or get you? Coffee perhaps, or tea? *Anything?*"

"No, thank you, Ahmed. I'm just fine."

Sandra was as civil and even pleasant as Sam had ever heard her. Of course, he'd heard her sexier, but never more civil and pleasant. The young lad reached in and gave her a freshly opened pack of the cigarettes she favored and a book of matches. The cigarettes were a brand called "Cocktail" by Sobrani. They were pink.

"Thank you, Ahmed. Oh, Sam, this is Ahmed. He's a messenger boy on the lot. Ahmed Ishibu."

"Very pleased to meet you, Mr. Marlow," said Ahmed Ishibu.

"Likewise." Sam started to drive off. "See you later, Sabu."

Adam Mellon's office was large, almost Victorian in decor, more tasteful than not, except for an oversize oil painting of the "Major" reflecting him a mite more glamorously than he looked many years ago in the uniform of the U.S. Army Air Force. In the portrait he gazed skyward, probably toward some air action in which he never participated.

Mellon approached from behind a teak desk that was as big as a bed. He was tall, immaculately tailored and groomed with a voice that could drip caramel or cyanide. Right now it was caramel. He looked like anything but his father. More like Walter Pidgeon. His mother, Aaron's second wife, was a movie actress. There used to be rumors around town about Adam's paternal lineage. But the rumors had talked themselves out a long time ago. After a while even Hollywood forgets.

Also in the room beside Sam and Sandra was a fat balding stooge in charge of publicity. His name was Frazer Fisher, but everybody called him Fresh.

Sandra Kent knew what was coming as Mellon walked closer.

"Sandy, you've got to stop and think of the consequences of what you're doing to yourself and to all of us who love you."

"Love?" smiled Sandra. "That's the phoniest four letter word in this town."

"Well, we do love you, Sandy, whether you choose to believe it or not. We care about what's happening to you. And it's happening more and more often. Three times this year."

"Two—so far." Sandra put a Sobrani between her lips and Fresh Fisher was there in a flash with a flaming solid gold lighter. "Thanks, Fresh. You're a love. Everybody's a love."

Mellon walked to a red velvet–lined sideboard that held three rows of Oscars, seven to a row. One was about two-thirds the size of the others. He picked it up and carried it back toward Sandra. More caramel.

"Remember the night you won this? A special Academy Award for a kid your age. How grateful you said you were? Well, Sandy, you're grown up now."

"Up and down. In and out."

"Then act like it, Sandy."

"Will you quit calling me that. It's Sandra. Remember? You changed it when you *first* told me I was grown up."

"That's right." The caramel was losing its flavor. "And *where* did you grow up? Right here on the lot. We've been mother and father to you. Sheltered and protected you. You know we've been shooting around you for three days. I've got a crew of a hundred people shooting goddamn inserts!"

"I needed therapy."

"Sonofabitch! I've got a producer who's a fugitive from analysis, a director with bleeding ulcers, and a star who's—"

"Who's *what*?!"

"Who needs steam and a rub." Mellon smiled and snapped a button on the intercom. "Jo, tell Orlando to come in."

"Yes, sir," an efficient female voice responded. "And Mr. Flint is still waiting."

"He can wait." Mellon snapped off the button and looked back at Sandra. "Maybe you can get into some kind of shape so we can get a shot this afternoon of something besides inserts."

The door opened and a square, squat fellow wearing blue pants, a blue T-shirt, and a sympathetic smile across a bulldog face appeared and looked at Sandra.

"Hello, Baby."

"Hello, Orlando." She rose. "Well, come on, Orlando, let's pound the pills out of me." Then Sandra gave Sam one of her aureole looks.

"See ya, Sam. And maybe next time you'll feel like marrying me." She left and Orlando followed.

Mellon's eyeballs swelled until they looked like brass doorknobs. "She wants you to marry her?!"

"Has Jo got my dough?" Sam inquired.

"Yeah, she's got it. By God, Sam, why don't you do it? You could keep her in line. Why don't you?!"

"She's too big for me."

"Damned ungrateful bitch. I remember when she was a fat little snot-nosed kid."

"So do I."

"I signed her. I'm responsible . . ."

"Yeah, Major, you're the one." Sam picked up the stunted Oscar. "You tossed her onto the fastest merry-go-round in kiddieland. So fast she needed pills to slow down—and pills to pep up. Then it was pot and men and booze—and more pills. Yeah, I guess maybe you *are* responsible."

Mellon was mad and made no secret of it. "I don't need any lectures from the hired help, Marlow. You just get paid to pick her up. That's all!"

"You're right, sweetheart. That's all I get paid for. And next time it'll cost you twice as much. Take good care of this."

Sam let the statuette drop. It narrowly missed the Major's instep.

As the door slammed shut, Mellon kicked the statuette halfway back to the velvet-lined sideboard.

"Fresh!"

"Yes, Major."

"Pick that damn thing up!"

In the outer office, Josephine Bramer was counting a series of hundred-dollar bills and placing them in Sam's palm. Sam wasn't paying any attention to the money. He was looking into Jo's sensitively sculptured face. She was almost as tall as Sam and she wore a masculine suit in an effort to conceal some of her curves. It was a waste of effort. There was nothing masculine about her. The curves were camouflaged a little but far from concealed. She had long, slender but strong hands. A clean, clear California complexion with brown eyes that didn't have or need much makeup—and copper colored hair.

Also in the outer office was John Flint—a double hyphenate, writer-producer-director. At first glance he could've been mistaken for John Ford. At second glance, too, when Ford was alive. Flint's age was hard to bracket. He had grey hair and grey eyes that were shaded with sunglasses, wore a slouch hat, tweed sport coat with patch elbows, Khaki shirt and pants, and brown boots. He puffed on a Peterson pipe and was purely out of patience.

"What the hell's he doing in there?" Flint flared. "I'm not going to wait all week."

"It was an emergency," Jo said in an efficient but soothing voice. "I'm sure he'll be with you shortly, Mr. Flint."

"Emergency?!" Flint looked at Sam and the money. "What are you, his bookie?"

"No," said Sam. "I saw your last few pictures and I'm

getting my money back."

"Listen, wise guy—and where'd you get that face? You don't kid me. I knew the real Bogart."

"Was he really shorter than me?"

"He was—"

Mellon's voice interrupted over the intercom.

"Jo, get me Goldstein. If he's not in his office, try Twenty-One."

"Yes, sir." She looked at Flint. "And Mr. Flint is—"

"Get me Goldstein!" Mellon croaked and clicked off.

Flint almost bit through the stem of his Peterson pipe. Sam put the three Gs in his trench coat pocket and headed for the door.

"Well, so long, folks." He walked past Flint and twitched. "They just don't make movies the way they used to."

CHAPTER
5

PANTHEON Pictures was about a fifteen-minute drive to Sam's Larchmont office. During the drive, Sam reflected on the fact that it had been a good year. Except for two deaths. Gena Anastas, a girl he probably was in love with, had died. She liked to drive fast—and she died fast. There was a quote from a Bogart movie, *Knock on Any Door*: ". . . live fast, die young and have a good-looking corpse." Gena's corpse wasn't good looking. It was just about midnight when she pranged her seventy-five-thousand–dollar sardine can into a boulder in Malibu and bounced down a cliff into the Pacific Ocean. They couldn't get to her untill noon the next day. Not a good-looking corpse.

And there was another death. Duke bought the farm. John Wayne. There was no doubt that Sam loved him. He went to see the Duke at his house in Newport when everybody, including Duke, knew there'd be no more friendly campfires for the big man.

Duke lifted his right hand. On his emaciated wrist there was still the brass bracelet given to him by the Montagnard guerrillas of Vietnam. And he managed to grin at Sam.

"You glorious sonofabitch." Duke's voice was even coarser than usual. "You got away with it, didn't you, Trooper? Wait til I tell Bogey. He'll laugh like hell. You always were a glorious sonofabitch. Weren't we all—glorious sonsabitches!"

Sam bounced the Plymouth's front tires against the curb of the "No Parking" zone on the corner of Larchmont and Beverly smack in front of the mailboxes.

As Sam walked across the sidewalk toward the door leading up the stairs, the blind newsie called out with his familiar flourish. "Hey, Sam. Keepin' banker's hours, huh? Checkin' in kinda late, aren't ya, pal? Waddaya hear, waddaya say?!"

"You do a lousy Cagney." Sam responded.

"Ain't it the truth—you doity rat."

The door to Mother's Gym was ajar. As Sam reached the top of the stairs he thought he heard Duchess giggling from inside the gym. Then he recognized her unmistakable high-pitched but sexy voice.

"O-O-O-Ohhh, that tickles."

"You'll get used to it," Nicky Kalamavrakinopoulos' voice assured her.

"Gee, I don't know," Duchess twittered.

Sam walked to the door and opened it wider. Duchess held a five-pound dumbbell in each hand and she wore a pair of leotards that were meant for a female two sizes smaller and much less developed. Matter of fact, it was hard to think of any female *as* developed. There were four other ladies of assorted sizes in the gymnasium, but Nicky's complete attention was concentrated on Duchess. His walrus mustache only half hid the satisfied smile on the sly Mediterranean face.

"Duchess, what're you doin'?" Sam inquired.

"Taking my lunch break."

"It don't exactly look like you're having lunch," Sam pointed at the dumbbells, "unless you're eatin' iron these days."

"That's the point," Duchess giggled. "I'm in training. Instead of eating, I'm going to work out with Mr. Kalamavra-kinopoulos. He pointed out to me that I was putting on poundage in certain places. He signed me up for a course."

"Where'd you get that outfit?"

"Belonged to one of the other girls. Mr. Kalamavrakinopou-los loaned it to me—but it's freshly cleaned."

"Uh huh," said Sam.

"And he gave me the once-in-a-lifetime discount, too."

"I see. Does Mother know?"

"Does Mother know what?!" It was a voice that could stop a cape buffalo, coming out of a face that would scare the buzzards off a garbage can. Mother filled up the doorway and was holding her pet Pekinese. Both she and the Pekinese looked at Nicky, who shrank a couple of sizes he couldn't afford.

"Oh, hello, Mother," Sam said. "We were just discussing the international situation. What's your opinion?"

"I don't give a damn about any international situation." Her businesslike brown eyeballs burned under caterpillar eyebrows. "The only situation I'm interested in is what goes on around here and what's Miss Banana doing in that outfit. It ain't decent."

"Nicky'll explain the whole thing. Come on, Duchess, we got to get back to the detective business."

"Thanks for everything," Duchess said as she placed a dumbbell in each of Nicky's unsteady hands. "Hope I get used to it so it don't tickle. See you tomorrow instead of lunch."

As they were crossing the hallway, Sam could hear Mother's guttural growl. "Awright, Buster, start talking."

Nicky did, in his native tongue—until Mother interrupted.

"And talk English. None of that damn Greek gobbledy-gook."

The door to Duchess's office was already open.

"I'm going to go into the girl's room and put back my dress. Sam?"

"Yeah."

"Do I . . . offend?"

"What?"

"You know," she pointed to herself, "smell of prespera-tion?"

"No. Just bananas."

"I'm going to quit hot turkey."

"Cold turkey. Quit what?"

"The bananas. Uh, while I was in training you got a call from, let me see here," Duchess held up a piece of paper from her desk, "Pan. Pan-something-or-other Pictures."

"Adam Mellon?"

"No."

"Sandra Kent?"

"No."

"OK, Duchess, I've run out of guesses."

"A man named Flynn."

"Flint?"

"Yeah, Flynn. Here's his private number. Wants you to call post-pronto. In other words, right away."

"Gotcha." Sam took the paper and headed for his door.

"Oh, and Sam. There's a cock-a-roach waiting in your office."

The thin sallow fellow in an expensive suit was standing reading a letter. He dropped the letter on Sam's desk when he heard Sam enter. Sam left the door open.

Sam walked past the man, tossed the three Gs on his desk and started to dial the phone.

"Oh, hello, Mr. Marlow. Barry Barrie," the thin sallow fellow muttered nervously. "It's been a long time."

There was a lack of reaction from Sam.

"I've, uh, been waiting for you. You do remember me, don't you? A few months ago you helped me out of . . . a tight little hole."

"John Flint," Sam said into the phone.

"I've got a job I want to talk to you about."

"Shut the door."

Barry Barrie smiled and moved to close the door.

"From the other side."

"What?"

"This is Sam Marlow," Sam said into the phone. "Flint called me." Then to Barry Barrie. "That's all. Blow."

Barry Barrie started to say something, but the flat look on Sam's face changed Barrie's mind. He left, slamming the door with a curse he wouldn't have used except he knew Sam was out of earshot on the other side.

"Marlow," Flint's voice came through, "how soon can you be at the studio?"

"I just left the studio."

"There's something on my desk for you."

"Yeah? What?"

"A thousand dollars."

"I'll be there in half an hour."

"That's better."

"By the way, did you ever get in to see Mellon?"

Flint hung up.

Sam picked up the three grand and walked toward Duchess's office.

She was now wearing one of those sheer synthetic polka dot minidresses that, come to think of it, didn't cover up much more than the leotard.

"I'm going out," he said.

"You just came in."

"I'm still going out."

"Where were you all morning?"

"In the desert."

"What did you do there?"

"I shot the breeze with a guy named Hobby Lobby."

"Sam, make sense."

"I'll try. Here, take this down to Crocker and put it in the account."

"Ohhh, monies!"

"That's what it is. Put it in the account."

"Alrightee. The manager down there is so nice. He's teaching me how to make out a deposit slip and everything."

"Everything?"

"It's complicated."

"What is?"

"Deposits and withdrawals. He says there's a penalty for early withdrawals."

"I got to go."

"I forget. Where did you say you were going?"

"To the movies."

"Have fun. And don't eat too much popcorn."

"See you later, Duchess."

CHAPTER

6

FIFTEEN minutes later Sam was approaching Pantheon Pictures' main gate again. He felt like he was on a yo-yo where the studio was concerned. He also felt hungry. He'd had nothing but bourbon for breakfast and no lunch, liquid or otherwise.

As Sam neared the studio gate a fuchsia Mercedes 450-SL screeched around a corner and cut in front of the Plymouth, missing the coupe only because Sam slammed on his brakes.

The fuchsia Mercedes 450-SL was driven by a woman. Sam recognized her just before he started to call her a dumb broad. But that was no dumb broad. That was Mona Hyland, the reigning love goddess of the fifties and early sixties. She was still beautiful. Didn't look more than forty. But it was more than just beauty. She had that gift given to few mortals—men or women. Call it glamour or radiance. Call it "it" or sex appeal. She had it and knew how to handle it.

Even though she'd left the screen years ago—without as much as a single TV appearance except for those old movies—

she still dressed like a star. All done up in fuchsia: silk turban, sunglasses, silk blouse, perfectly tailored slacks. All fuchsia.

She damn near ran into the young guard who was blocking the entrance.

"Yes, ma'am?" The young guard asked politely. "Can I help you?"

"You can get the hell out of the way, sonny." Her voice and demeanor were sangfroidal but sensual.

"Where did you want to go, ma'am?" the young guard still played it polite.

Mona Hyland pointed to the sign. "To the auction, you damned infant."

"Have to park on the street, ma'am, and use the north entrance—unless you got a pass."

"Pass my ass!" She hit the accelerator and the Mercedes roared past the startled young guard. The senior guard smiled and waved at Mona as she drove by.

"Hello, Miss Hyland."

"Hello, Ken," she motioned back toward the young guard. "Where do you find 'em? Nursery school?"

As Sam was pulling up, Ken approached the young guard.

"When were you born, Jim. Last Thursday?"

"You told me not to let anybody—"

"Mona Hyland isn't just *anybody*."

"OK, OK, I didn't recognize her." The young guard leaned down toward Sam's window but was still watching Mona drive away.

"Yes, sir," he said absently.

"Got a pass to see John Flint." Sam twitched. "Name's Valentino, Rudolph."

Ken, the older guard who had seen it all, was just shaking his head and scratching at an imaginary itch on the back of his head.

The outer office of John Flint's bungalow was plain enough and so was his secretary.

If Josephine Bramer only partially succeeded in camouflaging her contours, then Flint's secretary Jane Lane, succeeded

110 percent—if she had any contours. You couldn't tell by looking. The way Jane Lane was groomed and dressed would make a nun look like Mae West. She could've been thirty or less—or forty or more. Hueless hair tied back in a bun. No makeup. None. Her complexion, if you could call it that, was unblemished but pallid. Her facial features were straight enough and seemingly symmetrical but mostly sheltered by thick horn-rimmed glasses, also colorless. Her dress, if you could call it that, was tight at her throat and loose every place else—ashen in color, light wool in composition, it hung straight down past where her knees must've been. The shoes were buttermilk and flat. So was her voice.

"You must be Mr. Marlow."

"Check. Aren't you lonesome under that outfit?"

"Mr. Flint is in a meeting, but he left instructions to let him know as soon as you arrived."

"Then go ahead and blow the bugles."

Jane Lane was already on the phone.

"Mr. Flint, Mr. Marlow is here."

"Send him in," came the blustery response.

Jane Lane looked at Sam and started to speak.

"I heard him good. Say, pal, what's your name?"

"Jane Lane."

"Lane, huh? That was Duke's last name in a picture called *Hondo*." Sam headed for the door. "It's a good name."

Flint's office was bigger than it looked from the outside. Sam stepped in and let his eyes sweep across the walls. The room was a collage of props and souvenirs from Flint's pictures. Rifles. Spears. Shields. Stuffed animal heads. Even a Gatling gun. And there were posters—one-sheets from his films, including *Cross Fire in Cicero, The Big Broadcast, Hickok, Sodom and Gomorrah, Song of Solomon, Lucretia, Salome, Lincoln,* and more than a score of others.

The furniture was leather and heavy walnut. Red, black, and brown. It was a man's room and the man was puffing on his Peterson and pacing. Flint held a swagger stick in hand, waving and jabbing it for emphasis.

Mostly he was waving and jabbing toward another man in the room. Ten or fifteen years ago Charles Wentworth would've been played by Patric Knowles. Wentworth wore a venerable corduroy Norfolk jacket and was surrounded by books, magazines, notes, and clipboards. Flint leaned over him like Barton MacLane grilling a gangster in the back room of a Warner Brothers police station.

"No, Charlie," Flint barked, "you're spinning your wheels—wasting your time and mine."

"Well, Mr. Flint," Wentworth muttered, casting a cautious glance toward Marlow, "during our last meeting you were rather, well—"

"Well *what?!*" Flint shot back with his swagger stick.

Sam slammed the door with a pretty good bang.

"Miss Calamity out there said you were dying to see me."

"Yeah, come in, Marlow. Sit down. I'll be right with you."

Sam didn't sit. He stood.

"Well, go on, Charlie." Flint waved the swagger stick back at Wentworth. "After thirty years you don't have to measure your words with me."

But Charlie did anyhow.

"Well, Mr. Flint, during our last meeting you were rather, well, vague I guess is the word." Wentworth took a breath and bit off the last part. "It's one thing to research the past, but the future—the year 1997—"

"Yeah." Flint went to his desk, poured some water from the carafe into a glass and chugalugged. "Yeah, you're absolutely right, Charlie. I'll get specific. You come in at ten o'clock tomorrow and I'll have a hundred questions written out. When you bring me the answers to those, I'll have a hundred more—and a hundred more. Think that'll work?"

"Yes, sir," Wentworth replied eagerly. "Yes, sir, I do!" He was already gathering his paraphernalia.

Flint turned to Sam who was looking at one of the posters. "You seen many of my pictures?"

"Yep."

"Everybody has."

"Everybody over forty."

By now Wentworth, with his hands full, was fumbling at the door. "See you tomorrow at ten, Mr. Flint."

"Yeah." Flint responded without looking at Wentworth.

"Nice visiting with you, Charlie," Sam said.

"Uh, thank you." Wentworth nodded awkwardly and managed to close the door as he left.

"Charlie Wentworth. He's my researcher. Been with me a long time."

"Shows a lot of spirit."

"Marlow, you check out first rate."

"Gee thanks, Mr. Flint."

"Even though you are a wise ass. You got a reputation for being a little screwy and plenty tough."

"OK, I'm a little screwy and plenty tough. I got a hangman's knot for a heart and I can spit icicles in hell—now should we talk about you?"

"Look here, Marlow, I know what they say. They say I haven't got another picture left in me."

"Is that what they say?"

By now Flint was walking around the room working up steam. He was old, but he still had drive, energy, and strength—a certain crude but regal manner. And he didn't act like he was ready to abdicate the royal robes.

"Well, I made 'em eat their words before." He swept his scepter toward a poster. "When they said Westerns were dead I made a picture called *Hickok*—started the Western cycle all over again."

He strode to another poster. "When the Hays office said we couldn't put sex on the screen anymore, I went to the Bible and made *The Song of Solomon*."

Another poster. "When people started listening to radio I made a picture called *The Big Broadcast*, so they came to see as well as listen. You know who made the first color picture? Who was the first director to use a boom, split focus?"

He slammed the swagger stick across the back of a leather chair. "Well, now they think to make a picture you've got to be twenty-two years old, have a beard, and smell of marijuana or sniff coke. Why in my time—"

"It's not your time."

Flint jabbed the stick toward Sam's chest. "Oh, yeah?! Well, I'm still one jump ahead of Mellon and the whole front office. I got a firm contract and I'm gonna make a picture called *1997*."

"Sure you are," said Sam. "You're a walking historical monument, and what was that you said about a thousand dollars on your desk?"

"There it is," Flint pointed. "Pick it up and put it in your pocket. That's a retainer just for the time being."

Sam picked up the money and put it in his trench coat pocket. "Consider me retained—just for the time being."

"I thought so."

"Now, what am I retained for?"

"I've got a wife."

"Number four, isn't she?"

"Five. I'm not an easy man to live with."

"No?" Sam pulled at his ear lobe.

"No. I want to get rid of number five."

Sam took the money out of his pocket. "If you want her shot, that's a little out of my line."

"Not shot. What're you doing?"

Sam put the money back on Flint's desk. "I won't frame her either, Flint. You got the wrong boy."

"No, Marlow. You got the wrong idea. Put that money back in your pocket. She doesn't need to be framed. She's a tramp. We're gonna get a divorce."

"And you want some heavy guns in court, that it?"

"That's it."

Sam looked back at the money. "I don't usually take that kind of case either."

"You don't usually get a grand for openers."

"I get two hundred a day. Plus expenses."

"OK, OK! You got it! And you don't have to do anything that'll offend your code of ethics or tender sensibilities."

"Well, in that case, I'll take the case." Sam put the money back in his pocket.

"Just nail the bitch!" Flint slammed the swagger stick across the back of the chair again.

The intercom buzzed. Flint clicked down the button.

"Mr. Flint," Jane Lane's voice came through, "I tried to tell Miss Hyland that you were—"

That's as far as Jane Lane got when Mona Hyland swept into the room.

"Hello, hello, hello, hello!!"

"It's OK, Jane. She never paid any attention to anybody." Flint snapped up the intercom switch and looked at Mona. "Not even me. Did you, Funny Face?"

"Especially to you." She moved directly past Sam, put her arms around Flint and kissed him full on the lips. "You still smell of stale tobacco."

"And you still smell like —"

"Never mind." Then she acknowledged Sam. "Did anyone ever tell you—"

"You haven't seen anything yet. I got a Balinese dancing girl tattooed on my back."

"He talks like him, too." Then back to Flint. "I've decided to let you take me to dinner."

"I'm busy."

"So am I. *Just* dinner—that's all. Then I'm going to come back and do some bidding." She held up a handful of proxies from the auction.

"OK, Funny Face. I want to talk to you anyhow. About *1997.*"

"Jack, I quit this business a long time ago. Before it quit me. I don't need it."

"But I need you. Listen, Funny Face, there's just two women left in the whole world—you and your daughter—and a hundred million men."

"I got a feeling," said Sam, "that you two can get along without me."

"Tomorrow," Flint nodded. "Four o'clock. Be here. We'll talk some more."

Sam moved toward the door. "Nice meeting you . . . Funny Face."

Before Sam closed the door, Flint was back pitching the part in his picture to Mona Hyland.

Jane Lane sat behind her desk and glasses, typing away as if Sam weren't standing there, so Sam took a step closer and cleared his throat. That did it. She looked up and stopped typing.

"Say, Jane, have, uh, you worked for the pride of Pantheon Pictures very long?" Sam pointed back toward Flint's office.

"Three years, nearly."

"Must like it, then."

She nodded slightly.

"Do you like *him*?"

Jane Lane seemed in no hurry to say anything.

"OK, we'll skip that. But say, you're not all that long on conversation, are you?"

"What would you like to converse about, Mr. Marlow? Mr. Flint?"

"No, *Mrs.* Flint. Do you know the current Mrs. Flint?"

"Yes."

"Has she got a first name?"

"Cynthia."

"Cyn, huh? Cyn Flint. Well, Jane, I guess that about does it. Thanks for everything."

The outer door opened and in walked Ahmed Ishibu with a stack of mail. His brown face was beaming sunshine and smiles. "Good afternoon, Miss Lane."

"Hello, Ishibu." Jane Lane pointed to the pickup tray. "Just those two letters and I'll be finished with this in a minute, if you can wait."

"Of course, and these are for you." He put the mail on her desk, then spoke to Sam. "Oh, hello, sir. I saw you earlier today with Miss Kent. Remember?"

"Yeah, sure, Sabu, I remember. But you weren't looking at *me* much. You're a big fan of Sandra Kent's, huh?"

"The biggest," he beamed. "But one of the shortest," he shrugged.

"Yeah, well, a man's reach should exceed his grasp—or what's a heaven for?"

Sam figured that was as good an exit line as any. He silently thanked Browning for the loan of it and left.

CHAPTER
7

Silhouetted against the smoggy sky above the second-story rooftop of a warehouse, two uniformed L.A.P.D. cops were in a running gunfight with three pug ugly characters who looked like they had nothing on their minds but murder.

As they traded lead, one of the pug uglies took a slug in his liver, dropped the .38 and keeled over onto the edge of the roof. Then a cop bought one in the belly and fell forward on his face. The second cop squeezed off a round that caught a crook between the eyes. The crook's head snapped back like a slingshot and he fell in a heap. The third man, with narrow green eyes and a knife blade of a mouth, fired again and wounded the cop in the side. But it was the crook's last shot. He ran out of ammunition. The cop kept coming, but he was out of ammo, too. The crook threw his gun at the cop but missed, and the cop leapt onto him.

It was a classic fistfight. Powerful punches, looping lefts and rights to the faces and bodies of both men. Then the fistfight turned into a wrestling match.

They grunted, groaned, grappled, and rolled toward the edge of the roof. Then they broke apart. The cop stood teetering, holding his side as the man charged straight at him, flinging them both off the roof and down toward the pavement twenty feet below. They both crashed through an awning and landed on a stack of boxes in the street.

Neither of them moved until the applause started to fade. Then both stuntmen got up, shook hands and smiled at the spectators who burst out with another round of applause.

Sam stood watching as a beautiful tour guide, with short tawny hair and long tawny legs, addressed the group of tourists.

"And that, ladies and gentlemen, concludes our tour of Pantheon Pictures. As you all know, many of the props and costumes from our most famous films are being auctioned to the public. Many of these items are on display on Stage 22. Please feel free to visit Stage 22 and inspect these fabulous items—and then come back and bid on whatever strikes your fancy. If you care to make a proxy bid, you may do so. It is not necessary for you to be present when the item comes up for auction. Thank you, and Pantheon Pictures hopes you enjoyed your tour and will tell your friends."

The people did seem to enjoy it and probably would tell their friends—back in Toledo and other exotic places. As they started to disperse, a lot of the tourists looked at Sam and whispered to each other, most concluding that he was one of the tour attractions.

One woman—tall, thin, and toothy—with a bag of popcorn in one hand and flanked by her overweight husband, approached Sam and asked for an autograph.

"Beat it, sister." Sam twitched, turned, and started to walk away.

"Should I punch him in the nose, Adeline?"

"Oh, Homer, don't be silly. It's all part of the act."

Husband Homer didn't seem altogether convinced but settled for saying, "Well, he still didn't have to be so damn snotty."

Sam was walking by Stage 7 when he heard her voice.

"Hey, Sam, wait up a minute."

He turned and saw Sandra Kent, Mellon, and Jo Bramer coming out the door. Sandra wore a pink terry cloth robe with a hood over her blonde hair and dark glasses over her big blue eyes.

"Well, I see you punched in all right," Sam said.

"Yeah, and Adam came down to see that he got his money's worth. I didn't think you'd hang around this long."

"He didn't," Mellon said. "He came back to see Jack Flint."

"You know everything that goes on around this fun house, don't you, Major?"

"That's how I got to be boss."

"No. That's how your father got to be boss."

Sam looked around.

"Auctions, tour guides, popcorn, and candy. You *are* still in the motion picture business, aren't you, Major?"

" 'Shoemaker, stick to your last.' I'll run Pantheon."

"Well, hello, hello! Hello!! Hello!!!" came Mona's voice as she and Flint walked up. Flint was still carrying his riding crop and Mona was as imperial as ever. "If it isn't mellonhead—of the studio. I mean, Mellon, head of the studio."

At the mention of Mellon's name, three young persons, males, who had been on the tour, reacted and sidled closer. All three had long hair and weren't recently barbered or manicured.

Mellon was all smiles and caramel. "Mona, my dear, you never could read lines. Slumming?"

"Buying out some of your junk. Lock, schlock, and barrel."

"A lot of it is from *your* old pictures."

"They made you a lot of money, remember? Hello, Sandra, you look . . . splendid."

"I just hope I look as good as you when—"

"—you get to be my age. Why, thank you, *dear*." Mona was good at beating everybody to the punch line.

Flint barely touched Mellon's elbow with his swagger stick. "Adam, I'm trying to convince this stubborn broad to be in *1997*."

"You are, huh?" Mellon didn't seem interested.

By now the three young males had made themselves part of the group. The leader was a string bean in jeans, gold chains, and Gucci bag. "So you're Mellon," he smirked. "I been trying to get in to see you for a month. Why don't you give us a chance, goddammit?!"

"Who the hell are you?" Mellon barked.

"Steve Steilburg is who the hell I am. I'm a director, but you—"

"How'd they get in here?" Mellon demanded of anybody.

"With the tour," Sam smiled.

"Yeah, I'm a director, but your tight-ass secretary won't let me talk to you."

"Take it easy, bones." Sam wasn't smiling.

"Holy Christ!" Steve Steilburg looked from his comrades back to Sam. "What is this, a masquerade?" Then back to Mellon as he pointed at Flint. "You let the walking dead here make pictures. I got film. I'm a cinema graduate. Take a look at what's happening out there!"

"Some other time." Mellon started to walk away.

"No, pisher, now." Steve went after him. "Let's talk about it, *now*!"

John Flint moved toward Steve Steilburg.. "You heard him, punk. Beat it!"

Steilburg shoved Flint, who lost his balance and almost fell.

"Get some security here!" Mellon hollered as Steve screamed at Flint and stepped toward him.

"You scared of the competition, old man? You've had it! You're out of it! You're dead!!"

Sam moved fast and pinned Steilburg's arms behind him with just enough pressure not to break both of them. But Sam wasn't prepared for what happened next. John Flint moved almost as fast and lashed out with the swagger stick across Steve Steilburg's face. Sam maneuvered himself between Flint and Steilburg.

"That's enough!" he said to Flint.

At the same time a couple of studio cops and Will Catcher, the stuntman who fell from the roof with the counterfeit cop, moved in and grabbed hold of all three youths. "I'll get rid of this garbage for you, Mr. Mellon." Catcher, who looked like

William S. Hart, knew exactly how to do it. So did the studio cops.

All three youths were screaming and yelling, but Steilburg screamed and yelled the loudest. "I'll get you, Flint. You sonofabitch! You too, Mellon! We'll burn down your whole goddamn studio. We'll be back and get all you dirty bastards."

Ahmed Ishibu, Fresh Fisher, Charles Wentworth, and several other studio personnel appeared. Fisher went to Mellon and Wentworth went directly to Flint.

"Are you all right, Mr. Flint?"

Flint nodded as Sam stepped toward him.

"You're pretty fast with that horse whip."

"I'm sorry I did that."

"You'll probably get a chance to apologize—in court."

"We'll take care of it," Mellon said.

Mona partially succeeded in changing the mood. "Jack, let's go eat."

"Right, Funny Face," Flint nodded. "So long, you people." Then to Mona, "Chasen's."

"No," Mona replied. "Perino's."

"OK, OK. No wonder we couldn't stay married." Flint looked back at Sam. "She was wife number three."

"Miss Kent," Ishibu almost whispered, "there's hot tea in your dressing room, and may I take your script, please?"

"Sure, thanks, Ahmed. Just leave it on the table."

Ahmed Ishibu was on his way.

"Who is that little guy?" Mellon asked.

"He's a messenger boy," Jo Bramer answered.

"I see him every place I go except my toilet."

Sandra walked up to Sam. "Want to take me to dinner?"

"You're going home," the avuncular Mellon instructed, "get another massage and go to bed so's we don't have to shoot you through burlap again tomorrow."

But Sandra was still waiting for an answer from Sam.

"Sorry, Sandra," Sam answered, "already got a date—with Josephine."

It was tough to tell who was the most surprised. Sandra. Mellon. Or Josephine.

CHAPTER
8

Sᴀᴍ couldn't take it anymore. His innards were grumbling and he had a hunger headache. He stopped at Pink's on La Brea Avenue and put down two hot dogs with chili, mustard, and onions and two RC colas. Not exactly gourmet but it quelled the revolution in his belly and brain.

The door to Duchess's office was halfway open and Nicky Kalamavrakinopoulos was contritely concocting a cock-and-bull story, obviously at the behest of Mother Superior. "So you see, Tootsie, right now we can't take any more members. We're fulled up."

"Gee, it don't look so full in there."

"Well, but we have to give each member special attention."

"Like you were giving me?"

"Uh, sorta."

"So that means I have to miss out on the once-in-a-lifetime discount, don't it?"

Nicky looked back at Sam and beyond, to where Mother stood tall in the hall.

"Gee," Duchess said, "I'm really disappointed."

"Me, too," Nicky gulped.

Mother motioned with her massive head and Nicky headed past Sam.

"Hello," said Nicky.

"Good-bye," said Sam. He could hear Mother from across the hallway.

"Did you tell her?"

"I told her," the little Greek squeaked.

"Now I'll tell you something," Mother barked. "Get in there!" The door slammed.

"Well, Duchess," Sam twitched, "looks like it's back to the bananas."

Duchess shrugged, opened the center drawer of her desk, produced a banana and started peeling. "Yeah, lucky I saved one just in case the hot turkey didn't take."

"Cold turkey. Any calls?"

"Any what?"

"Calls." Sam pointed to the phone on her desk. "The Ameche."

"Ameche? What language is that?"

"Never mind."

"Oh, speaking of language, remember the guy who used to call up and talk dirty? Well, I hadn't heard from him in a long time. I thought he was sick or something—anyhow, he called up this afternoon."

"Duchess, I told you before, all you do is encourage him."

"I don't think so. I let him talk for a while and then I just asked him a couple of questions and you know what happened?"

"What?"

"He hung up on me."

"I'm gonna go wet my goozle."

"Do what?"

"Take a hit from the office bottle. This conversation's getting to me."

He started for his office. She picked up a piece of paper from her desk. "Oh, Sam, somebody from Pan—Pan-something-or-other called."

"Flint?"

"No."

"Mellon?"

"No."

"Sandra Kent?"

"No."

"Duchess, do you mind telling me who it was?"

"Of course I don't mind, silly. That's part of my duties. It was, uh, Josephine Kramer."

"Bramer."

"Right."

"Get her on the . . . never mind, I'll do it."

Sam walked into his office and headed straight for the bottle of Wild Turkey.

"Ameche," Duchess twittered. "Sounds eye-talian."

It wasn't the best French restaurant in town, but it sure as hell wasn't the worst. The worst part was that by the time they got there it was almost ten P.M.

Sam had washed down about a pint of bourbon and gargled three times in a not altogether successful effort to get rid of the acerbating effect of the afternoon's hot dogs and their accoutrements. But right now the music was playing, the romantic table for two was set, the dinnerware sparkled, and Josephine Bramer looked beautiful as the waiter hovered in attendance.

"Would you care for a drink, Monsieur Marlow?" he inquired in more French than English.

Sam looked at Josephine. "You a gin man, sister?"

"Gin will be fine," she smiled.

"A brace of martinis—Gordon's. Double and dry. With anchovy olives. Up."

The waiter nodded and was off with his message to Garcia.

Josephine looked at Sam as if she were going to paint him.

"What're you looking at, angel?"

"At you. Sam, you are a tonic. I was just trying to figure out what you might've looked like before."

"Oh, I was a handsome devil. Six feet four. Two hundred and twenty pounds. Blonde wavy hair."

"All right, I get the picture. But you know, Sam, I think this is the first time I've seen you without that trench coat.

"Saves a lot of wear and tear on the suits." Sam lit a cigarette. "You always work 'til nine o'clock at night?"

"Mr. Mellon had some important dictation to get out."

"I think he was just trying to discourage you from having dinner with a certain private eye."

"Mr. Mellon's not like that. Why did you say we had a date?"

"To find out if we did."

"Or . . . to make Mr. Mellon mad?"

"I don't want to make Mr. Mellon anything. It's his secretary that I'm—"

"Please. *Executive* secretary."

"Say, what is the difference between a secretary and an executive—"

"About a hundred dollars a week."

"I see. Well, don't tell Duchess."

"Tell who?"

"Ahhh, booze!"

The waiter set the drinks before them.

"Thank you, my man," said Sam. "Now, count to a hundred and bring two more just like them."

"One more," instructed Josephine.

"Certainement," said the Gaul and took his tuxedo toward another table.

"Well," smiled Sam, "confusion to the enemy."

They clinked glasses. She sipped; Sam drank.

"Are you working for John Flint?" she asked.

"Who wants to know? You or Mellon?"

"Forget I asked."

"Yeah, I'm on retainer. Don't know for how long. He's a feisty old—" Sam drank some more, "—bastard."

"He's a terror on the set. A maniac. My father worked for him on some of his pictures."

"Your dad an actor?"

"No, he was a craftsman, an artist really. They called them prop makers in those days."

"Yeah? You ever know a prop man named Horst Borsht?"

"No, but I read about him in the paper last year. He was murdered, wasn't he?"

"Yeah, he was a client of mine—for about five minutes. But I usually have better luck with clients. Tell me more about your father."

"He died on location on one of Mr. Flint's pictures."

"Oh, I'm sorry."

"Flint never missed a beat. Kept right on shooting. It didn't matter to him. Nothing matters to Mr. Flint except his films."

"Yeah, I guess we all have our priorities. His is pictures instead of people. Well, hello!"

The waiter was back with another double Gordon's while one of his assistants in a red jacket wheeled over a chalkboard with the menu, written in French.

The waiter waved at the chalkboard with a flourish. "Potage? Poulet? Poisson? Un gigot de mouton? Trés bien, Monsieur Marlow?"

"Yeah, OK, Capitaine," Sam said, "and we'll eat it in French, but could you chew it in English first?"

Two hours later, Sam was kissing Jo Bramer in front of the Griffith Observatory. They were in the front seat of her car. Matter of fact, it only had a front seat. A 1980 Mercedes 450-SL. He kissed her again.

"Say, why don't you people buy American cars?"

"I didn't buy it. Somebody gave it to me."

"Yeah, why?"

"Because I was good."

"At what?"

This time she kissed Sam. "You sly devil," she whispered. "You knew we'd be too late for the Laserium Show."

"So did you."

She nodded.

A million Los Angeles lights, both stationary and moving, glittered below, and a million stars glittered above.

"We can still look at the heavenly bodies," he pointed toward the stars and planets, "and I can tell you everything you always wondered about the observatory."

"I'll bet you can."

"The place was built in 1935 as a public education facility. They got a Zeiss telescope. And more than a million and a half people visit every year. The director is a pal of mine named Dr. Edwin Krupp and Griffith Observatory was *not* named after D. W. Griffith."

"No?"

"No. It was named after a fellow with the unlikely name of Colonel Griffith Griffith."

"Heavens, heavens."

He kissed her again. "And right over there, they shot the climax of *Rebel Without a Cause*. The scene where Sal Mineo died."

"I remember," she nodded. "I was a bit of a teenage rebel myself. We all must have gone to see that picture a dozen times."

"James Dean was already dead when it was released. Strange thing about that picture. Three of those kids died young. Dean, then Nick Adams and Mineo. But, at least Natalie Wood is happily married again. Corey Allen is directing pictures himself now. And Dennis Hopper—well, he's had his ups and downs. And haven't we all?"

Sam leaned over to kiss her again. That's when the bell rang and the light went on. "What the hell is *that*?" Sam twitched.

"The phone," she smiled.

"Now I know why you wanted to take your car. Damned executives."

"Hello," she paused.

Sam could hear a man's voice, but not what it said.

"Oh." She seemed to tremble. "When? Where? Yes, sir. I'll be right there." She placed the phone back on its cradle.

"Was that your man Mellon?"

"Yes."

"More dictation?"

"Not exactly."

"Then, what's up?"

"John Flint is dead."

"Damn," said Sam, "he didn't last much longer than Horst Borsht."

CHAPTER
9

THE smell of death. Yes, death has a smell. Life has many smells. Death but one. Life smells of spices and sweat. Of tobacco and perfume. Of foods and flowers. Of grass and garlic and gasoline and even rust. Life is a revolving door of different smells, good and bad. But death only smells bad. It smells of rot. That's why morticians try to cover it up with flowers and embalming fluid as fast as they can. But the morticians hadn't taken over yet. The coroner, Saul Selvin, was there still doing his number. And Sam could smell the smell of death as soon as he and Jo Bramer walked into Flint's office.

The place was alive with a lot of people, except for John Flint, who was being carried out under a sheet and on top of a stretcher.

Lt. Marion Bumbera, Homicide, was in charge. Bumbera was built like a welterweight fighter and at one time he had been. But his face looked like it had absorbed a lot of punishment from a few heavyweights. Sam and Bumbera had been swapping favors ever since Sam's first case, when he was searching for a set of sapphires known as "The Eyes of Alexander," and trying to keep some of his clients as well as himself alive.

Sam was surprised that Sgt. Horace Hacksaw wasn't around. Instead, a young detective named Tim Foley took notes. Foley was six foot two, well built, and you couldn't draw a better picture of a sunny-faced leading man.

Also present: Mellon, Sabu, Fresh Fisher, a studio cop, the coroner's photog, and a few supernumeraries. No press—yet.

Selvin, the coroner, was his usual carefree self.

"Poison," he said. "Three, maybe four hours ago. I'll have to make some tests. Give you a report in the morning, Lieutenant."

Selvin leaned across the white tape on the carpet that outlined the spot where Flint had fallen. An empty glass lay where Flint's hand had extended. Selvin picked up the glass professionally with a clean handkerchief as his photog snapped another photo.

"All right, Fanoudas, that's enough film. Let's hit the peg." Selvin started legging it toward the door.

As the coroner and company were leaving, Bumbera spotted Sam. "Well, Mr. Sam Marlow. And I'd like to know what you're doing here."

"So would *I*," said Mellon.

"I'm with her." Sam nodded toward Jo. "She's taking me home."

"Right," Bumbera nodded back. "And who's she?"

"Mr. Mellon's secretary," Jo replied.

"*Executive* secretary," Sam corrected. "Incidentally, Flint was a client of mine."

"What was the case?" Bumbera asked.

"I don't know exactly. He was going to tell me tomorrow."

"That sounds like a lot of bull," Mellon snorted.

"Don't it, though. But Bummy'll buy it for now. Won't you, Bummy?"

"Sure, sure. For now. All right, let's take it from the top. Who found the body?"

"I did," Ahmed Ishibu stepped forward.

"And who are you?" Bumbera inquired further.

"Messenger boy."

"You deliver the midnight mail?"

"No, sir," Sabu beamed. "I was working on a project of my own in the research department. On my way out I saw a light. I thought Mr. Flint was working late and there might be something I could do for him. The door was unlocked, so I walked in."

"But there wasn't anything you could do for him, was there?"

"No, sir. He was dead."

"How did you know he was dead?"

"He wasn't breathing."

Bumbera arched an eyebrow toward Tim Foley, who took more notes and tried not to smile.

"Did you touch anything?" Bumbera walked closer to Sabu.

"No, sir."

"What *did* you do?"

"I called the gate."

"With what?"

"With the phone."

"Then you touched the phone."

"Yes, sir, I touched the phone."

Bumbera turned away from Sabu and walked toward the studio cop. "OK. We got your story from there."

"Mr. Bumbera," Fresh Fisher moved forward, "how are you going to handle this?"

"*Lieutenant* Bumbera, and who are you?"

Mellon made answer. "He's Fisher. Fresh Fisher, head of our publicity department."

"Lieutenant, what do you think?" Fisher pursued. "The studio'll have to release a statement. Is it suicide? An accident?"

"That's *two* strikes," said Sam.

"Marlow," now Fresh Fisher walked toward Sam, "you don't think that—"

"I think that somebody punched his ticket." Sam lit a

cigarette. "What do you think, Bummy?"

"I don't know what I think—yet."

"We better put our heads together," Mellon scratched at his cheek. "Fresh, Jo, let's go up to my office."

"So ends our night," Sam said to Jo.

"Oh, Mr. Mellon," Bumbera added, "I'd like to have a meeting in your office at 10:30 tomorrow. And have the people there who worked directly with Flint. Secretaries, assistants."

"Yes, of course," Mellon was most cooperative.

By now Sabu was at Mellon's side. "Mr. Mellon, sir, is there anything further I can do to help you, sir?"

"Yes. Go home and let me run the damn studio."

"Yes, sir, thank you, sir."

The place thinned out fast.

"Bummy," said Sam, "can I bum a lift home?"

"Yeah, sure. I'll substitute for the secretary."

"Just to the front door," Sam smiled. "Young Tim, how's the shiny new detective?"

"Still polishing my badge and keeping my mouth shut."

"You'll make a first class cop," Sam replied. "Say, where's Hacksaw?"

"He's recovering from surgery," Tim answered with a smile.

"Brain?"

"Not exactly." Bumbera looked at Tim Foley.

"Oh, I get it," Sam nodded. "He finally got those hemorrhoids taken care of."

Bumbera pulled up in front of Sam's apartment on the five-hundred block of Larchmont. Sam got out of the back seat, closed the door and leaned in toward Foley and Bumbera. "Thanks for the lift, coppers."

"OK, Sam," said Bumbera, "and thanks for the dope on Flint."

"Say, what about that would-be director that Flint smacked?"

"Checked him out. Alibied up and down," Foley answered.

"What about his friends?"

"Them, too," said Bumbera.

"*All* his friends?"

Bumbera just shrugged.

"By the way," Sam asked, "how did the widow Flint take the news?"

"Who can tell over the phone?" Bumbera shrugged again. "She could'a been laughing or crying."

"Yeah. You boys wanna come up for a snort? I just bought me a case of first-rate Scotch."

"No, thanks." Bumbera pointed to Foley. "*He's* still got a sheet to fill out."

"Ain't he thoughtful?" Tim smiled.

"Yeah, he's the berries. Good night, Bummy. Good night, young swain."

It was past two A.M. As Sam started for the stairs that led to his second-story apartment, the thin sallow fellow stepped out of the shadows.

"I told the landlord the joint needed fumigating," Sam said to Barry Barrie.

"Look, Mr. Marlow. I need to talk to you."

"No dice." Sam started to move.

"Maybe this'll change your mind."

Barry held up five one-hundred-dollar bills, and at the same time another fellow stepped out of the shadows. This fellow was neither thin nor sallow. He was huge and healthy. Looked like Mike Mazurki in *Murder, My Sweet.*

"Well, well," said Sam, "if it ain't Moose Malloy."

"The name's Dumbrouski," said Dumbrouski through a big blue jaw.

Sam looked from the money to Dumbrouski. "A little persuasion, huh? Friendly and unfriendly."

"It's about that tight little hole you got me out of a few months ago. Well, you see, I'm in trouble again and you're the only one she'll listen to."

"I see." Sam took the money from Barrie with his left hand and with his right he slugged Dumbrouski just as hard as he could on the side of Dumbrouski's blue jaw. A quick, curious look came across Dumbrouski's eyes. He teetered a tenth of a second and fell like a shot buffalo.

It looked like Sam was going to slug Barry Barrie, but instead Sam slapped him twice, back and forth, then tore up the five yards and let the pieces flutter down on Dumbrouski. "Pick up your laundry and blow."

Sam stepped over Dumbrouski, started up the stairs, and then added, "I'll talk to the kid."

"Thank you," Barry Barrie muttered as he wiped the blood from his mouth. "Thank you."

Sam opened the door, turned on a small lamp and walked to the rolltop desk that served as his sideboard. He twisted the cap off a brand new bottle of Glenfiddich and knocked back the double Scotch. In that instant he thought about Gena Anastas, Duke Wayne, and John Flint. All three dead. But the difference was that Sam knew Flint had been murdered. Flint might not have had too much longer to live but he had a right to live it. Somebody cheated Flint out of a chunk of life. Sam didn't like to see anybody cheated like that. Specially a client.

Sam poured another double, tossed it back and headed for the bedroom. Just as he snapped on the bedroom light he felt that he wasn't alone. When the light came on, the Luger was already in Sam's hand and prepared to make its point.

Sandra Kent—miniskirted, lovely long legs crossed—sat in the big leather chair. The way she looked, there wasn't a grown man in America who wouldn't have given his right eye to be standing in Sam's shoes.

"I couldn't sleep."

Sam put the Luger back in his trench coat pocket. "John Flint's dead."

"I know," she shrugged. "But that isn't why I couldn't sleep."

"How did you know?"

"It was on the radio."

"Don't you have an early call on the set?"

"I promise I'll be there. On one condition."

"What condition?"

She looked at the big brass bed. "That you let me spend the

night here.''

"Precious, have you been sniffing that nose candy again?''

"No. But I'll do worse than that—I promise—unless you say yes.''

She rose and came toward him with all she had— everywhere. She put her arms around him and pressed that soft, warm, wavy body right where it would do the most good.

"Well, Sam?'' She licked her lips and murmured "What do you say?''

"I say . . . what the hell. I'm only human.''

CHAPTER
10

WHEN Sam woke up the next morning, Sandra Kent was gone. But he could still smell her perfume and she had left a note on the bedstand:

> YES! YES! YES! YOU ARE HUMAN!!
> I'll make my call on time. Pantheon
> Pictures thanks you—and so do I.

He went to the kitchen, poured out a bowl of Cheerios, put on a fresh pot of coffee and had breakfast. Half an hour later, after a shower and a two nick shave with his straight razor, Sam pulled the Plymouth up to the "No Parking" zone on the corner of Larchmont and Beverly.

The blind Newsie handed Sam a paper and announced, "John Flint's dead."

"That's a hard one to hear," Sam responded.

"Ever meet him?" the Newsie asked.

"Once or twice."

"Good or bad?" the Newsie prodded.

"Yes and no," Sam said and kept on going.

He didn't need any more dialogue. But he got it. Mother was waiting for him at the head of the stairs. She stroked her hawser hand through a hairdo that looked like a mess of spun steel. "Would you mind stepping into my office?" she commanded.

"Not at all."

"Your lease is up," she intoned in a hanging-judge voice. "Would you want to sign up for another year?"

"Yup."

"Have to raise your rent fifty dollars a month."

"OK."

"I meant sixty."

"OK."

"Say, why don't you get rid of that jiggly secretary of yours?"

"Why should I?"

"She's making passes at Nicky."

"She is?"

"She *is!*"

"I got a better idea."

"What?"

"Get rid of Nicky."

"She can't even type."

"Neither can Nicky."

"But I love him"

"Mother, it looks like we're all gonna have to learn to live together."

"You said what?"

"Figuratively, that is," Sam said and headed toward his office, "and Happy New Lease."

Duchess was breakfasting on banana and Coca Cola. "Oh, Sam, good thing I got here early. Some foreigner called."

"What foreigner? From where?"

"From long distance, of course. I didn't get his name but he sounded like that guy in *Dr. 'Shravago'.*"

"What did he say?"

"He said he'd call back later."

"Good work, Duchess." Sam started for his office.

"Are you going to wet your foozle again?"

"Yeah. Goozle."

"Sam."

"Yeah?"

"What's a goozle?"

"It's your throat."

"Oh, good. I was hoping it wasn't something dirty. Oh, and, Sam."

"What?"

"Friendly advice: You're getting bags under your eyes again. You've got to quit staying up so late at night."

"Thanks, Friendly."

Sam went in and poured a stiff one from the office bottle. He lit a Lucky and headed back to Duchess. "I'm going out."

"You just came in."

Sam put Flint's thousand dollars on Duchess's desk.

"Oooh, monies!" Duchess twitted.

"Yeah, Crocker time."

"What time?"

"Drop in at the bank again and make a deposit."

"Sure, Sam, but remember what the manager said: 'There's a penalty for . . .'"

". . . early withdrawals. Yeah, I know, Duchess. Pantheon Pictures."

"What about them?"

"That's where I'm going."

"Say," she pointed to the newspaper on her desk. "That's where that man Flynn died last night."

"Flint. That's right." He started for the door.

"Sam, what are you going to do there?"

"Find out who done it."

That was easy enough to say—especially to Duchess. But it would be a lot harder to find out—and prove—to the world. Well, by the yard it's hard; by the inch it's a cinch. Sam would take it by the inch. And the next inch began with that 10:30 meeting in Mellon's office.

Lieutenant Bumbera was talking and waving around the newspaper with the headline story. "John Flint Dead— Hollywood Mourns Passing of Pioneer. Flint's Body Found at Studio. Mystery Surrounds Death of Writer-Producer-Director."

Bumbera let the newspaper drop on Mellon's desk. He pulled a small notebook from his jacket pocket, referred to his notes from time to time and kept talking. The people in the room included Tim Foley, Sam, Mellon, Josephine Bramer, Fresh Fisher, Sabu, Jane Lane, and Charles Wentworth. Wentworth seemed a little more slumped and paler than the day before. Jane Lane hadn't changed a jot. Just her clothes. But they were the same style, if you could call it that. Everything else about her was just the same.

"He died from some fast-acting poison I can't pronounce," Bumbera recited. "There was enough left in the carafe to kill a mule. He took the dose around 10:30. Before that, he had dinner with Mona Hyland at Perino's." Bumbera was talking to everybody and nobody. Mostly he was talking to himself.

"Got back to the studio just before eight. Went to Projection Room A and ran a picture called *Lucretia*, by himself. Got to his office a few minutes after ten and a few minutes after that, poured some water from the carafe into a glass, drank it and dropped dead. Looks like a case of homicide."

"I still don't see why you rule out suicide," Fresh Fisher wanted to know. "He could've poisoned himself."

"Mr., uh, Fisher, is it?"

Fisher nodded at Bumbera.

"Mr. Fisher, if you were going to poison yourself, why would you drop the stuff into a jug, *then* pour it into a glass?"

"I don't know. But anyone contemplating suicide can't be thinking too logically."

"Good point," Bumbera walked over toward Jane Lane. He looked her in the eye. She looked him right back. They were the same height. "You're Mr. Flint's secretary?"

"I am—was."

"Flint's first appointment was a ten o'clock this morning.

Andrew J. Fenady 61

That right?"

"Yes, it was."

Bumbera walked toward Wentworth. "With you, Mr.— Wentworth."

"Charlie." Wentworth nodded. "Yes, sir."

"What was the meeting about, Charlie?"

"Some research I was doing for a picture."

"Uh-huh." Bumbera shot a look at Jane Lane. "And what was the rest of his day like? Appointments, I mean."

Jane Lane's voice was efficient—and flat as her front and backside. "Mr. Flint was going to run two pictures today in Room A. He was going to have his lunch brought in, and he had an appointment with Mr. Marlow at four o'clock and a meeting with Mr. Mellon at 5:30."

Bumbera to Mellon: "To talk about a picture called *1997*?"

"That's right."

"Uh-huh." Bumbera then inquired of Fisher, "Sound like a man contemplating suicide?"

Fisher just shrugged.

"Sam," Bumbera continued, "you've usually got something to say about everything. What do you say about this?"

"In a word—murder."

"Now, just a minute," Mellon said. "Jack Flint was a, well, a sort of tyrant. But who'd want to kill him?"

"A lot of people." Sam pulled at his ear lobe. "And now there's a studio that doesn't have to make a picture it didn't want to make."

"Marlow, you've got a mouth!" Mellon snapped.

"Ain't it the truth."

"Keep talking, Sam." Bumbera took a step.

"Pantheon's turned out nothing but bombs for a couple of years now, except for Sandra Kent's pictures. That's the reason for the auction, the tours, the candy and popcorn. There's a stockholder's meeting coming up pretty soon. Word is that some of the stockholders are sick of seeing red. Word also is *1997* would've been not-so-hotso, another bomb—an expensive bomb."

Bumbera moved toward Mellon. "Did you want to make the

picture or not, Mr. Mellon?"

"No, I didn't."

"Uh-huh."

"But there are a lot of ways to get out of a contract."

"Murder's one of 'em," Sam smiled.

"Marlow, I suppose I should throw you off the lot."

"I suppose you should."

"But I'm not going to. You've got my permission to poke that screwy kisser of yours around here as much as you want. Day or night. Stick your snoot any place you like. See what you come up with."

"Thanks."

"And on top of that, I'll personally put up a reward of ten thousand dollars for Flint's killer. What do you think of that?"

"Could be a very noble gesture," said Sam. "Could be a lot of canal water."

"All right, folks," Bumbera pointed toward the door, "that's all for now."

"Josephine," Mellon instructed, "get hold of Mrs. Flint. I want to talk to her about the funeral arrangements."

"Yes, sir." Josephine was on the way to her office.

"Have your boys finished with Flint's bungalow?" Sam asked Bumbera.

"Yep."

"I'd like to poke around in there," said Sam as he looked at Mellon, "before they auction off the furniture."

Sam was walking out the door of the Mellon building toward the back lot when Sabu caught up to him.

"Mr. Marlow," Sabu smiled his scrutable smile, "if there is anything I can do to help you . . ."

"Yeah, there is. You know what stage Sandra Kent's working on today?"

"Yes, sir. Same as yesterday, Stage 7. If there is anything else . . ."

"If there is, I'll send up a smoke signal. In the meanwhile, do everything you can to keep the endangered species of this jungle safe and sound. Got that?"

Sabu's eyes widened. "Yes, sir," he said automatically as Sam turned briskly and walked away.

On Stage 7 Sam stood in the shadows and watched Sandra Kent, in a bikini, kissing her leading man, who was in a beach robe. His name was Biff Brock and everybody in town knew he was acey-deucey, but most of America and the rest of the free world considered him mighty macho. It didn't seem to matter to Sandra one way or the other. She was gobbling him up like he was Gable.

"Cut—print. Fine!" said the director as one of his stooges handed him a double dose of Maalox.

Sandra immediately spotted Sam and walked up to him. "Good morning, Sam. Did you get my message? I left it—"

"Yeah, I got it." Sam took the note from his trench coat pocket, tore up the paper and let the pieces fall to the stage floor. "There's an old saying, precious: 'Never put it in writing.' "

The wardrobe woman walked up with a pink terry cloth robe. "Sandra, do you want this?"

"No, Voulee, let the bastards gawk. Besides, it's too damn hot on this stage. Come on, Sam, let's go to my dressing room. It'll take Ulcers another hour to figure out the next shot, which'll end up being a close-up of my boobs."

Voulee, the wardrobe woman, went back to the set and Sandra led Sam toward a twenty-foot trailer that had been driven onto the stage. She opened the door and pointed inside.

"As the Spider Lady said: 'Come into my parlor.' "

"This is as far as I go."

"We've got plenty of time," she teased.

Sam couldn't get over how fresh and beautiful she looked— like a two-week vacation. "You forgot something last night," he said.

"Really? I can't think of *anything* we forgot."

"I'm talking about this." Sam pulled a lady's wristwatch out of his pocket. "Looks like the band got broken."

"I think I remember when that happened," she smiled. "Aren't you a prince to bring it back."

"Yeah, I'm a prince. See you around, Princess." Sam put the

timepiece in her hot little hand and walked off.

Outside, in a not too conspicuous spot, a stuntman dressed in an L.A.P.D. uniform was playing liar's poker with Will Catcher. Five bucks a clip—and the law was losing plenty of Abe's cabes.

"Six aces," Catcher smirked. "Count 'em up."

"Damn!" said the cop. "Don't you ever lose?"

"Once in a while to Jack Elam, every day to the bangtails."

The cop gave Catcher his last five. "See you on the roof." As he walked away, Catcher called out to Sam, "Say, Marlow, got a minute?"

"Make it two," Sam replied and lit up a Lucky.

"My name's Catcher. Will Catcher. I'm a stuntman."

"I know," said Sam, "and a damn good one. Cars, boats, falls, fists. You got a damn good reputation. Been at it a long time."

"Yeah, too long. The bones are gettin' brittle and the skin is gettin' thin."

"Then quit," Sam shrugged, "while you're still all together."

"I can't—the horses, that is. And there ain't no way I can make a better payday. And speakin' of pay, I understand that Mellon's offered ten Gs for Flint's killer."

"You mean it's in *Variety* and *The Reporter* already?"

"No." Catcher smiled and the knife blade of a mouth became the edge of an ax. "But news travels fast in this business, and I keep my eyes and ears open. What I mean is, if I come up with something that helps you nail him— splitsville?"

"Well, I'll tell you something, Will. I keep my eyes and ears open, too. And I usually work alone, but if you come up with something that's worth some geetis, you'll get it. Got it?"

"Yeah, sure." Catcher folded the fistful of fins and stuck them in his pocket. "You know, I did a few pictures with Bogart almost thirty years ago. Some of my first and his last. Well, I got to go fall on my ass."

"Happy landings," said Sam, "to the both of us."

CHAPTER
11

At noon Sam was inside Stage 22 where the marathon auction continued. The auctioneer banged his gavel on the table and warned, ". . . going once, twice, three times—sold! One hundred sixty-five dollars to number 1818C."

The barnlike bunker was stocked with thousands of items of all sizes and all tagged and numbered. The auctioneer moved around on a raised platform and conferred with his assistants in front of rows and rows of folding chairs, about half of them occupied.

"Next item is number 1401 in your catalog," the auctioneer announced. "Four gold-framed portraits, assorted sizes, from the motion pictures *The Duke of Detroit* and *A Time to Love*. I have no proxy bid. I want an opening bid of two hundred dollars."

More than a dozen hands shot up.

"I have two hundred, two-fifty, three hundred—no, lady, I need fifty-dollar bids. Three-fifty—do I have four? I have four. Ladies and gentlemen, the *frames* are worth—four-fifty, five,

five-fifty. Do I have six? Six? Five-fifty once, twice—fair warning." He banged the gavel. "Sold at five-fifty to—hold up your number, sir—to number 88A."

Sam started to make his way toward the exit as the auctioneer droned on.

"And now ladies and gentlemen, from one of the greatest sea stories ever made, *Captain's Orders:* a ship's desk, item number 1402 in your catalog. I have a proxy bid of two thousand dollars. What do I hear? Silence? We've got to move along. The proxy bid is two thousand. Do I have a bid? Fair warning."

As the auctioneer hit the gavel, Sam hit the door.

He walked past the warehouse where the stuntmen were putting on the show again. Catcher and the cop fell through the awning. The audienced applauded and Sam kept walking toward Flint's office.

Jane Lane was monkeying with the strap on one of her flat shoes and Sam almost got a look up one of her legs, but she heard him come in and straightened out like a soldier on sentry duty. Well, what the hell. Sam thought; she's no three-alarm fire anyhow.

"Who do you think killed him, Janie?

"Mr. Marlow, do I look like a detective?"

"Hard to tell. Sometimes looks are deceiving. Besides, detectives aren't supposed to look like detectives."

"It seems to me, *you* go out of your way to look like one."

"See, you *would* make a good detective. Mellon said I could poke around." He pointed toward Flint's office. "Do you mind?"

"Not at all. But I'm going to lunch."

"OK. If anybody comes looking for you, I'll tell 'em you're in the commissary."

"I won't be."

"You won't be *what?*"

"In the commissary."

"Food bad? Or the company?"

"Both." Jane Lane walked toward the door. "I hope you

find what you're looking for."

"Same to you, sister."

Half an hour later, Sam was lying on Flint's leather couch reading a leatherbound loose-leaf notebook with an embossed cover:

OUTLINES AND NOTES FOR
1997
by
JOHN FLINT

Sam lowered the notebook as Charles Wentworth entered the room and looked around somewhat bewildered.

"Step right in, Charlie. Step right in."

"Oh, Mr. Marlow."

"Right again, Sir Knight. How goes the search for the Holy Grail?"

"I'm . . . supposed to help Miss Lane."

"She could use some."

"Help her gather some of Mr. Flint's personal effects, but—"

"But what?"

"Well, she doesn't seem to be here."

"No, she doesn't. It's her lunch hour, Charlie."

"Oh, I see." Wentworth pulled a watch from his vest pocket and studied it. "So it is. I, well, I've sort of been in a daze since—I still can't believe it. Just yesterday, Mr. Flint was so—"

"Alive. Yeah, it's hard to believe."

"Yes. You were here; you saw—"

"That was yesterday, Charlie. Today he's dead as a sardine."

Wentworth nodded and looked around. "So many yesterdays."

Wentworth's attention was drawn to the swagger stick on Flint's desk. He stepped a couple of steps over and touched it almost reverently. The mood wasn't quite the same after Sam inquired, "He ever hit you with that, Charlie?"

Wentworth seemed wounded by Sam's query. There was a

sincerity and warmth in Wentworth's quavery voice. "Mr.
Flint always treated me . . . decently. There were times when
the studio wanted to lay me off. Mr. Flint always found some
work for me to do, some projects to keep me on."

"Yeah, he oozed over with charm and compassion."

"I know you're being cynical, Mr. Marlow, and that's your
prerogative. But Mr. Flint had great perspicacity. He knew
what the audience wanted. He was much more intellectual
than he let on—and sensitive."

"OK, I second the motion. He was a cinema saint."

Sam held up the notebook. "You know, this ain't half bad."

"He would have made another great picture, in spite of—"

"Mellon? We'll never know."

Sam walked over and picked up the swagger stick as three
big men and a fair-sized woman walked in. The woman was
pushing a mover's dolly. The biggest man had a beer barrel
belly and a flatiron chin.

"Lunch hour must be up," said Sam.

"We get to work early, buddy," said Flatiron,"take an early
lunch."

"Swell," said Sam. "What can we do for you?"

"Nothin'." Flatiron looked around. "Is this where he
croaked?"

"Another fan. Yeah, right where you're standing."

Flatiron spat at the carpet. "I wasn't any fan of that rat's. I
was on his crew once. That was enough."

"For you or him?"

"You got something against labor, buddy?"

"Why no, buddy. My mother went through it."

"Bright boy," said Flatiron and looked to one of the other
big men. "He's a bright boy."

"Hmmm, dialogue right out of Hemingway," Sam remarked.

"Out of what?" Flatiron asked.

"Skip it," Sam twitched.

"Hey," Flatiron suddenly said to everybody in the room,
"look at this guy's face. Did you notice he's a ringer for
Bogey? Talks like him. You know, I liked Bogey."

"Swell."

"The hell with him," said the other big man. "Let's start moving this junk."

"Yeah," Flatiron agreed. The movers began taking down the pictures and one-sheets, but Flatiron kept looking at Sam and muttering, "Goddamn, just like Bogey."

Sam, still holding Flint's riding crop, walked over to Flatiron. "Hey, buddy—I apologize."

"You do?" Flatiron was still a little wary.

"Yeah. Say, uh, where you fellows taking this stuff?"

"Over to Stage 1."

"What for?" Sam asked.

"Search me, Bogey. We don't ask questions. We just do what we're paid to do."

"That's a good policy." Sam walked to Wentworth. "Buck up, Charlie, it ain't the end of the world."

Wentworth looked around the room that was being dismantled and almost whispered. "In a way it is."

Sam turned and walked toward the door. As he did, he almost bumped into the female moving person. " 'Scuse me, Mac," said Sam.

"Up yours!" the female moving person replied.

CHAPTER
12

Sam drove a little out of his way and stopped at Tommy's on the corner of Alvarado and Fourth. He did a repeat of yesterday's lunch at Pink's. Two hot dogs with chili, mustard, and onions and two RC colas. The repeat was a lot better.

When Sam got to the office, Duchess had one foot on her desk drawer and was painting her left set of toenails.

"Duchess, why don't you go to the bathroom and do that?"

"Because, Sam, I don't have to go to the bathroom. Besides, the phone might ring by someone important."

"I see. Well, did it?"

"Did it what?"

"Did the phone ring today by someone important?"

"I don't know."

"Well, let me put it this way. Did anybody call?"

"I don't think so. But I had to go to the bathroom—twice."

"Get Pantheon Pictures. I want to talk to Josephine Bramer."

"Wait a minute, Sam." She put aside the toenail brush. "Let me write that down."

"Never mind. I'll get her."

Sam took a hit from the office bottle. The Wild Turkey tasted warm and smooth in his stomach. He got Jo Bramer on the phone and asked her for Mrs. Cynthia Flint's phone number. She gave it to him and then told Sam that Flint's funeral services would be held tomorrow on Stage 1 at Pantheon Pictures. There would be a big story and an announcement in the morning trade papers. She said she'd see Sam there.

"Wanna go to dinner again tonight?" Sam asked. "We never did finish our dessert."

"Sorry, Sam. I've got a date."

"Oh, I'm sorry, too. With Adam Mellon?"

"Please. He's a happily married man."

"Aren't they all?"

"Bye-bye, Sam."

"So long, sweetheart."

Sam dialed Mrs. Flint's number. A man answered.

"Hello," said Sam. "I'd like to talk to Mrs. Flint. My name's—"

"Mrs. Flint isn't talking to anybody."

The man hung up. So did Sam. Duchess buzzed him.

"Yeah, Duchess."

"There's a man on the line."

"Who is it?"

"It's that good-looking policeman. Hmmm, yummy."

Sam mashed the button. "Hello, yummy."

"What did you say?" Tim Foley asked.

"I said, did you shoot anybody today, copper?"

"Yeah, two innocent bystanders and a teenager."

"About par. That's enough with the lip flap. What do you want, swain?"

"Sam, you gonna work out at the gym tomorrow?"

"Yeah."

"OK if I meet you?"

"Sure."

"Same time?"

"Same time. Say," Sam asked, "wanna have dinner tonight? Take in a movie?"

"Sorry, Sam, I got a date."

"See you tomorrow morning."

Sam hung up as Duchess walked in.

"I can't even get a date with a cop," Sam muttered.

"What did you say?"

"I said, would you like me to take you to dinner tonight?"

"No. That's what I came in to ask you."

"Ask what?"

"Can I leave early? I've got a date with somebody else tonight and with you tomorrow night, if that's OK?"

"That's OK. You going out with that musician again?"

"Yeah, the tuba player."

"He must have some pucker."

"Yeah," Duchess twittered, "and he kisses good, too."

Sam took another hit from the office bottle.

A little while after Duchess left, the phone rang. It was Hobby Lobby calling from Palm Springs. Hobby Lobby said that Shah Tabriz would like to speak to Sam.

"Let him speak," said Sam.

"Mr. Marlow," Shah Tabriz said, "we seem to have some difficulty getting through to you. Is your secretary new?"

"At what?"

"What I meant was—"

"Yeah, I get your drift. What can I do for you, pal?"

"Oh, no, I want to do for you. I'm giving a little party this weekend. May I send Abu Lobi to pick you up tomorrow?"

"Tomorrow I'm going to a funeral."

"Oh, I'm sorry."

"Yeah. I usually don't go to funerals. Didn't even go to my own. But this is business."

"May I inquire what time is the funeral?"

"Noon. High noon."

"May we pick you up in the afternoon?"

"I guess you may."

"Very good. Tomorrow afternoon, then."

"Say, Shahny, can I bring a date?"

"Certainly. Good night, Mr. Marlow."

"Adios."

Well, it looked like a very big weekend and a very little tonight—unless Sam called Sandra. The hell with it. He didn't know if he could go through that two nights in a row. Besides, he didn't want her to become habit forming. She was doomed. Like Monroe and Garland. She was cool and smooth and beautiful on the outside, but that engine inside had to be overheating—burning itself out and her life with it.

Sam walked south on Larchmont and crossed the street to where Phil's Phresh Fish and Poultry had moved. He bought five dollars worth of smoked salmon, went to his apartment and opened a nice cool bottle of Budweiser beer. Ah, that first swallow tasted swell. So did the rest of it.

Sam put the salmon on a plate, sliced up an onion as thin as he could, squeezed on some lemon, oil and vinegar, added some capers, got out another Bud and clicked on the Quasar to see if he could find an old movie.

He found something else when he opened the door after the knock. He found Sandra Kent. She stood there with a look on her face that would knock a monk out of his socks. She was standing still. But she wasn't. Everything about her seemed to be moving a little. Not really moving. Vibrating.

"Great thunderin' hallelujah," said Sam.

"Sam."

"Yeah."

"I'm hungry."

"Does this look like a McDonald's?"

"I wasn't thinking of hamburger."

"Would you settle for smoked salmon?"

"You mean like lox?"

"Yeah, like lox."

"I love lox."

"Then don't just stand there vibrating, come in."

She did.

"Don't you get tired?" he asked.

"Of what? Besides, I only have to work half a day tomorrow. Mellon's closing the studio at noon for his side show."

"Want a drink?"

"I'll have what you're having."

"I'm drinking beer."

"I love beer. I'm a peasant at heart."

"I never would've guessed." Sam went to get her a Bud and a knife and fork. He reached for another plate.

"Never mind that, we'll eat off the same plate. Like peasants. Let's be peasants, Sam."

They sat at the table, ate out of the same plate and drank beer from the bottles.

It turned out not to be a little tonight. It was big. Very big. After they ate, Sam found out that he could go through it two nights in a row—and then some. Not only was she great, she was grateful.

Sandra was inexhaustible. Sam figured he could rest up over the long weekend in Palm Springs.

But he figured wrong again.

CHAPTER
13

A_T seven the next morning Sam was wearing sweat pants and shirt, ten-ounce gloves, and headgear. Tim Foley was stripped to the waist with the same style headgear and gloves. They were boxing in the new gym at Paramount.

Sam sped two left jabs that landed on Foley's head, snapping it back both times.

"This the way you're going to spend your vacation?" Sam asked.

"Doesn't start 'til next week."

"Keep your left hand higher," Sam instructed, "and your legs closer together." He whipped a left that clipped Foley's chin and a right that churned into his midsection.

"I'm going to quit the force," Foley grunted.

A lightning left-right combination sent Foley down to one knee.

"I said left higher and the right closer to your chin. Left high—chin low. You're wide open. And circle away."

Foley shrugged off the blows and staggered to his feet.

"Why do you wanna quit?"

"Why?!" Foley swung and missed. "Why?! You know how much money a Detective One makes?"

"Yeah, about the same as a garbage man."

"Less a lot of deductions." Foley threw a right that Sam took on the forearm. "Witholding tax, pension plan, off-duty medical care . . ."

Foley landed a series of pretty good punches as Sam back-pedaled. "Medical insurance, Police Relief Association, Police Protective League, Credit Union, Charities Plan, Dental Plan, and by the time I make my car payment and pay the rent, and take care of my mother who needs a nurse to take care of her, I can just about get by on eighty-eight varieties of hamburger every month—if I don't rip a pair of pants making somebody on a bum beef."

"So you'd rather be rich. Well, I've had it rich and I've had it poor. Rich is better." Sam landed a jab. "Keep moving to your left more."

"Right. That ain't all of it, Sam. They practically defy you to make an arrest even if you catch a guy with a smoking gun." Foley circled to his left and landed a left. "To be a cop today you got to have the patience of Job and be a Philadel-phia lawyer to boot—listen to everybody hollering 'police brutality.' " He swung and missed. Sam tapped him twice with jabs.

"You're dropping your left."

"Yeah—go to court on your own time. You know a cop has to buy his own bullets?"

"So, what are you gonna do?"

"Take my vacation, then take out a license to be a private eye." He got in a good left-right. "Live a little, like you."

"You're sick." Sam landed a hook.

"Sick of all the guff. A favor?"

"What?"

They circled and traded light jabs. "In the next couple weeks maybe I can sort of help you out."

"I been making my way through life without you." Sam

feigned a left and landed a hard right on Foley's heart.

"All right. Help *me* out. So I can get the hang of it."

"In two weeks?"

Foley stuck Sam with a left. "Got to start sometime . . ." he swung and missed, ". . . someplace. Will you, Sam?"

"Don't call me; I'll call you." Sam hit him with a double left hook and crossed with a right that knocked Foley to the canvas. "*If* I need some muscle minus brains. Time!"

Sam helped Foley to his feet.

"I told you you were dropping your left."

"Thanks, I'll remember. Where'd you learn to hit like that?"

"Johnny Indrisano taught me. See you at the funeral."

Half an hour later Sam pulled the Plymouth into the "No Parking" zone on the corner of Larchmont and Beverly and walked past the blind Newsie.

"Hey, Sam, I see in the trades Flint's funeral's gonna be over at Pantheon."

"Yeah."

"You goin'?"

"Yeah."

"Oughtta be a lot of laughs."

"Yeah."

Sam started up the stairs. As he got near the top he could hear voices from Duchess's office.

"Oh, thank you very much, Mr. Kalamavrakinopoulos," Duchess twittered, "but as you can see it's not even half full."

Nicky could see all right. He was watching as Duchess leaned over the wastebasket while her abundant breasts swayed, heaved and almost tumbled out of the spaghetti-strapped synthetic dress. His beady brown eyes bounced from her breasts to her creamy white legs that were also in abundant evidence.

"Okey-dokey," Nicky leered. He was carrying a couple of loaded wastebaskets from Mother's gymnasium. Stacked on top of each other, they'd be about as tall as he was.

"Oh, good morning, Sam. Mr. Kalamavrakinopoulos here was just asking if he could take out the banana peels and stuff. Isn't he sweet?"

Nicky leered some more and blushed as much as a Mediterranean can.

"Yeah," Sam sneered. "He's about the sweetest and shortest Greek I ever seen."

"*Nicky!*" came the caterwaul from across the hall. "What the hell are you doing in there?"

"I'm coming, Mother!" Nicky scrambled out and barely managed to balance the wastebaskets and close the door behind him.

"You finished with the trade papers?" Sam pointed to *Variety* and *The Reporter* on her desk.

"Uh-huh." Duchess nodded and handed Sam the papers. "Big doin's today, huh, Sam?"

"Yeah. I'll be going to the funeral in about an hour." Flint's death was bannered on both papers.

"Who died?" Duchess asked.

Sam looked at the headlines and back at Duchess.

"Adolph Hitler," said Sam.

"Gee, that's too bad," Duchess shrugged. "I didn't even know he was sick."

Sam headed for the office and the bottle.

He went through both papers in less than ten minutes, separating the so-called hard news from the press agent puffery planted by PR men on behalf of their clients—actors, actresses, producers and directors, singers and swingers. All about "Six Pix Indie—Prod Deals," "Brando doesn't know it yet, but he's being paged by Roger Corman to star in *World War III*," "Aren't all three networks nagging Tina Louise to star in a series?" Harmless stuff—a touch of truth mixed in with a dash of hogwash and hope. Still it was the best way to keep abreast of what was happening or could happen in Hollywood.

Duchess buzzed on the intercom. "Sam, there's two men here to see you."

"Tell me a little something more about them."

"Well, one's small and the other's big—very big."

"Tell Lieutenant Bumbera and Sergeant Hacksaw to come right in."

"Gee, Sam, how'd you know their names?"

"From here I can read the names on the back of their badges."

"You can?!"

"Shoo 'em in, Duchess."

"OK, Sam."

The door opened. Bumbera sauntered in with his usual banty-rooster walk, but Sgt. Horace Hacksaw followed gingerly; he walked as if he had a raw egg between his legs. He was as big as ever, like an oversize jukebox, but there wasn't any bounce in his step.

"Well, well, come in, coppers. Want a hit from the office bottle?"

"Way too early, Sam, but thanks," Bumbera replied.

"Well, I'll sail again." Sam poured himself another drink and pointed to a hardbacked chair. "Sit down, Hack. That's a nice comfortable chair over there."

Hacksaw looked like he'd just been gassed. "I'll stand, wise guy."

"OK, anything you say, but it's good to have you back on the beat." Sam looked to Bumbera. "Anything break on the Flint case?"

"No, Sam. This is not official."

"OK, then what is it? You boys didn't just happen to be passing through the second story of Larchmont and Beverly."

"It's about Tim." Bumbera had a habit of frequently adjusting his shoulders as if he was trying to set them just right. A lot of fighters do that.

"What about Tim?" Sam asked.

"Well, I know you been talking to him."

"No. He's been talking to me. So what? What are you telling me, Bummy? Put it on the plate without the lettuce."

"I know he's been thinking about quitting the force and for some cockeyed reason he thinks being a private eye is chock-full of glamour, dames, and dough."

"Well, isn't it?" Sam lisped.

"He's a good cop." Bumbera adjusted his shoulders again. "It's hard to get good cops these days, and harder to keep them."

"Yeah, I know what you mean." Sam glanced at Hacksaw, then back to Bumbera. "But what're you telling me?"

"I'm telling you not to give the kid any bad advice."

"Or what?"

"Or the road could get bumpy for you, Marlow," Hacksaw said. "That's what! You bend an awful lot of rules as it is. So you're liable to get a little bent, too. Find yourself without a badge to put in that goofy trench coat."

"Oh, so *that's* the way it is?"

"Yeah, Hacksaw grunted, "that's the way it is!"

"Now wait a minute, both of you," Bummy said.

"No, I'm not gonna wait a minute. In the first place, I don't tell anybody what to do unless I'm paid for it. In the second place," Sam looked at Hacksaw, "where the hell do you think you are, in some smelly back room of some police station sweating out some two-bit bag man?"

"I know where I am!" Hacksaw shot back.

"In the third place, I don't meddle in the internal affairs of the police department. Don't meddle in mine. And I'm going to show you something else: There's the door!"

"OK, Sam. We know where it is. Look, there's no need to fly off the handle," Bumbera placated. "We, uh, well, we just like to take care of our own. You going to the funeral?"

"Yeah."

"Wanna lift?"

"No."

"OK, Sam, see you there."

"Yeah. Oh, and Hacksaw, be sure you take those stairs one at a time."

As Bumbera and Hacksaw came out of the door on the street corner and walked toward the blind newsie, Hacksaw spied a meter maid who was passing by on her motorized tricycle.

"Hey, you!" Hacksaw commanded. "Park that thing and come over here!"

She did.

The meter maid was a flat-nosed blonde with a florid face, thin pale lips, whale-wide hips and heavy leather-booted legs. Hacksaw flipped out a wallet and flashed his shield. "I'm Sergeant Hacksaw."

"Yes, Sergeant." The meter maid assembled herself to attention. "What can I do for you?"

Hacksaw pointed to Sam's Plymouth in the "No Parking" zone. "You see that car?"

"Yes, sir."

"Ticket it!"

"Yes, sir."

"And it better be plastered with tickets every time it's parked there or you'll pull duty someplace where it takes you three hours to drive home."

"Yes, sir."

Bumbera and Hacksaw walked toward their car as the meter maid hurriedly wrote out a ticket, slipped it under the Plymouth's windshield wiper, saddled her tricycle and drove south on Larchmont.

Sam came out the door, spotted the ticket and nodded toward the blind newsie. "Seen enough cops for the day?"

"Yeah," the blind newsie nodded back. "It sure got fuzzy out here this morning. Hey, Sam, I won't be around for a couple of weeks—going on vacation."

"Yeah, where you going?"

"The islands. I thought I'd like to see Hawaii."

"Sounds swell. Well, aloha."

Sam pulled the ticket from under the wiper, tore it to pieces, opened the door and got behind the wheel. The Plymouth butted out into traffic and chugged away, spewing a wake of blue-black smoke from its exhaust.

CHAPTER
14

ADAM Mellon had taken a leaf from an old Hollywood scenario. When Harry Cohn died, the services were held on Stage 12 of the Columbia lot. Danny Kaye did the eulogy. The stage overflowed with people. That's when someone was moved to remark, "Give the audience what they want and they'll pack the place."

Mellon had gone Columbia one better. He had built an exact three-wall duplicate of John Flint's office on Stage 1 of Pantheon Pictures. Everything was there. Pictures, posters, Flint's desk, chairs, the couch, sundry other personal effects. Even the carafe.

In front of the desk, on a slightly raised platform stood Ray Milland. To the right of Milland and the platform was a bronze casket. Immediately in front of the casket were stacks of film cans marked with the names of John Flint's pictures.

The place was packed. Movie stars, agents, writers, producers, directors, television cameramen, photogs, and the Hollywood Press, including Rona Barrett, Hank Grant, Army

Archerd, Frank Barron, James Bacon, Bob Osborne, Will Tusher, Regis Philbin, Marilyn Beck, Dick Kleiner, Vernon Scott, and a score more. And, of course, the people from Pantheon. Mellon looked somber and sincere, dressed dark right down to his cuff links. Sandra Kent was there in body, if not in spirit. So were Fisher, Wentworth, Jane Lane, and all the rest, including Will Catcher and Sabu, who both stood along a curtained wall. Sam sat on the aisle next to Josephine.

Bumbera, Foley, and Hacksaw were trying not to look like cops. Their act was a flop.

As always, Academy Award winner Milland was dignified and in beautiful voice as he began the threnody.

"Stage 1. There are those who will wonder at the choice of this final setting, where we have come to speak of, to remember—yes, to eulogize—one who walked as a giant among us. But it is altogether fitting and proper that we who worked with and loved Jack Flint should gather at a place where he guided so many of us. Stage 1.

"But this is not just Stage 1, a concrete edifice at Pantheon Pictures in a place called Hollywood. Because of men like Jack Flint it is many places and things. It is Noah's ark. A palace in Samarkand. It is the Old West. It is a lost ship on a stormy sea. It is a courtroom—yes, it is even a holy place.

"For what is a holy place? It is not built of stone and mortar, of brick and wood. It is built of love."

That's when a bunch of youths sprang to their feet with cries of:

"WHAT THIS TOWN NEEDS IS MORE FUNERALS!"

"GIVE US A CHANCE TO MAKE PICTURES!"

"FLINT DIED TWENTY YEARS AGO!"

That, plus a storm of obscenities.

Steve Steilburg pulled a Bolex out of his Gucci purse and screamed, "WE CAN MAKE BETTER PICTURES WITH THIS!"

The security guards scrambled to snatch up the youths while the TV cameras whirled to record the activity for the early news. Photogs' flashbulbs exploded like a Fourth of July jubilation.

A couple of the young protestors unfurled a banner proclaiming "RATINGS ARE CENSORSHIP" and "THERE'S NO SUCH THING AS DIRTY PICTURES."

The studio police and Will Catcher were turning the tide and carrying the day as they hustled the youths outside, still screaming obscenities and slogans.

"FAT CATS MOVE OVER!"

"TEAR DOWN THE STAGES!"

"ALL THE WORLD'S A STAGE!"

"GO WHERE IT'S AT!"

"FIND OUT WHAT IT'S ALL ABOUT!"

"TO HELL WITH EVERYBODY WHO WEARS UNIFORMS!"

As Steve Steilburg was being escorted up the aisle, he saw Sam. Steilburg managed to break away from the cop and came at Sam screaming and swinging. Sam sidestepped and hooked a right into Steilburg's rib cage that broke three bones. Steilburg collapsed like a snapped copper coil. The cops carried him out while he tried to pump air into his lungs.

When order was restored, Mr. Milland proceeded extemporaneously:

"We were speaking of love. Perhaps in view of what just happened here we should also speak of ambition—and manners. *Ours* was an ambitious generation. We, too, wanted to make the world a better place, but not by screaming, not by obscenity, not by desecration. There are other ways. Leadership ought to be earned . . ."

Sam leaned closer to Josephine. "Know what, angel?"

"What?"

"Wives number three and five did a no-show."

CHAPTER
15

I⊤ was still early afternoon when Sam got back to the office. Duchess was reading the funny papers and finishing off the last of three scoops of ice cream with sliced bananas out of a bowl.

"Oh, hi, Sam. How was the funeral?"

"It got mixed reviews."

"Oh, good. A man came up to see you. I shooed him into your office."

"What sort of a man?"

"He looks like he's mad at somebody. Hope it's not me." Her nose wrinkled. "Or is it 'I'?"

"It's neither one of you. He's mad at the world."

Abu Lobi was his usual scowling self when Sam went in and took off his hat and trench coat.

"Well, he did send his number one boy," said Sam. "Who's guarding the Shah's body?"

"My men are seeing to his safety. Besides, the Shah is incommunicado."

"Oh, I thought he was in Palm Springs. How long you been at this job?"

"Many years."

"Yeah?" Sam tugged at his chin. "You fellas have a lot of laughs together? Like the other day in the desert? Say, who were those gunsels?"

"Who knows? The Shah's enemies are everywhere."

"Yeah, I heard that song before. Say, when do you want to grease the skids?"

"Do what?"

Sam picked up the phone and buzzed the intercom. "Duchess, shoo yourself in here, will you?" Sam put the phone down and answered Hobby's question. "Saddle up. Take off. Leave."

Duchess entered. "Is there anything I can do?" she asked.

"Immediately," Hobby Lobby answered Sam's query.

Duchess was puzzled. "Immediately is a *when,* not a *what.* What's he talking about Sam?"

"About our date, Duchess. It starts now." Sam looked at Hobby Lobby. "But we'll have to stop by and pick up clothes, shirts, slacks—stuff like that—and a toothbrush."

"Yeah," Duchess nodded, "even though neither Sam or me wears underwear."

That remark seemed to throw the Arab a little.

"Everything will be provided." Hobby Lobby smiled a scimitar smile that still came out a scowl.

"For me, too?" Duchess inquired.

"Definitely for you," Hobby Lobby responded. "The Shah has a predilection for blondes."

"Sam," she asked, "is that a dirty crack?"

"Probably," said Sam. Then to Hobby Lobby, "Well, let's hit the road. I hope you're not driving one of those exploding limousines."

No, the Arab wasn't driving anything—on the ground. But he *was* piloting the Shah's personal customized Jet Ranger helicopter, and Sam and Duchess were aboard and wafting their way toward Palm Springs.

Ol' Hobby Lobby knew how to handle that machine and he went out of his way with a couple of fancy but unnecessary maneuvers just to do a little hot-dogging.

You have to see the Palm Springs area from the air to really appreciate it. And a helicopter is the best way. Barren mountains, red rocks, and the beige desert decorated with date trees, orange groves, and grapefruit gardens. The country clubs with their evergreen golf courses and blue green swimming pools. A veritable oasis blossoming out of hell's hard land.

The Shah had picked himself a prime spot all right, all right. About sixty acres between Palm Desert and La Quinta— all walled. With trees and gardens and tennis courts. With a nine-hole golf course, three swimming pools of assorted sizes and temperatures, jacuzzies and saunas, stables and riding trails, and a palace that would make the Caliph of Bagdad look like he was on welfare.

Then there were the guest houses. Six. Count 'em, six separate structures for people who wanted to sleep over in private.

Hobby Lobby set the bird down on Shah Tabriz's personal helicopter pad right where he was supposed to, somewhere on the south sixty. That's where one of the limousines, a Mercedes, idled, waiting to whisk Sam and Duchess to adjacent guest houses where a set of servants awaited with wardrobe, whiskey, and the heart's desire of each guest.

An hour later Sam lounged in a terry cloth bathrobe next to the Shah, who watched fascinated at the sight of a polka-dot bikinied Duchess walking onto a diving board at swimming hole number three. Actually, the sight of a bikinied Duchess would have fascinated a eunuch.

Her long golden hair glimmered in the sun and curled around her smooth white shoulders and bouncing breasts. Her full-scale upper body triangled to a small circle of waist, then she valentined into healthy undulating hips that tapered down well-turned alabaster legs to tiny feet. She'd have more effect on a coronary case than a charge from a defibrillator.

Standing on either side of the reclining Shah was a set of

identical blonde beauties, also bikini clad. How this brace of blonde dynamite had escaped Hugh Hefner's centerfold confounded Sam. They served the Shah spirits, lit his cigarettes and anticipated his every whim. But right now Shah Tabriz's attention was turned toward the divine and diving Duchess. She knifed into the warm pool, surfaced on her back and swam while her beauteous breasts bobbed in the water.

Shah Tabriz stared in awe and unabashed admiration as Sam remarked, "I'd say you lean toward blondes."

"Blondes. Yes! Blondes!" the Shah responded.

"There's an old saying in my country," said Sam. "Blondes are fickle."

"In my country," said the Shah, "blondes are scarce."

"I see what you mean."

Hobby Lobby scowled in the background as Shah Tabriz pulled a thick envelope out of his pocket and handed it to Sam.

"Mr. Marlow, there is twenty-five thousand dollars—American—in this envelope. It is for you, on account."

"On account of what happened out there in the desert?"

"Precisely. And there will be more. Much more. Later tonight I want to talk to you about an errand you might care to perform back in Los Angeles."

"I'd say this makes me the highest paid errand boy in the world." Sam took the envelope. "You know this is gonna put me in one hell of a tax bracket."

"There are ways of avoiding the bothersome tax situation altogether. If you like, I can have one of my specialists show you how to—"

"No thanks, Shahny, I'd prefer to stay on the square with Uncle Sam."

"As you wish."

Just then one of the twin blonde beauties arrived with a fresh beverage for the Shah while the other blonde bookend put a fresh cigarette in his holder, produced a flame from a gold lighter and lit him.

"Say there, Shahny, can you tell these two apart?"

"Melanie and Melody? Oh, yes."

"How?"

"I have my ways."

"Even in the dark?"

"*Especially* in the dark."

"I see. Say, this party tonight—little party or big party?"

"Hmmm," the Shah shrugged, "big party."

"Anybody I know?"

"I think you might be surprised."

Sam patted the envelope in his robe pocket and sipped on his gin and tonic. "After the twenty-five Gs, nothing could surprise me."

CHAPTER
16

B UT Sam did get surprised that night. More than once. First at the number of people who showed up—about two hundred. Second at some of the people themselves. They weren't exactly strangers.

People like Adam Mellon, who did not show up with Mrs. Mellon. No, he escorted a radiant Josephine Bramer. Fresh Fisher turned up alone. And Pantheon's biggest asset, Sandra Kent herself, made an entrance. She wore a practically transparent shimmering pink dress that made you want to run, not walk, right over and tear it off. Every man jack there made it his business to get as close to her as possible. She knew it and was teasing the juices out of every male in the joint. Hard to tell who Sandra was with, if anybody. It might even have been Sabu. Yes. He was there too, all five feet of him, all dressed in white silk like a coffin lining.

The area around swimming hole number one had been converted to look like a set out of the Arabian Nights. Tents, torches, even live camels and a lot of dead lambs and goats roasting on spits—and, of course, the nearly naked slave girls serving hors d'oeuvres and drinks. The hors d'oeuvres included the ordinary stuff such as caviar, terrapin, crab, shrimp, and some stuff that wasn't so ordinary. Tabbuli, kibbeh naye, dolmas, hummus bi tahini, borek, and sfeeha.

And, of course, there was entertainment. All kinds—from the obligatory belly dancers to acrobats to elephants that did tricks. And music right out of Port Said.

Hobby Lobby and about a dozen other beefy bedouins circulated with bulges under their coats making sure everything and everybody was secure—especially Shah Tabriz. The bodyguards were toting enough lead to make them bowlegged.

Yeah, it was your ordinary hundred-thousand-dollar party. And most people seemed to be getting the Shah's money's worth.

It didn't take too long for the old gang to get together. The Shah with his bookends, Sam and Duchess, Mellon and Josephine, even Sandra and Sabu.

"Say, who invited you?" Mellon asked Sabu.

"I did," said the Shah as he strolled up, braced by the blonde bookends.

"Oh, you two know each other, then?" Mellon surmised.

"We are . . . countrymen," Shah Tabriz nodded.

So did Sabu.

"Say there, Mellon," Sam inquired, "you goin' into the oil business, or is Shahny here going into show business?"

"That's none of *your* business," Mellon replied.

"Miss Kent," the Shah dripped of Oriental oil, "I'm so happy you accepted my invitation. I have admired you from afar."

"Yes, well . . ." Sandra gave him a look and body movement that would blow the lid right off an oil derrick, "How do I look close up?"

"Fabulous."

"Then why don't we get better acquainted? Maybe you'd care to show me your—parlor."

"I would care very much."

They moved off together, but it didn't look like they were

heading for any parlor. Sabu stood there with a sort of sick smirk on his bedimmed face. The blonde bookends had obviously been ditched by the Shah before. They didn't bat an eyelash.

"Oh," said Sam, "Mr. Mellon. I don't believe you ever met *my* executive secretary. This is Duchess. Duchess, meet Mr. Mellon and his executive secretary, Miss Bramer."

Josephine gave Sam a look that wasn't too friendly. He returned the austerity.

"Pleased to meet you both," Duchess curtsied.

"Yeah," said Sam, "Mr. Mellon gives good funerals. Well, Duchess, what do you say? Should we go and . . ."

"Wet our foozles? Let's!"

"Maybe we'll see you later," said Sam. "Oh, and Mr. Mellon, give my regards to the Mrs."

Toward the wee hours, the party was still going strong. The Shah and Sandra had done a vanishing act for nearly three hours. But they were back now. It was easy for Sam to imagine what went on—and off—in the interval. After those two nights, Sam was pretty well acquainted with Sandra's boudoir repertoire. From the look in Shah Tabriz's eyes, she must've pulled every trick in the book.

Now Sandra was sitting on one side of the Shah, who made himself comfortable in an oversize wicker chair, and Sam and Duchess sat on the Shah's other side. They, along with about a hundred others—including Mellon, Josephine, Sabu, and Fisher—were seated poolside watching the entertainers perform on a slightly raised platform that served as a stage.

The act consisted of three people and a lot of cutlery. Knives of assorted sizes, including a scimitar the star kept waving around and swinging dangerously close to his two featured players. The star was a bronze giant of a man wearing a turban, a vest on his naked buffalo chest, and Oriental silk pantaloons. He was barefoot. The featured players were two beautiful, full-bosomed, full-hipped Arabian dancing girls. They swayed and heaved to the music while

Star threw knives, narrowly missing the girls' feet and bodies as they danced around three columns on the stage.

The tempo of the music became faster, the dancing became wilder and the knives came closer. It was a good act. With a wow finish.

As the music crescendoed to a climax, Star spun and threw his heavy scimitar straight at Shah Tabriz's head. Sam saw it coming barely in time and knocked the Shah, who had been gazing at Sandra, right on his ass. The scimitar split the wicker chair almost in half. But Star wasn't finished with his act. He pulled an automatic out of his baggy silk pants and pointed it at the Shah on the floor. That's just as far as Star got. Sam's Luger cracked fire and blew a hole the size of a quarter through Star's forehead. The hole out the back of Star's head was about the size of a splattered eggplant.

The two beautiful featured players had something in mind beside a curtain call. They each snatched up a knife, screamed some slogan in a foreign language and charged at the stunned Shah.

Sam hesitated a split second. Hobby Lobby and company didn't. They riddled both beauties with lead. One beauty almost made it to the Shah. Almost. Instead she dropped the knife and died as she fell bleeding into the pool.

Hobby Lobby and his storm troopers hurried toward the Shah as the spectators were just about through screaming, sobbing and running for cover.

Sam was already helping the Shah to his unsteady pins.

"Once again," the shah stuttered to Sam, "I am in your debt. My . . ."

"Yeah, I know," said Sam, "your enemies are everywhere. Say, who books your acts? John Dillinger?"

A few minutes later Shah Tabriz, Sam, and Hobby Lobby were convened in one of the Shah's more intimate rooms. It was only the size of a modest public library. The Shah was still pale as his collar—trembling and guzzling ouzo. He was also giving Hobby Lobby a few choice dirty looks. "Mr.

Marlow," he said, "name your price."

"For what?"

"For coming to work for me exclusively."

"Naw, Shahny, I couldn't do that. I've got to work for myself. There's just something in my system."

"Don't give me your answer now. Think about it."

"I already have. On both counts."

The Shah took a piece of paper out of his pocket. "That errand we spoke of earlier. May I retain your services for that?"

"I don't know. What is it?"

"Simply this." The Shah handed Sam the paper. "Be at this place at this time. A package will be delivered to you by someone who has possession of the other half of this."

Shah Tabriz handed Sam part of a foreign currency that had been torn in a jagged pattern.

"What am I supposed to do with this package?"

"Just call me when you have it. I will tell you then."

"Sounds easy as eating gravy."

"You will do this for me?"

Sam glanced at Hobby Lobby, who was looking at Sam and oozing hate out of every pore. "Sure, Shahny. We got a deal."

"Good. Very good."

"Yeah. Too bad the party had to break up early—but it coulda been a lot worse. About the cops: I, uh, s'pose you'll handle 'em again?"

"Rest assured," the Shah nodded.

"Yeah," said Sam, "that's the best way to rest all right. Well, I'm going to go find my foozle friend." He started to walk out. "Oh, and I'm sorry your pool got bloodied. But then, you've got other pools."

CHAPTER
17

WHAT with all the knives, bullets, blood, and bodies, the weekend broke up early. The survivors headed for home after a sort of somber Saturday brunch. Except for Sandra. She and the Shah spent the weekend.

Hobby Lobby helicoptered Sam and Duchess back to L.A. in sullen silence. Duchess didn't notice. She kept telling Sam how much she enjoyed the acrobats, elephants, and sword dancers. She told Sam she had a better time with him than with the tuba player. In a way Sam felt flattered.

Sam spent most of Saturday and Sunday in bed with a bottle of Glenfiddich and a novel by Dashiell Hammett. By Monday morning he was ready to bounce a corpse down the street and see what would happen. It was ten A.M. in Holmby Hills and all was well with the world.

Her toenails were lacquered and professionally manicured. Her trim ankles ascended into well-turned thighs revealing the lower part of a black bikini, then upward toward a flat belly.

She blossomed into an ample bosom, a fine smooth stem of a neck, and finally a beautifully sunglassed face of about thirty years framed by an expensive coiffure.

The lady relaxed by a swimming pool, sipped a Bloody Mary and read *Playgirl* magazine.

Sam surveyed the environs—about the size of a soccer field—and the lady. She remained unaware of his presence until Sam spoke. "That the latest thing in widow's weeds? Black bikini?"

She turned. "How'd you get in here?"

"I came in the alleyway."

"Go out the same way. Now—or you'll regret it."

"Better to have something to regret than nothing to remember." Sam looked around. "So this is the house that Jack built?"

"Who are you?"

"Name's Marlow. Sam Marlow."

She stared at Sam's face. "Are you wearing a mask?"

"Yeah, I'm really the Lone Ranger."

"OK, Mr. Marlow, if that *is* your name. You've got thirty seconds before you get tossed out. Or maybe shot."

"Ever try poison?" Sam twitched.

She rose and took off her sunglasses. She had hawklike hazel eyes and an erect, high-breasted body. "What does that mean?"

"I worked for your husband."

"Then go see him about getting paid. And good luck."

"Already been paid."

"Then blow."

"Plain talk. Sorry you missed the funeral. It was a hell of a show."

"I caught it on the late news. You haven't got enough class to be a lawyer. You must be a shamus—or a fugitive from Camarillo."

"Beauty *and* brains." Sam picked up the *Playgirl* from the table. "You subscribe to this or pick it up on the newsstand?"

"Listen, eyeball, I already explained to the cops, Mutt and Jeff, or whatever their names are. Nobody knows what's in the old bastard's will. I'd probably be better off with a divorce."

"Not the kind of divorce he had in mind."

"OK, now you'll see what *I've* got in mind."

Sam had already spotted the man. Handsome. Dark complexioned. Over six feet. Right at two hundred pounds. Big knuckles on big hands, and he looked like he didn't mind a fight now and then. Especially now. He was walking directly toward them from the garage-apartment building.

"Handsome little devil," Sam nodded toward the man.

"He's not so little up close," she smiled.

The little devil did in fact get bigger as he got closer.

"What's the problem, Cynthia?"

"Ah," said Sam, "the old family retainer."

"No problem, Leonard. Just a trespasser. Says he's a shamus and asks a lot of dumb questions, mostly about Jack."

"Since we're on a first-name basis, you can call me Sam."

"I'll call you turd head."

"Please, there's a lady present." Sam held up the *Playgirl* magazine.

"Yeah," said Leonard. "Well, *you* ain't gonna be present much longer."

Leonard grabbed Sam by the shoulder and spun him. Sam kept right on spinning, did a 360, and landed a left on Leonard's nose. Busted and bleeding. A fast right to the stomach and the coup de grace—a solid left hook to Leonard's jaw that knocked Leonard into the hot jacuzzi.

The widow Flint came flailing at Sam. "You sonofabitch!!" She swung a roundhouse right. Sam ducked deftly. She was off balance. Sam booted her in the bikini. She joined Leonard in the jacuzzi, with another "sonofabitch!!!"

"Thanks for your hospitality," said Sam. "I think I can find my way out. And have a nice day."

Sam took it on the heel and toe.

So much for widow number five. Sam's next stop was widow number three.

Mona Hyland was doing her exercises along a ballet workout bar in a room mirrored on three walls. Sam watched her appreciatively. Even if she were a dozen years younger, Mona Hyland could've been proud of her leotarded figure. At her age, "phenomenal" was not an exaggeration.

Her home was high on a small plateau. In the background, through the sliding glass doors, were the Hollywood hills. Mona Hyland continued her exercises while they talked.

"I appreciate your seeing me, Miss Hyland."

"Mona. Jack liked you."

"He didn't know me very well." Sam looked at and past her. "Nice view."

She got the point and smiled. "It's an older neighborhood but still a good one. Did you want to talk about Jack?"

"No, to listen. And everybody I listen to has a different opinion. Like they're all talking about different people."

"That was part of Jack's charm. It was hard to find the real Jack."

"How did *you* find him?"

"Charming—in small doses. We couldn't get along *too* long. Too much alike. Too competitive. We had to outdo each other. But I'll miss the competition."

"You didn't show up at the funeral."

"That was no funeral."

"What do you think of Mellon?"

"The 'last tycoon'? I stopped thinking about him years ago."

Mona seemed somehow different in private than in public. Not imperial at all. Oh, she still had style and grace, but there was a calm, a warmth and casualness that Sam had never seen before.

"You know," said Sam, "this is gonna sound silly and you've heard it a million times before, but I'm gonna say it anyhow."

"Go ahead."

"I like the movies, specially the older ones—back when stars didn't look like garage mechanics and the ladies didn't want to be plumbers and box with each other and drive trucks, when there was glitter and glamour, when people cared how they looked and smelled. When pictures had class. You were a part of all that. A big part."

"I suppose I was." She finished exercising and picked up a towel.

"In fact," Sam added, "after Rita Hayworth married the Khan and retired for a while . . ."

"Yeah, then it was my turn to be the sex goddess. God, how I hated that slogan Mellon made up: Mona begins where Rita left off. But I was just a dumb kid in a candy store."

"Angel, you didn't look like any other kid on my block."

"Thanks."

"And you still don't."

"In this town, when people start telling you how good you look—it usually means you don't."

"Not in this case. Don't you, uh, miss it?"

" 'When I was a child I understood as a child, thought as a child, but when I grew up I put away childish things'—from the Good Book."

"Yeah," said Sam, "Corinthians, Chapter 13, Verse 11. It was also Burt Lancaster's last speech in a picture called *Elmer Gantry*—won him the Academy Award."

"You know your Bible and your movies." She smiled.

"You think Flint could've killed himself?" Sam asked.

"No more than I could."

Sam walked over to the window and pretended he was eyeing the view. "The last thing he did was run one of your pictures—*Lucretia*."

"He told me he was going to."

"Why didn't you watch it with him?"

"Just saw it on television. I liked the commercials better."

"How long were you married?"

"Three or four years, off and on. I don't remember. It was a long time ago."

"But you still saw him—off and on."

"Off and on, now and then." Mona Hyland smiled again and nodded. "Well, if you'll excuse me, I've got to take a fast shower and get to the hospital."

"You don't look sick to me," Sam said.

"Volunteer work. Children's Hospital."

"Ah, a Good Samaritan."

"Only three times a week."

Sam pointed at her leotards as she started off. "You favor the color burgundy, huh?"

"That's not burgundy, it's fuchsia."

"Uh-huh." Then Sam pointed to the phone. "Can I make a call? Local."

"Help yourself. And maybe we can talk some more—now and then." She started out of the room again.

"That'd be swell. Oh, and Miss Hyland . . ."

She stopped and turned around.

"You've got a good figure!"

"Thanks, Mr. Marlow," she smiled. "I've got good habits."

Sam called Duchess. She was still all giddy about how much fun she had had over the weekend. Sam could hear Nicky in the background, then Duchess giggled and got even giddier. Duchess did manage to say, "Josephine Kramer called from Pan-something-or-other Pictures." Sam let it go at that and told Duchess he'd see her in an hour.

He was in no hurry to talk to Josephine. He'd stop at the bank first. He was still hefting the twenty-five grand. Then he'd go to the office and call Ms. Bramer.

He walked to the Plymouth that had protested the steep winding climb up to Mona's house, got in and fired up the six cylinders. Sam lit a Lucky and started the long winding descent on the narrow road. In less than a minute, from behind him, he heard the sound of another car's horn and then the Plymouth was being passed by Mona's Mercedes. She was turbaned again and looked fresh as a spring garden. She smiled and waved as she roared past Sam. He waved and smiled back.

But at that moment, Mona's smile changed to a crease of concern and then a look of panic erupted in her eyes as she rounded a sharp curve.

Her foot hit the brakes. The pedal hit the floorboard. She tried to pump some pressure into it, but the pedal lay flat and impotent. She looked back at Sam and silently pleaded for help as the Mercedes gained momentum with the descent. Sam motioned for her to scrape against the rocky side of the hill. He tossed out his cigarette and gunned the Plymouth to try to force her into the wall.

She turned the steering wheel sharply but the Mercedes failed to respond. The steering mechanism was also gone. Sam could hear Mona scream as the Mercedes dove off the curve—twisted and somersaulted—bounced again and again on the sharp jutting rocks and crashed into the canyon below.

Sam's foot slammed on the brakes. His fist smashed onto the dashboard—and he sobbed.

CHAPTER
18

HER blanketed body was being strapped onto the helicopter.

Bumbera stood next to Sam, who was still not under complete emotional control and fighting not to show it.

There were over a dozen police and paramedics around the wreckage of the Mercedes. The copter roared to life—the blade whirled and left a dusty downdraft in its wake as it lifted Mona's broken body from the bowels of the canyon.

"Bummy," said Sam, "if I'm around when they catch whoever did this," he took a breath, "you better . . .''

"Take it easy, Sam. It happens like this now and then."

"Yeah—now and then."

"We'll get him, Sam."

"I never wanted to get anybody so much in my life." Sam squeezed the words out. "Yeah, we'll get him."

Hacksaw approached. He carried a carton containing Mona's purse and personal objects from it. Also in the carton was Mona's turban. It was smeared with a pattern of dried blood.

"Bummy, we've picked up whatever we could find," he said. "You want to go over this stuff now?"

Bumbera glanced at Sam. "Later."

Tim Foley walked up holding a couple of slips of paper in his hand. "Here's a couple more," he said.

"What are they?" Bumbera asked.

"They're—let's see—says, 'Proxy Bid—Pantheon Pictures Auction.' I guess . . ."

"Later," Bumbera repeated.

"I remember her when I was just a little kid," Foley mused. "She sure was a beauty."

"*Was* is right," said Hacksaw and glanced back at the wreckage.

"*OK*, you two!" Bumbera snapped. He motioned for Hacksaw and Foley to leave. Hacksaw shrugged and started to turn away.

"Just a minute," said Sam. "I'll take that." He looked at Bumbera, who nodded and led the other two men away.

Sam held the turban in both hands. He looked at it for a moment, then tried to flake off some of the dried blood.

CHAPTER
19

Fɪʀsᴛ Sam was sad. Then he got mad. Feeling sad and mad is poor medicine. Sam finally got hold of himself.

When he came into the office, Duchess was gazing at one of the posters of Burt Reynolds she had pinned on the wall. "Hi, Sam. Hey, what's the matter? You look like you just lost your best friend."

"A long time ago," said Sam.

He pulled out the envelope with the twenty-five thousand and dropped it on Duchess's desk.

"Ooooh, look at all that monies! Where did we get it?"

"From Shah Tabriz. We won the door prize at his party."

"You know, Sam, somebody at that party said he was worth a billion dollars. Is that true?"

"Well, he's got it. I don't know if he's worth it."

"I don't understand."

"Neither do I. Get Josephine Bramer."

"Who?"

"Never mind, I'll get her."

Sam did.

Josephine already had heard the news of Mona Hyland's death and seemed genuinely saddened. Sam said he'd be at Pantheon Pictures in half an hour.

He was.

Mellon was beside himself. "Good God, Sam, these killings have got to stop! This whole thing is giving Pantheon Pictures an unsavory reputation. Right, Fresh?"

Fresh Fisher had only two responses to Adam Mellon, "yes" and "indeed." This time he used both.

"Marlow," Mellon pounded on his desk. "This studio has become an abattoir. You've got to find out what's at the bottom of this."

"I can only go so far," said Sam, "and a little farther."

"Name your price!"

"I've had two offers like that," Sam twitched. "This one intrigues me. I'll do what I can."

"As soon as you can," Mellon emphasized, then added, "I suppose we'll have to handle the funeral arrangements for Mona. I don't think she had any relatives."

"No, you won't," Sam said emphatically.

"Won't what?" Mellon questioned.

"You won't handle a goddamn thing to do with Mona Hyland's funeral," Sam said. "Not a goddamn thing. Or I walk off. You got that?!"

"OK, OK, I just thought—"

"Don't think anything about Mona Hyland. She stopped thinking about . . . just never mind." Sam turned and walked past Josephine Bramer.

"Marlow?" Mellon questioned. "Where are you going?"

"Projection Room A." Sam answered and kept on walking. "After I make a couple stops."

The door to Flint's bungalow was open. Sam walked in. Plain Jane Lane and Charlie Wentworth were transferring scripts, letters, notes, and other material from the filing cabinets in her office into moving cartons.

"Hello there, Jane," Sam said. "You being evicted?"

"I'm being transferred to the secretarial pool starting next week, Mr. Marlow, so you and I won't be seeing much of each other."

"Just when we were falling in love. Too bad. What about you, Charlie? They got a pool for you?"

"I haven't heard yet. I don't know what I'll be doing."

Will Catcher walked in the door.

"Hello, Mr. Marlow, I saw you come in here."

"Well, you said you'd keep your eyes and ears open."

"Yeah, but so far bupkis—nothing. You think there's a connection between Flint and the Mona Hyland gig?"

"I don't think anything, yet. Say, Jane, do me a kindness will you? Have a print of *Lucretia* sent over to Projection Room A soon as you can. And book the room for the rest of the day for me."

"Yes, sir." Jane picked up the phone and made the call.

Catcher walked toward Wentworth, who was working over some cartons marked "Research." "You gonna take that stuff back to research?"

"Yes, I am."

"Want me to give you a hand?"

"Thanks, but we're not permitted to carry anything; there's a union. We have to call the department."

"Oh, yeah, I forgot."

Sam walked to the partially open door leading to Flint's office and poked his head in. The room was bare. Outlined on the walls were slightly lighter imprints where the pictures, posters, one-sheets, and trophies had hung. Sam closed the door and walked back into Jane Lane's room.

"They sure picked it clean. Thanks for making the call, Jane. See you around the pool. So long, boys."

Sam went out the door and walked toward Projection Room A.

Three hours later he was still in Projection Room A running *Lucretia* for the second time.

Mona Hyland wore a diaphanous nightgown of the Renaissance. She was the quintessence of sex—her look, her walk, her every motion. She moved closer to the figure of a man who stood waiting. Mona gently touched the man's face with both her hands and slowly, sensually pressed her glistening red lips to his. "That was good-bye, Alphonso."

"Lucretia, I will give you anything, if you stay."

"Anything?"

"Yes."

There was a pause in the dialogue as the camera moved closer to Mona's glowing face. "Then give me your name, Alphonso. I want the House of Ferrara." She waited for his answer. Her eyes promising, taunting. He lowered his head.

Sam rubbed at his eyes, pulled at the lobe of his ear, lit another Lucky and kept watching.

Just outside the front gate of Pantheon Pictures, Steve Steilburg and his contingent were marching in an elongated circle shouting slogans and carrying hand-lettered placards telling their side of the story: "YOUTH MUST BE SERVED," "MELLON IS A BIGOT," "PANTHEON PICTURES IS PREJUDICED," "THE GESTAPO CAN'T STOP US," "OUR CIVIL RIGHTS HAVE BEEN VIOLATED," "WE'LL SEE YOU IN COURT," "MELLON IS A FASCIST."

Several policemen were there trying to make sure the demonstration remained reasonably orderly.

Mellon was at his office window watching the proceedings below. He turned to Josephine and Fresh Fisher. "Can't we get rid of those bums?"

Fisher shook his shining head. "Not so long as they, *quote,* demonstrate in an orderly manner, *unquote.*"

"Goddamn rabble! Direct pictures!! Somebody ought to direct 'em to a bathtub. Put 'em in the Army and delouse the bastards."

Mellon walked over to his desk, started to pour some water from his carafe into a glass, then stopped when he realized what he was doing. "Jo, did you put in a call to that Lieutenant . . ."

"Bumbera? Yes, sir."

"He never called back?"

"Not yet."

"Damn police. All they care about is their pensions. Anyone of us could be next. Don't they understand that there's some maniac running around loose? Speaking of maniacs, what's Marlow doing? Is he still in the projection room?"

"Yes, sir."

"He could've run the picture twice by now."

Josephine looked at her watch. "He just about has."

Sam closed his eyes a moment and listened to Mona's voice coming from the screen. She made the dialogue sound a lot better than it was written.

"Alphonso, because of what I've done, men have died in a senseless war. And the only man I've ever loved has poisoned himself. It's too late for us."

"No, it's not too late, Lucretia."

"I am no longer Lucretia."

"Yes, you are. You're still the same woman in the same body. The House of Ferrara is yours—if you choose."

"I have already chosen—another house."

Mona was wearing the habit of a nun. She smiled a beatific smile and held up a heavy carved pectoral cross suspended from a simple chain around her neck. The camera moved in on the cross, the music swelled and THE END dissolved onto the screen.

The lights came on in the projection room and a voice from the booth came through the speaker.

"I go on overtime in five minutes. You want to run it again, sir?"

As the projectionist spoke, the door to the room opened and Sandra Kent came in. Sam clicked down the speaker button. "I'll let you know in a minute."

Sandra seemed pensive—at least for Sandra. She walked a couple of steps and looked with her silver blue eyes toward the imageless screen. "There's a superstition in Hollywood that death comes in threes. Think I'll be next, Sam?"

"How'd you know I was here?"

Sandra smiled and moved closer to Sam. "Mellon's not the only one who's got spies."

"The ubiquitous Sabu," said Sam. "I think that little monkey's with the CIA."

Now she was very close to him. "Sam, you've never tasted my lamb chops, have you?"

Sam didn't look at her or respond. She touched his face. "You know what I feel like?"

Sam shoved her hand away rudely. "Cut it out!"

There was a look of genuine hurt in Sandra's big blue eyes. "Hey, I'm sorry. I thought maybe you'd want a little dinner, a bottle of wine—forget about what's happened for a little while. That's all."

"I'm sorry, Sandra." Sam stroked at his chin. "Sounds swell." He pressed down the speaker button. "That'll be all. Goodnight and thanks."

There was the sound of two clicks of acknowledgment from the booth. Sam rose. His mood changed. "Can you really cook?"

They started to walk out.

"Ever hear of an Italian who couldn't?"

"Kent—Italian?"

"Cantori, signori."

"A blonde Italian?"

"In northern Italy they breed 'em blonde. By the way, Sam, what's *your* real name?"

"Put-in-tame," said Sam, "Ask me again and I'll tell you the same."

CHAPTER
20

THEY had the dinner and the bottle of wine. Sam wasn't nuts about lamb—ate too much of it when he was a kid. But Sandra was a good cook. She knew her way around the kitchen as well as the boudoir. But that night there was no boudoir. They just ate nice and talked nice. Sam did ask if she and the Shah were going to become an item around town— and the world. She said no, the Shah was OK the first night, but over the weekend he got too kinky. Sam let it go at that and thought, well, back to the bookends for the Sheik of Araby.

And it was back to the office for Sam. He had to do a little mulling. And he mulled better with the office bottle than at his apartment. Somehow there had to be a link between Flint's and Mona's murders. So far it was the missing link.

He parked the Plymouth, unlocked the door to the building and walked up the dark stairway toward his office.

There's something about an old building at night. Somehow it's never absolutely silent. There are always some sounds that seem to come from somewhere. The attic or under the stairs, around some corner. Maybe it's ghosts—or just the beams groaning and complaining with old age. As his footsteps took him to the top of the stairs, Sam seemed to imagine more sounds than usual tonight.

But it wasn't just his imagination. He unlocked the door and opened it. Before he could turn on the light, a hand holding a sap came down hard at Sam's head.

Sam barely managed to move his head in time. He took the blow on his shoulder and dropped to one knee right in front of a shadowy figure. The sap came down at him again, but Sam beat it to the punch with a right uppercut that contained all the power he had. The shadowy figure fell backward on the floor.

But as Sam snapped on the light and saw Duchess and Nicky bound and gagged in a couple of chairs, two other figures sprang at him, one from across the dark hall and another from around a corner. Both men were wearing stocking masks that squashed their features into mutantlike monsters and both charged with saps in their hands.

Sam just didn't have time to get to the Luger in his trench coat pocket. He made do with both fists and feet. He hit them hip and high. He kicked and ducked and jabbed and hooked. Missing some and connecting some.

One of the attackers swung the sap at Sam's head. Sam ducked and the frosted glass window on the door shattered. The attacker screamed and pulled his bleeding hand away.

Sam kicked the third man in the groin and then nailed him with a left and right.

The man on the floor stirred until Sam kicked him in his stockinged head. He stopped stirring.

The man with the bleeding hand ran toward the stairs yelling, "This sonofabitch's crazy!"

Sam caught the second man at the top of the stairs, spun him around and landed a right square on his jaw. The man flew back and dropped ten steps down onto the fleeing bleeding man. They both bounced crazily all the way to the bottom and crashed through the plate glass window of the door.

Duchess was bound body and breasts with clothesline. Sam untied and ungagged her first, then Nicky. Each of them had bruises—Duchess a blue welt on her forehead and Nicky a corking black eye.

"Oooh, Sam. They made me so mad. They tied me and hit me and then, well, I won't tell you what else they did. It wasn't nice. And poor Mr. Kalamavrakinopoulos, he was just an innocent sidestander."

Sam walked over to the unconscious man in the stocking mask and tore it off. "Well, waddaya know?! If it ain't Leonard, the houseboy!"

Leonard had a piece of tape across his broken nose. Sam pulled out his Luger, grabbed Leonard with his other hand and forced the dazed man to his wobbly feet.

"Duchess, call Lieutenant Bumbera."

"OK, Sam." She started for the telephone, then turned and slugged Leonard with a perfect right hand punch on his broken nose. Leonard almost passed out again. Duchess looked at Sam. "He hit me first—and did things that weren't very nice."

Mother bellowed from halfway up the stairs. "What the hell is going on! Is that goddamn Greek up there?!"

She filled up the open doorway next to the shattered glass. "That breaks it, Marlow! You're moving out! You and that banana-eating sex maniac!" She looked at Nicky. "And I got half a notion to throw you out, too!"

She noticed the bruises on Nicky's and Duchess's faces. "Have you two been fighting? Or, or, what?"

"Take it easy, Mother," said Sam, still pointing the Luger at Leonard. "These two were both innocent victims of this gorilla. The police are on their way. Now here's five hundred dollars for your trouble, and I'll have the damage repaired first thing in the morning."

Mother hung fire for a moment. "You will?"

"I will."

She grabbed the five yards fast. "Well, in that case, come on honey pot, let's go home."

"Okey-dokey," said Nicky, and winked through his black eye at Sam as he went to Mother.

"You go home too, Duchess," Sam said. "I'll stick around here with laughing boy and wait for the gendarmes."

Not too much later the gendarmes were in Sam's office. Sam, Bumbera, Hacksaw, and Tim Foley all stood. Leonard, with fresh blood on his bandaged nose, was seated on the hardbacked chair in the middle of the room. Bumbera was gently whacking the palm of his own hand with Leonard's sap.

"You can't do this," said Leonard.

"Can't do what?" Bumbera asked.

"Just keep me here like this."

"Can't we?"

"Well, for how long?"

"Just a few more minutes."

"What about my rights?"

Bumbera whacked his palm a little harder with the sap. "What about 'em?"

"I want to call my lawyer," Leonard said emphatically.

"You can call the Supreme Court—in just a few more minutes."

"Hey, Tim," said Sam. "I thought you were on vacation."

"Starts tomorrow."

"It *is* tomorrow."

"Tim, you wanna shove off, go ahead," said Bumbera. "We'll wrap this up."

"Naw, I'll stick around."

Another officer escorted Mrs. Cynthia Flint into Sam's office.

"Oh, thanks for cooperating, Mrs. Flint."

"You said it was urgent, Lieutenant. If it's about Jack, I've already . . ."

Hacksaw moved a couple of steps to his right, revealing Leonard. "You *are* this man's employer, aren't you?" he asked.

"He works for us, yes." She was a little nonplussed now.

"*Us?*" Bumbera adjusted his shoulders again.

"My husband and me. My *late* husband."

"Uh-huh." Bumbera stepped toward Leonard. "Well, to-night your employee and a couple other goons attacked Mr. Marlow with . . ." Bumbera let the sap drop with a thud onto the coffee table, ". . . with a deadly weapon."

"Call our lawyer, Cynthia," Leonard blurted.

"*Our* lawyer?! Listen, you two-bit torpedo, don't try to get me mixed up in this mess. I told you to forget about him." She looked at Sam. "But no, you had to show how tough you are. Well, you showed it, all right."

"Cynthia."

"And how *dumb* you are, too. Look, Lieutenant, I had nothing to do with this. Don't know anything about it. Do whatever you want with him!"

"Uh-huh," Bumbera grunted.

"Listen, Cynthia," Leonard spat out. "You can't get away with—"

"With what, you ass hole!" She turned to Bumbera. "I didn't like my husband, Lieutenant, but I didn't kill him. The truth is, I don't think he did it either." She nodded at Leonard. "He's too damn dumb. But that's for you to find out—like I did. Can I leave now?"

"Sure, sure," said Bumbera with a smile.

Two hours later Sam rubbed some more liniment on his sapped shoulder, pulled his third Bud of the night from the fridge and called Tim Foley's place. Foley was in bed asleep. "You enjoying your vacation so far?"

"It's terrific."

"You want to do a little private eyeing tomorrow and make five yards?"

"Sure," Foley replied with eagerness.

"You know the old Rickenbacker Air Field?"

"Yeah, it's abandoned, isn't it?"

"Not quite. Be there at noon."

"OK. Where'll I find you?"
"You know the answer to that one."
"Yeah, you'll find me."
"Check. Oh, and Tim."
"Yeah?"
"Bring your hardware."

CHAPTER
21

It was eleven fifty-four by the watch on Tim Foley's left wrist. He got out of his pride and joy, a 1965 Mustang convertible, and stretched his arms, legs, and back.

Foley looked around at the abandoned airfield. Another relic of the second world war. The field had been operative until about fifteen years ago. Since then it had fallen into disrepair. Of the dozen or so buildings still standing, most were windowless, some were roofless and the corrugated hangars were peeling and rusted. The landing strips were gnarled and rutted, with weeds growing out of the furrows. A ghost station for the sky.

Tim Foley waited and looked back at the road he had driven. The road Sam Marlow would be driving. A warm Santa Ana wind sang its soft song, rattling whatever was loose and flaking more rusty particles off the hangars. Somewhere a piece of glass fell from a window and Tim Foley inadvertently touched the Smith and Wesson on his hip. Then he heard it. He looked again for Sam's car on the narrow road. But the sound wasn't coming from the ground. Tim realized it was coming from the sky.

It was a plane, all right. But nothing like Tim Foley had ever seen before except in old movies on television. A World War II fighter plane that looked like a phantom searching for a lost haven out of a lost time.

The plane buzzed low just over the Mustang and Foley instinctively ducked, even though the aircraft was a hundred feet over his head. It tipped its wings in a salute, banked and made a perfect landing on the imperfect field, then taxied toward Tim. The cockpit was a two-seater but only one man was sitting there.

That man was Sam Marlow. He slid back the cockpit cover and stepped onto the wing. Foley was astounded. He couldn't believe his eyes. But just for an instant. He realized this was typical of Sam Marlow—not to be typical.

Sam Marlow wore an old-fashioned aviator's helmet with goggles, and a World War II bomber jacket, topped off with a flowing white silk scarf. Sam jumped down from the wing and lifted the goggles from his eyes to his forehead as Tim walked up smiling and shaking his head. "Well, I got to say one thing, Sam, you do do things with—"

"Panache, my boy, panache."

"I didn't even know you could fly."

"Sonny boy, there's a lot of things you don't know." Sam looked around the skeletal airstrip. "This looks like the opening shot of *Twelve O'Clock High*. The only thing missing is Dean Jagger."

Foley stood back and looked at the plane. "Where the hell did you ever dig this up?"

"In a graveyard. She's a Republic P-47 Thunderbolt right out of WW II—completely restored with a converted two-man cockpit and ready for WW III."

" 'Beautiful Darlin' Betsy.' " Tim read the inscription on the front of the fuselage. "Who's that?"

"That, my young fugitive from the kindergarten, is the name of McMasters and Sands' first oil well."

"McMasters and Sands—never heard of 'em."

"Gable and Tracy in *Boomtown*—named their first well after Claudette Colbert."

"Yeah?" Tim grinned. "You look more like something out of *Test Pilot*."

"Ah, you saw that one, huh?"

"On television. That was Gable and Tracy, too, wasn't it?"

"Yeah, Tracy died in the end and Gable cried. So did I." Sam's eyes searched the sky. "Well, looks like they're late."

"Sam, what's this all about?"

"Never mind. Did you bring your piece?"

Tim patted the Smith and Wesson on his hip. "Are we gonna have to shoot somebody?"

"Never can tell. It's a warring world." Sam pulled the Luger from under his bomber jacket and checked the clip.

"I still think I'm cheating you out of five hundred bucks," Foley grinned. "You don't really need me at all, do you, Sam?"

"Son, there's one thing you'll have to learn about being a private eye."

"What?"

"There are some one-man jobs and some two-man jobs. This is a two-man job. And thar she blows." Sam pointed toward the sky in the east.

Another plane. But this one wasn't out of the past. It was very much part of the present. A spanking new Lear jet catching the sun's shiny reflection and sparkling against the brazen sky. It was piloted by somebody who knew his stuff. It wasn't easy to land that machine on this poor excuse for a field, but that son of a pelican did it.

"Well, pardner," Sam motioned, "let's go meet the stage-coach." He started walking and Foley followed.

The door of the Lear opened and out came three men. The sky jockey and two other fellows you'd want to have for friends. Big and with the look in their eyes that said Green Berets. One of the men carried a suitcase, a heavy suitcase constructed of some kind of strong metal. They were all toting artillery. The pilot looked at Sam and almost smiled. "You'd be the one."

"How did you guess?" Sam twitched.

"That face." The pilot pointed. "There's only one face like that."

"No," Sam twitched again. "There's been two already."

"Yeah, right," the pilot responded and pulled a piece of foreign currency out of his pocket. "If you've got something for us, we've got something for you."

Sam took out his half of the bisected bill and handed it to the pilot. The pilot put them together. "That's a good fit," he smiled.

"Yeah," said Sam, "just like in the movies." He glanced at the two men, then back to the pilot. "Say, what do you feed those two, cement?"

The man with the heavy case put it on the ground.

"I was only kidding, pal," said Sam.

"Sure, pal," said pal. "I hope you can carry this."

"Oh, he does the carrying," Sam pointed toward Tim. "I'm just vice-president in charge of potatoes."

The pilot pointed to the P-47 Thunderbolt. "You going up in that relic?"

"Yeah, the latest thing in space travel."

"Well, good luck," said the pilot. As he and the two men headed into the Lear, he added, "And keep 'em flying."

"Yeah," said Sam, "and buy bonds."

They watched the Lear take off, then Tim turned to Sam and asked, "What now?"

"I'll tell you what now," Sam twitched. "Now we got company."

A black-and-white police car was on the road and coming toward them fast. The red lights flashed, but sans siren.

"Sam, you think we're breaking the law?"

"That depends on what's in this suitcase; or it could be something else."

"Such as?"

"Such as Bumbera checking on his little chick. He warned me not to give you any bad advice."

The car pulled up close and slammed to a stop in a swarf of dust. The uniformed police jumped out with their hands full of guns and nightsticks.

"Take it easy, boys," Sam suggested.

"Shut up!" one of the cops commanded.

It all happened faster than you can tell it. But whoever choreographed the caper had it timed to the titmouse. Sam remembered seeing the helicopter as Tim got clubbed across the head, then Sam took one right above the ear. He remembered one other thing. All three cops were dark complexioned. Then the black pit opened up and he dove in. Of course, it had no bottom.

Actually, the leather aviator's helmet must have absorbed much of the blow, because Sam was stirring even before the three counterfeit cops with the suitcase got to the helicopter that had landed less than forty yards away. The helicopter started to take off and the people inside had to have seen Sam getting to his knees, because they let fly with a barrage of bullets that whistled all around Sam and the still unconscious Tim Foley. The helicopter people were soon out of range and safely into the sky—so they thought.

Sam was mad enough to bite the leg off a lion. He shook the hell out of Foley. He slapped Tim across the kisser a couple of times until Tim came to and grunted, "Hey, Sam, cut it out. What the hell are you doing?"

"Come on, son. We got to get going."

"Where to?" Tim wobbled to his feet with Sam's help.

"Up!" Sam jerked his thumb toward the sun. "We're going *up!*" He shoved Tim toward the Thunderbolt. "Get in! We're going up and get those bastards!"

They both climbed into the cockpit, Sam into the front seat, Tim the back. As Sam slammed the cover shut, he hollered, "Put on the ears so we can talk!"

He hit the starter. The Thunderbolt's two-thousand-horsepower Pratt and Whitney engine kicked over. The propeller rotated, slowly at first, then faster into an invisible circle and Beautiful Darlin' Betsy bumped and buffeted, then skitted and skimmed along the pocked and pitted strip, and finally flew into the wild blue yonder with one hell of a roar.

The wheels folded under the wings and Betsy banked to the right and toward the speck in the sky that held the heavy

suitcase and those thieving sonsabitches who'd be sorry they
ever slugged Sam Marlow.

"Can you hear me, Tim?"

"Yeah, yeah, Sam, I hear you. Christ Almighty, I've got a
headache! It's killing me!"

"Hold onto your belly button, buddy boy. We're going to
nail those bandits!" Sam sliced gracefully to the side, reversed
bank and aimed his nose at the enemy.

"Sam, Sam. Lissen to me! I gotta get outta here! I got no
stomach for this. I get air sick in an elevator!"

"You're sittin' pretty, son. Just relax and enjoy the view."
Sam turned the P-47 on its side, then upside down, righted it,
and gunned full throttle toward the helicopter that loomed
larger just above the horizon.

That's when the helicopter pilot and passengers realized
that they weren't safely away—that they should've killed the
two men on the airfield when they had the chance. But the
odds were still with them. The latest, liveliest, most agile
helicopter against a pristine plane that had no more place in
today's sky than a lead bathtub.

But Sam had other ideas. Beautiful Darlin' Betsy was all he
believed in. A piece of the last glorious war that would ever be
fought on earth or heaven. Of Pearl Harbor. Mindanao.
Guadalcanal. Midway. Of John Wayne in *Flying Tigers*.

Once again Sam was one of Hell's Angels; he was Errol
Flynn in *Dive Bomber*. Dana Andrews coming in on *A Wing
and a Prayer*. Tyrone Power in *A Yank in the RAF*. John
Garfield in *Air Force*. Gregory Peck in *Twelve O'Clock High*.
Clark Gable in *Command Decision*.

Yeah, once again it was like the old days—with clients,
cases, danger, dough—flags and causes and dames worth
fighting for. He would touch the face of God and fill the
heavens full of lead. He pressed his finger on the trigger and
the P-47's guns sent a stream of lead through the sky toward
the helicopter.

They were now over the City Hall of Los Angeles, near the
freeway interchange. There had never been a show like this

and the people on the sidewalks, in their cars and trucks on
the streets and freeways, soon were aware that something
beautifully bizarre even for Los Angeles was taking place that
extant moment.

The helicopter was a four-passenger Jet Ranger—light, fast,
and maneuverable. Sam's Thunderbolt was heavier than most
fighters. In the glory days they called her "the flying milk
bottle." She was used to escort bombers. Heavy though she
was, the Thunderbolt maneuvered well and could outdive
Japan's and Germany's best.

First the helicopter tried to outrun Sam but found out that
was hopeless. The Jet Ranger's top speed was 150. Beautiful
Darlin' Betsy cruised at 250 and dove a lot faster. The
helicopter pilot then decided to outmaneuver Sam and get to
somewhere the plane couldn't land. Sam knew that game
plan, so it was up to him to shoot the helicopter down before
that happened.

Sam made another pass, pressed the trigger and peppered
the sky with metal, but missed the helicopter again. The
helicopter shot off toward the north. Sam did an Immelmann
and caught up to the bird right over Dodger Stadium. Forty
thousand fans stood on their feet, but not because Steve
Garvey hit a home run. Even the players quit playing—there
were two men on base—and looked upward as the Thunderbolt leaped toward the copter with guns blazing.

In desperation, the men inside the bird poked their guns out
and fired at the flying anachronism. Sam dove straight at them
and came within an ace of colliding. He cut close enough for
them to count the stitches on his wings.

The bird twisted, twirled and turned, and Sam twisted,
twirled and turned right with it in a maze of maneuvers. The
copter pilot tried every trick he knew but couldn't get shed of
Sam. Sam twitched and grinned and let go another spurt. Tim
paled, grimaced and groaned and tried not to let go of
everything in his stomach.

They were over Bronson Canyon now and heading for the
valley. Sam couldn't allow the bird to land in one of the

narrow canyons. He wanted to force it out into an open area. Out toward Lancaster or Palmdale if he could.

Word of the dogfight was all over town. In fact it was the talk of the town. All the radio and television stations were interrupting their regular programs to tell about the only dogfight ever to take place above the City of the Angels.

Sam spotted Bruce Wayne in his KFI "eye in the sky" airwatch helicopter. Brucey was keeping a discreet distance while telling his radio listeners about the aerial goings on.

Sam came in at six o'clock and closed the gap. He pressed his finger on the trigger and the Thunderbolt chattered a castanet of death, belching blue fire at the helicopter. The Thunderbolt's eight guns kept thundering and the recoil shook Beautiful Darlin' Betsy's every bolt. Her motor sobbed and wailed—and so did Tim Foley.

Betsy's wing went up and her nose went down. Sam's next burst tore some of the feathers off the bird, but not enough to affect its flying.

"I'll get 'em next time, Tim. Just watch!"

"You're gonna get us all killed!" Tim yelled.

"Nobody lives forever," Sam grinned.

"What the hell do you suppose is in that suitcase?"

"That's what we're gonna find out."

"Whatever it is, it can't be worth it."

"I ain't had so much fun in years. Come on, Betsy, bite 'em in the ass!"

Betsy did.

The next burst caught them where it hurt. The copter started to smoke and lose altitude. The pilot struggled for control. He had no choice but to set down on an open field. The space looked too small for Sam to land. But Sam had other ideas.

Before the burning bird bounced to the ground, Sam was coming in.

"Sam," Tim yelled. "You can't land here."

"Who says I can't?"

"The field's too short. You can't make it!"

"Made to order."

"Your wheels aren't down!"

"That's why we're gonna make it!"

The men were getting out of the burning bird as Sam set Betsy down on her belly with a final burst of her eight guns that cut two of the counterfeit cops to pieces. Betsy plowed a fifty-foot furrow across the field kicking up a wake of dirt and debris. It seemed she was going to crash into the bird, but fifteen feet short she buffeted to a stop—almost did a cartwheel but didn't.

Sam threw back the cockpit cover, had the Luger in hand and sprang onto the wing and ground with Tim right behind him. The two survivors near the fiery bird were blasting away with everything they had.

One of the survivors ducked for cover and still had hold of the heavy suitcase. Between shots and ducks, Sam recognized him. "I'll be damned," he said. It was Hobby Lobby.

"What's the matter?" Tim hollered from his cover between the gunfire. "You know him?"

"Yeah. It's Judas."

Tim's next shot took the counterfeit cop and Sam's next shot hit Hobby Lobby. Lobby sprawled to the ground still gripping his gun. Tim rose and started toward the two fallen men.

"Tim!" Sam screamed, but too late. The gun in Hobby Lobby's hand went off twice and Tim took two in the belly, then fell to the ground.

Four helicopters from the Sheriff's Aero Bureau were landing on the field.

But not before Sam ran over and emptied the Luger into Judas.

CHAPTER
22

THERE's something about the smell of a hospital that is unhealthy. The undertakers use flowers to cover up the odor of death. The hospitals use antiseptics to cover up the odor of sickness. But somehow the real smell comes through in both places.

Tim Foley had been on the operating table for two hours. Sam was in a private waiting room. So were Bumbera and Hacksaw. So was the heavy suitcase. Sam still wore his bomber jacket, but it was unzipped now as he lit his tenth cigarette. Hacksaw poured out two more cups of coffee, handed one cup to Bumbera and took a gulp from the other. Nobody in that waiting room had spoken a word during those two hours.

The silence was broken five minutes later when a nurse who Bumbera recognized passed by the doorway. "Excuse me, nurse," he asked, "is there any word from the operating room? Is he still in there? Can you tell us anything at all?"

"No, there's no word. Yes, he's still in there, and I'm sorry I can't tell you anything more than that."

"OK, thanks."

"Lieutenant."

"Yeah."

"The doctor knows you're waiting. He'll stop by as soon as the operation is over."

"Yeah, OK. Thanks again." Bumbera crumpled the Styrofoam coffee cup and let it drop into a wastebasket.

That's when Shah Tabriz showed up with a new brace of bodyguards. The Shah stepped into the room. The bodyguards waited in the hall. "Mr. Marlow. I arrived as soon as I could."

"Yeah. This is Lieutenant Bumbera and Sergeant Hacksaw. They were with me when I called."

"How do you do, gentlemen? I am very sorry."

"What have you got to be sorry about?" Bumbera pointed to the suitcase. "Nothing happened to that. All those uncut diamonds. How much are they worth?"

"Five million dollars," the Shah shrugged.

"Well, they're not worth as much as that kid's life in there. Not to me."

"Nor to me, Lieutenant. I have instructed the hospital to spare nothing, nothing to save that boy's life."

"We don't need you and your oily money. We'll take care of him!" Bumbera flared. "You hear?! We take care of our own!"

For once it was Hacksaw who restrained Bumbera. "Bummy," he said quietly but with strength.

Bumbera nodded and pointed to the case again. "There it is. Take your five million and get the hell out of here. I wish there was something illegal in what you did, but there wasn't. I checked on that, you can bet. Or I'd have seen you in jail no matter how much money you've got. So take it and get the hell out of here."

Shah Tabriz picked up the suitcase and started out. He paused near Sam and whispered, "Mr. Marlow, I deeply appreciate what you've done. Abu Lobi was a traitor and deserved to die. About your compensation—"

"Give it to the kid," said Sam.

Shah Tabriz nodded, handed the suitcase to one of the bodyguards at the door, and left.

"Hack, get outta here a minute, will you?" Bumbera asked. Hacksaw nodded and walked through the doorway.

"And close that door, huh?"

Hacksaw did.

Bumbera walked close to Sam, threw a right cross that caught Sam on the jaw and knocked him against the wall. A trickle of blood leaked from Sam's mouth.

"I'm gonna tell you somethin', Mister. If Tim Foley doesn't make it, there won't be any secret of Sam Marlow because there won't be a Sam Marlow. First I'll tell the world all about you." Bumbera pulled the .38 police special from his hip and pointed it at Sam. "Then I'm gonna give you two in the belly just like he got. And I'll make mine count. You got that?"

"Yeah, I got it."

"Then you get the hell outta here, too. I don't want to see that face of yours again." Bumbera's gun hand trembled. "Go on, beat it or I'll give it to you right now."

Sam opened the door and walked past Hacksaw and down the hallway. The doctor was just coming around the corner. "Oh, there you are, Mr. Marlow. I was on my way to see you. Well, it was touch and go for a while there, but your friend's going to be all right."

"Thanks, doctor," Sam started off.

"Mr. Marlow."

"Yeah?"

The doctor pointed to Sam's face. "You're bleeding."

"Not anymore."

Sam went to his apartment, showered, changed his clothes, then like a homing pigeon he headed back to his office. The damage to both doors had been repaired and the frosted window relettered. The office was dark and quiet. It was empty. Sam felt empty. He wanted to be where it was dark and quiet.

He sat in the shadows and went up against the whiskey

bottle. He downed four or five doubles of Wild Turkey. It got to him. Not just the whiskey. Everything that had happened the last few days. He lay down on the leather couch and went over it from the beginning. The plot and the people.

It started with Sandra Kent up in the desert. Then the thirty-foot Cadillac with the big bang. Shah Tabriz and Hobby Lobby. The desert rats blazing away and Sam sending them to a fiery hell with the sawed-off shotgun and the Armalite.

Then back to the heavenly hills of Hollywood and Mellon, head of Pantheon Pictures, and Fresh Fisher, the professional sycophant. Sabu—there was more to him than met the eye. Somehow Sam felt Sabu was deeper than he was tall. And the first fatality—Flint. Flint had his followers, too. Wentworth and Plain Jane Lane. Who knew what went on under that shroud she showed to the world? The meeting with Mona Hyland, all done in fuchsia, in Flint's office. First impressions *can* be deceiving.

Steve Steilburg and his squad of would-be successors to the old cinema. Will Catcher with his narrow green eyes, knife-blade mouth and open ears. Stunts and shows. Popcorn and poison. Observatory kisses and Josephine Bramer. Flint's funeral with flourish and fireworks. Tim Foley, a sweet kid and a sucker for a right. A Palm Springs orgy, Arabian Nights style, with a lot of familiar faces and a swimming pool soaked with assassin's blood.

Back to L.A.—Holmby Hills and the black-bikinied widow with her hawklike hazel eyes and her lover boy, Leonard.

Sam didn't want to think about Mona and the car crash off the cliff. But he did. A broken body. A bloody turban and murder. Of "now and then" and what might have been. Lucretia Borgia, Sandra Kent, and lamb chops with red wine and no sex this time. Leonard, his stocking mask and his muggers botching the business in Sam's sanctorum. The widow Flint kissing off lover boy Leonard. A five-million-dollar sky heist that didn't come off thanks to Beautiful Darlin' Betsy. And young Tim Foley taking a fall full of Hobby Lobby's lead but passing by St. Peter's pearly gates, and Sam Marlow with a lumpy lip and a whiskey head.

That just about brought everything up to date in Kansas City. But not in Hollywood. Sam still didn't know who killed Flint and Mona—or why—or whether the Arab business had anything to do with show business. Sam fell asleep trying to figure it out. He didn't know how long he slept; it could have been five minutes or fifty before the phone rang.

"Sam Marlow."

"I've been trying to reach you for hours." It was Josephine Bramer.

"Yeah, well I been hopping around here and there. You know how it is some days."

"Sam, quit clowning. Everybody in town has been talking about that stunt you pulled today. Are you all right? Did you get hurt?

Sam rubbed his lip. "Well, once I forgot to duck and I could use a soft shoulder to lean on, but other than that I'm shipshape."

"You mean that?"

"About being shipshape?"

"No, about wanting a soft shoulder."

That surprised Sam some. "Yeah, sure; you got any suggestions?"

"I've got a couple of soft shoulders—and a couple of steaks. How does that sound?"

"Sounds swell, but could we reverse the order? I just realized how hungry I am."

"The address is 608 Bentley. Just off Wilshire. It's a duplex. I'm on the bottom."

"You're wide open for a dirty crack," Sam said, "but I won't make it. See you in half an hour, sweetheart."

It seemed that there was something about Sam that brought out the cooking instincts in women lately. First Sandra and her lamb chops, now Josephine and her steaks. There wasn't any sex with Sandra's lamb chops. Sam wondered about Josephine and her steaks. Well, he wouldn't have long to wonder.

Sam took time out to stop at Bogie's Liquor Store on the

corner of Melrose and Vine to buy a bottle of Beaujolais. A couple of lady senior citizens saw him coming out of Bogie's wearing that trench coat and carrying a sack. They stared at him, then at each other, then back to him.

"I thought you were dead," one of the blue-haired ladies remarked.

"I am," Sam twitched and held up the sack, "but I still get thirsty." He tipped his grey felt hat and walked toward the Plymouth. "Goodnight, ladies."

He got into the grey coupe and started south toward Wilshire. Some spell it *Bogie* and some spell it *Bogey*. Sam preferred *Bogey*. No special reason, but then he didn't have to have one. A man or a woman can spell his or her own name any way he or she prefers. So that closed the book on that one.

Sam got to Josephine's when he said he would.

"I hope you don't mind," Josephine smiled. "I didn't get dressed."

"It's your party." Sam handed her the wine and took off the coat.

Josephine wore a kind of clinging housedress held together only by a sash and it didn't look to Sam as if she wore anything underneath. All those contours she concealed by day were revealed by night—at least this night. Her copper-colored hair fell long and soft across a set of round but widespread shoulders, then tumbled loose toward what turned out to be an ample, almost pendulous, pair of lightly harnessed breasts. Her waist was narrow enough and her hips filled out just right down to long strong legs that would've done pride to Juliet Prowse.

The steaks were done to pink perfection and Josephine backed them up with a baked potato, sour cream and chives, plus a neatly tossed green salad. The red wine went down warm and friendly.

Mostly she asked about what had happened that day and if the police officer was going to survive. Sam told her the story with more than a modicum of modesty, said Foley was going to make it, and asked her about the connection between Shah Tabriz and Mellon. She said she didn't know of any connection except that Mellon told her he had been invited to a party in Palm Springs. His wife was out of town so he asked Josephine if she felt like spending the weekend in the sun.

"You spend every weekend with him when Mrs. Mellon is out of town?"

"That," she smiled, "is none of your business."

"You're right."

After that, Josephine suggested they move to the couch for an after-dinner drink. Sam moved to the couch. She moved to the sideboard.

"You like Grand Marnier?" she asked.

"I do, but it reminds me of somebody. I'll take anything else."

"Courvoisier?"

"Swell."

She brought the bottle and two snifters on a tray and set the tray on the coffee table. Sam poured two stiff ones to start. They clinked snifters.

"What'll we drink to, Sam?"

"To movies—and murder."

"*Just* to movies," she sipped.

He swallowed.

"Who was she, Sam?"

"Who was she who?" Sam twitched.

"You know who I mean. The Grand Marnier lady. Was she beautiful?"

"She was beautiful—when she was alive. She lived fast and died young."

"Did you love her?"

"I don't know."

"But she loved you."

"She needed me—for a while." Sam took another swallow. "Let's talk about movies."

"All right, Sam. You must be the biggest movie buff in town."

"Maybe I used to be. But they've changed."

"How?"

Sam shrugged and poured another dose into his glass. "First

2

they made them silent. Then they made them talk. Then they made them in color. Then they made them wide screen. Now they make them dirty, mostly."

"Not Pantheon Pictures."

"No, I've got to admit that even though Sandra Kent doesn't go around playing Queen Victoria, Mellon's still got pretty good taste. That's probably why he's losing money."

"You know, Sam, I was brought up in this business. My father lived it day and night. But it's gotten to the point where I want to get out."

"Why?"

"A lot of reasons. One, I'm sick and tired of seeing incompetent men get important jobs just because they're men."

"Ah! So besides being beautiful you want to be a producer, or a vice-president, maybe."

"Why not?"

"Yeah, why not? Sherry Lansing's beautiful and she got to be president over at Twentieth Century-Fox."

"She's the exception, but I think it's wonderful, don't you?"

"Oh, I don't think it's so wonderful. She probably took the job away from some poor incompetent *man*."

"Sam, quit kidding."

"OK, I will. Say, what's wrong with the husband-and-kids business these days?"

"Are you proposing?"

"No, just asking."

Sam let some more brandy leak into his belly. Either Josephine was getting to him or the brandy was. Or both. He began to get that glow.

"I had the husband business once," she purred and moved nearer. There wasn't that much distance between them to begin with.

"You did?"

"That was a long time ago."

There are times that you know a woman wants sex. Not love but sex. Her every look. Her every move. You can almost smell it on her.

"He was lousy in bed," Josephine whispered. "But I was

young and too dumb to know it." She kissed Sam with everything she had. Her soft warm mouth opened up and pressed right where Bumbera had smacked him. It hurt some, but Sam pressed back for a long, long time with everything he had.

"You've wised up some since then," Sam finally remarked.

"You'd be surprised how much."

That was an invitation if he'd ever heard one. "Maybe I would—and maybe I wouldn't."

As she rose, the sash came loose and the flimsy housedress fell open. She rolled a pair of naturals. The invitation became a warrant and Sam knew he was under arrest.

"Let's find out," she said and put her long, strong, lovely fingers around his hand.

"I thought I was supposed to do the seducing," said Sam.

"You did." She led him to the bedroom.

A night light was already on and the covers were already down. She let her dress ease off, stood naked a moment in the semidarkness just long enough for Sam to lick his lips and appreciate his good fortune. She was built along the lines of Anita Ekberg during Ekberg's ripest years. And Josephine Bramer was ripe right now. She glided onto the bed and waited with parted lips.

Sandra Kent was a sex kitten. Josephine Bramer was a cat. A tiger. A tiger, tiger, burning bright in the darkness of the night. A hungry tiger. A sweet savage. Gleaming and groaning. Giving and getting. With a seething tenderness and a raging tranquility. She was pleasure and pain. Softness and strain. Fang and fur. Fire and ice. She was flesh and claw. Fluff and fury. With bite and blood. With body and soul. She was more woman than Sam Marlow had ever met. She was all woman—and Amen!

That night Sam's cup ranneth over.

CHAPTER
23

THE next morning every blood vessel and bone in Sam's body ached. But it was worth it. He managed to get to the office by ten. It wasn't easy, but he made it up the stairs.

Duchess was in one of her ebullient moods. She held up a copy of the *L.A. Times* carrying a front page picture of yesterday's dogfight between the Jet Ranger helicopter and Beautiful Darlin' Betsy—with a banner proclaiming, "BO-GART LOOK-ALIKE IN DARING DOGFIGHT OVER L.A.—Sam Marlow thwarts 5 million dollar sky heist. Four killed. Police officer critically wounded."

"Oooh, Sam, isn't it sensational? Have you got any more monies for me to Crocker?"

"Not today."

"Hey, Sam, weren't you in great danger of getting killed to death up there?"

Sam went straight to his desk and took a turn at the Wild Turkey. Duchess followed him, still waving the newspaper

and her hips. "There've been a trillion calls. And a man
named Roger Dorman called and wants to do a movie about
your life."

"Corman," Sam said. "If he calls again, tell him I saw
Attack of the Crab Monsters. Thought it was swell."

"Sam, are you trying to be funny?"

"I don't think so."

"Neither do I. Did you have any breakfast?" she asked.

"Yeah, I had a live barracuda."

"Would you like a banana?"

"No, thanks. Say, Duchess, how are you and the tuba player
getting along?"

"We split."

"Why?"

"He's in love with the singer in the band."

"She can't be as pretty as you."

"She's a *he*!"

"You mean—?"

"Herbie's, as they say, gone gay." She wiggled all over.

"That's what they say, all right."

"But I don't see what's so gay about it," she observed.

"Neither do I."

Duchess leaned down and picked up a paper clip from the
floor. She still wasn't wearing any underwear. "Do you want
me to get Mr. Colman on the phone?"

"Who?"

"Mr. Colman, the man with the crab monsters."

"No, thanks, Duchess." Sam took another breakfast hit from
the office bottle.

"Sam, I have to tell you something for your own beneficiary."

"Yeah, who is it?"

"Huh?"

"I mean, what is it?"

"It's about whiskey."

"Whiskey, my precious, is the medicine of despair."

"What I mean is, Sam, you're getting to be a boozer."

"Yeah, I've turned drinking into a science. Bourbon in the

morning. Then beer. Gin in the evening and scotch after supper, with a bang or two of brandy on special occasions." He got up and started to walk.

"Where are you going?" Duchess asked.

"To the toilet."

"Oh! *Excuse me!*" Duchess sashayed back toward her desk. Sam found that shutting the toilet door invariably brought their conversations to a close.

He spent the rest of the morning on loose ends. He called the aviation outfit that had restored Beautiful Darlin' Betsy a few months ago. Don Deadpath, the man in charge, had already read about the dogfight. Deadpath said he'd go out there with a crew and haul Betsy into the shop, then call Sam with an estimate if the ship could be saved.

"Don, I don't care what it costs," said Sam. "Save her."

"Sure," said Deadpath. "All it takes is money."

Then Sam dialed the hospital to get a report on Tim Foley and talk to him, if possible. Foley's condition was improving, but, no, it was not possible to talk to him. Not today; maybe tomorrow.

Sam buzzed Duchess on the intercom.

"Sam Marlow's office."

"Duchess, this *is* Sam. You're on the intercom."

"Well, anyhoo," Duchess giggled, "what can I do for you now that I have you?"

"Want me to take you to lunch? Spaghetti over at Andre's?"

"That's very nice of you, Sam, but I sneaked across to Baskin Robbins and got some ice cream. It's in the bowl right now with the bananas."

"What ever happened to the cold turkey?"

"What cold turkey?"

Sam put on his hat and walked through Duchess's office. "I'm going to Pantheon Pictures."

"I thought you were going to spaghetti."

"First, I'm going to spaghetti. Second, I'm going to Pantheon Pictures. Enjoy your lunch."

"Thanks, I will." Duchess scooped out another spoonful of ice cream and banana.

As Sam went out the door into the hallway, Nicky came out of the Ladies' Gymnasium carrying two trash cans and two black eyes.

"Say there, Nicky, what happened to your other eye?"

"What do you think happened!" Mother bellowed as she loomed from behind.

"Well, well," said Sam. "It does seem that 'hell hath no fury.' "

"What the hell is that supposed to mean?" Mother challenged.

Sam just shrugged and walked down the stairs, whistling the song that Cary Grant always whistled in *Mr. Lucky*, "Something to Remember You By."

He let the gazers gaze at Andre's while he downed a plate of shrimp creole with spaghetti and garlic bread along with two bottles of cold Budweiser beer. Forty minutes later he was at Pantheon Pictures. Sam wasn't exactly sure why he had come or what he was going to do, but he sure as hell wouldn't solve the murders of Flint and Mona by sitting in his office and swapping non sequiturs with Duchess.

Since he was here he had to start somewhere. Sam figured Mellon's office was as good a place as any. Besides, that would give him his first daylight look at Josephine since they had jungled up together last night. Sam had left the duplex before dawn. He just couldn't take another go-around on Josephine and her sex machine.

But the way she said, "Well, hello, Sam. How are you this afternoon?" sort of got Sam's juices stirring again. Josephine was the picture of poise, elegance, and cool efficiency, but Sam knew that was just the outer layer. Under that veneer beat the heart of a wildcat. He wished now that he had taken one more ride on that madding merry-go-round. Well, there'd be other times and other rides.

"Did you wish to see Mr. Mellon?"

"That's not what I wish, but I'll settle for it."

She pressed the intercom. "Mr. Mellon, can you see Mr. Marlow?"

"Tell him to come in," decreed Mellon's unmistakable voice.

"Yes, sir." She nodded to Sam. "Sam, I'm glad I caught you in last night."

"You do a great steak."

"I thought you'd be a meat-and-potatoes man. We'll have to do it again."

"Just ask."

"I will."

"If you don't, *I* will. And next time, I'll make the dinner."

"You cook, too?"

"You better believe it."

"After last night, I believe you could do anything."

As she said it, Sabu came in with the mail and Josephine became all business again. "Go right in, Mr. Marlow."

Ah, yes, it was back to Mr. Marlow again. Mr. Marlow went right in.

"Marlow!" Mellon said. "It's a miracle you're still in one piece."

"It sure is," Fresh Fisher chimed.

"Don't you two ever agree on anything?" Sam cracked.

"I've got to tell you, Sam. The Shah is mighty appreciative. I'd say he's going to make you a rich man."

"I'm already rich—and beautiful. What's between you and the Arab? You buy your gas from him or what?"

"Doesn't everybody?" Mellon retorted. "Have you turned up anything on the murders?"

"No, but I'm questioning a lot of suspects."

"Like who? Flint's wife?"

"Yeah, and your secretary."

"Josephine?!" Mellon laughed. "You're wasting your time with her."

"I want to do a thorough job for you, Mr. Mellon. This is my chance to make good."

"I swear I never know when you're serious."

"Neither do I. About Charlie Wentworth—"

"What about him? You don't suspect that poor old soul too, do you?"

"I'd just like to know what your plans are for his future—what future he has left."

"Why?"

"Because I worry about him."

"Well, I hadn't thought about it," Mellon shrugged. "Now that Flint's gone, I suppose we'll have to let him go."

"I wish you wouldn't do that."

"Why?"

"I told you. I worry about him. He reminds me of my favorite uncle. And when I worry I can't keep my mind on the detective business. I wish you'd let him stay on, say in the research department, until he's ready to retire. That way I wouldn't worry about him and I'd keep my mind on the detective business and you and I would both feel better all the way around. How about it, Mr. Mellon?"

"Marlow, you're a marshmallow. OK, he stays."

"Good, and Fresh here can plant a nice story in the trades about Charlie's promotion—just to make it official."

"You don't trust me, huh? All right, Fresh, do it."

Of course, Fresh Fisher nodded.

"They're supposed to open up Flint's will sometime today," Mellon added. "That might give us a clue or a motive."

"It might," Sam nodded.

"Have you talked to that lieutenant friend of yours—what's his name?"

"Bumbera," Sam rubbed his lip with his thumb. "No, not today. But we got together yesterday."

"Well, find out what you can from him. He seems to be avoiding me."

"You're lucky," said Sam, soothing his lip again. "Well, I'd better get back to the bushes."

There were two agents from ICM waiting in Mellon's outer office, so Sam just tipped his hat to Ms. Bramer and went silently on his way.

Will Catcher had a pigeon and was taking him for a flock of fivers when he spotted Sam and peeled off toward him. "Hey, Marlow, wait up a minute!"

Sam did.

"I want to tell you I saw some of what you did in that plane of yours yesterday. Holy Jesus Christ!"

"Yeah," said Sam. "It's a sin to send us boys up in those crates like that."

"Any time you want to join the Stuntmen's Association, I'll sponsor you, my friend. That's all the guys've been talking about all day. Anything left of that Thunderbolt?"

"Sure, we fly the dawn patrol tomorrow. Say, have you seen Wentworth around any place?"

"Yeah, matter of fact, I did. He went into Flint's old office just a couple of minutes ago. You know how much we'd charge for that gag you did yesterday?"

"Is Calamity Jane still in there?"

"Search me."

"Later," said Sam and peeled off himself.

"Well, well, well," said Sam as he walked into the bungalow where Wentworth and Jane Lane were still working. "You two kids are getting to be an item on campus."

"Mr. Marlow," Wentworth crinkled a smile and pointed toward the sky, "You certainly are a man of action."

"And luck. But Jane here looks a little disappointed. Were you hoping for one more casualty in that little war?"

"I wasn't hoping for anything, Mr. Marlow."

"Uh-huh. Say, you didn't by any chance type up Flint's will, did you?"

"No, I didn't. I don't know anything about it."

"I see. Well, Charlie, they're going to open it up sometime today. What do you think?"

"I don't follow you, Mr. Marlow."

"He had a lot of money. Maybe millions. Who do you think he left it to?"

"I wouldn't have any idea. He never mentioned such matters."

"All business between you two, huh? You think he might've left something to you, Charlie?"

"I hardly think so."

"Well, we'll soon find out. So long. And good luck, Charlie."

"Thank you, Mr. Marlow."

Sam left without a parting shot for or from Plain Jane Lane.

It was inevitable that he bump into Sabu again. That little guy was all over the lot.

"Hello, Mr. Marlow."

"That's twice in a row I've seen you now without Sandra Kent. Are you two trying it apartsville?"

"Apartsville? I don't understand."

"That's because you don't read Hank Grant's column in *The Hollywood Reporter*."

"Did you want to know where Sandra Kent is working?"

"No, I think I'll skip Boardwalk," said Sam, "and go directly to jail."

Sam was spinning his mental wheels. He didn't need another scene with Sandra. He suddenly felt he ought to get away from Pantheon Pictures. From Sandra, Sabu, Mellon, Fresh Fisher, Bramer, Wentworth, Plain Jane Lane, Will Catcher—the whole bunch of them. He decided he'd leave all that behind and go do something different. He'd go to the movies. Catch a double feature at a matinee.

The Encore Theatre on Melrose was reprising a couple of Bogart classics. Actually, one was a classic—*High Sierra*; the other was a quasiclassic—*Key Largo*. Sam had seen them both dozens of times; he had lost count. But he plunked down his two bucks, picked up a pair of popcorn cartons for another singleton and sat in an aisle seat up toward the front.

High Sierra was made and came on first. Bogart played Roy Earle and got the part because Paul Muni turned it down. Mr. Muni didn't want to die in the end. It's been rumored that George Raft, who was a bigger star than Bogart, also turned down the part, but Raft always denied it.

Raft did turn down *The Maltese Falcon* and doesn't deny that. His agents advised him that there was a clause in his contract stipulating he didn't have to star in a remake. *The Maltese Falcon* had already been filmed twice. Once in 1931 with Ricardo Cortez as Sam Spade and again under the title *Satan Met a Lady* with Warren William as the detective and Bette Davis in the female lead. The agents also advised Raft that Huston had never directed a feature before and all the women in the movie—Mary Astor, Gladys George, and Lee Patrick—were too old and nobody would come to see the picture. Bad advice.

High Sierra was about an old-time gangster who had been sprung by Big Mac, played by Donald MacBride, to pull off a heist in Las Vegas. The gangster, Roy Earle, was hard as nails but had a soft spot for a crippled girl and a dog, a mutt named Pard. Earle was a crook, but he wasn't crooked. Not like a cop named Jake Krammer, played, naturally, by Barton MacLane. Earle also had a moll named Marie, played by Ida Lupino, who got star billing over Bogart. That was the last time Bogey ever got billed second. Bogart's dialogue included the immortal line: "I hope you're not trying to pull a fast one—'cause I don't like fast ones." The picture was raw, rugged, violent, sensitive, and sentimental. It also featured a hotel clerk named Louis Mendoza who was played by a Hungarian named Cornel Wilde who went on to bigger and better parts for a long, long time.

Bogart did die in the end and also went on to bigger and better parts. The dog and Ida lived, but not so happily ever after. It was a damn good picture written by John Huston and W. R. Burnett. Burnett also wrote the novel *Little Caesar*. *High Sierra* was remade as a Western in 1949 with Randolph Scott and Virginia Mayo and called *Colorado Territory*. Not bad. It was remade again in 1957 as a gangster picture with Jack Palance and Shelley Winters and called *I Died a Thousand Times*. Not good.

Ironically, the lead in *Key Largo* had been played on broadway by the same fellow who turned down *High Sierra*, Paul Muni.

Key Largo was suspiciously similar in plot and people to *The Petrified Forest*. A gangster and his boys take over a small isolated hotel and hold hostages until they make a deal and hotfoot it away. In this case they hot-boated it away—or tried. Bogart and Edward G. Robinson reversed the roles they had played plenty of times in the thirties. This time Bogart was the hero and Robinson the Mantee-like gangster with Mafioso overtones. And this time Bogey blasted Robinson full of lead instead of vice versa. Good cast—Lauren Bacall, Lionel Barry-more, Claire Trevor as the moll this time, who won an Academy Award mostly due to the lousy way she sang "Moanin' Low." Also Thomas Gomez, Marc Lawrence, and Harry Lewis, who now owns all the Hamburger Hamlets and is a millionaire.

The picture missed the mark a little, but Bogart and Bacall didn't. Sam had timed it just right. As the Max Steiner music swelled and Bogey steered the "Santana" back to Key Largo and Bacall, Sam ran out of popcorn. He called Duchess from the theatre lobby, told her to go home and did the same.

Sam poured himself a tumbler of Gordon's gin over plenty of ice, then touched it with tonic. He heated up the last of the weekend chili, sat in front of the Quasar with the hot chili and a cold Bud, watched Walter Cronkite and went to bed at eight o'clock—alone.

He figured he'd bag z's for a solid ten hours. That's right—once again he figured wrong.

CHAPTER
24

Sᴀɴᴅʀᴀ lay naked in one bed in one room. Josephine Bramer lay naked in another bed in another room. Sam ran back and forth every few minutes, sweating passion from every pore. From sex goddess to wildcat. It was just too much to ask from one man. As he was bucking wildly on the madding merry-go-round and running out of bucks, he was saved by the bell. He snapped on the light and looked at the clock. Midnight. Sam answered the phone and shook off the dream—both of them.

"Sam Marlow."

"Mr. Marlow, sorry to disturb you."

"I get two hundred a day plus expenses."

"This is Ahmed Ishibu."

"I know who it is. My midnight rates are even higher."

"Mr. Marlow, I'm with Sandra Kent."

"Congratulations."

"Not really with her, but in the same place."

"You want me to come beard for you?"

144

"I don't understand that, but I'm afraid there's going to be trouble. She's been drinking and worse. I think she is, what you call 'high.' "

"That's what we call it, all right."

"She has to work early tomorrow. She'll never make it and something very bad might happen to her. I thought—"

"OK, OK, I was just thinking about her myself. What's the name of this den?"

"The Disco Dis-Co. It's on Santa Monica near—"

"Yeah, yeah, I know the place. OK, Sabu, sit tight. Uncle Sam'll be right over."

Sam managed to park the Plymouth about half a block away and then walked to the Disco Dis-Co. He paid the entrance fee and joined the party. A few people looked at him in his trench coat and grey felt hat, but then they looked back at what everybody else was looking at—Cinema's Sex Goddess, Sandra Kent.

It was the sort of place Caligula would've loved—even without the lions. They should've searched you for weapons when you walked in and, if you didn't have any, they should've given you one. A squad of bouncers gracelessly threaded through the tapestry of intemperance.

It was your basic bacchanal. The kind of joint that was going out of style but still survived on the white suits, Gucci bags and boots, gold chains, silk shirts, and simple souls in search of saturnalia. It was everything Sam despised. The synchronized strobes slashing out their phosphorescent lightning bolts. Minutely mirrored globes circling and corruscating—machine-gunning a million moving flickers through the curdling haze of smoke and splattering the spectators, making them look even more like refugees from Kafka. A cavalcade of color and cacophony. The raised disco booth blasting out the bleeting beat—defying you to listen without going deaf or at least holding up both palms to your ears. And the poor pathetic people—not all that young—soaking in the sight and sound as if it were some magic balm from Gilead to blot out the inner thirst and hunger and loneliness. All hollow men and women forced to find fallow fulfillment nightly in noise and illusion.

Right now they were finding not so fallow fulfillment in looking at Sandra Kent. She was in the center of the floor, dancing. Not really dancing. She was having sexual intercourse with the sound and strobes—and spectators. She was taking on the whole damn place and more than holding her own. She made Rita Hayworth's dance in *Gilda* look like a Grandma Moses maypole.

Sandra wore a long, low-cut, sleek, white satin dress that looked as if it had been grafted onto her, with a slit up each side that reached nearly to her undulating hips. She undulated all over. Her long, wavy, blonde hair bounced across her milky, moving shoulders. Her pliant arms and hands weaved sensually around and across her perfectly molded breasts as they ascended and descended, bobbing with the beat of the music. Her cobalt blue eyes flashed fire with the frenetic rhythm. She glided and gyrated as if her middle and groin were urged on by some ingrained vibrator. Her supple, sweeping, bending legs quivered and throbbed. So did the audience.

Sabu walked up to Sam and shrugged helplessly.

As Sam started to move toward her, he was restrained by a gentle but firm hand belonging to Walter, the manager, who introduced himself.

"I'm Walter, the manager," he said. Walter looked about as mysterious as an open-faced sandwich. Everything about him could be summed up in one word—one syllable. Tough. "Can I help you?"

"No," Sam replied and took a step.

Sam was restrained by Walter again. This time less gently and more firmly. As a matter of fact, he got pushed into a corner. At least it was quieter.

"Where do you think you're going?" Walter wanted to know.

"Home," said Sam, pointing to Sandra. "And so is she."

"You go; she stays."

"We're a team."

"You just split up. We don't often get a movie star like that."

"No?"

"No. Can't you see she's having fun? And so are the customers."

"Not this customer."

"We can't please everybody."

"You could try."

Walter shook his head.

"And you could try to stop me from getting her," Sam added, "but don't."

"Mister," Walter asked, "do you imply violence?"

"No, I guarantee it."

Out of the darkness a familiar face appeared. A face with narrow green eyes and a knife blade of a mouth. Sam wondered whether he was glad to see Will Catcher, who had just come in with a lady. Sam got only a glimpse of the lady before she turned and melted into the crowd. She had a body that would stop traffic and there was something slightly familiar about her beautiful face. Maybe an extra or actress over at Pantheon, but Sam wasn't thinking about that. Right now he was thinking about whether he had gained an ally or stretched the odds. He'd find out soon, because no matter what, time was short and the odds were long.

"Hello, Sam," Catcher greeted. "What's the rumble, Walter?"

"This clown's trying to break up the party."

"He's a friend of mine, Walter."

An ally. The odds shrunk some. But not enough. Not in this joint abounding in bouncers.

"I don't care if he's the King of Bulgaria," Walter observed.

"Things are very bad in Bulgaria. The devil has the people by the throat," Sam remarked.

"What?" Walter looked puzzled.

"That's a line from *Casablanca*. You see there was this young girl . . ."

"This guy's nuts," Walter said to Catcher. Then, to Sam, "Out!"

As he said it, Walter snapped his fingers and out of nowhere two bouncers appeared. They were big square-built fellows who looked like they had crippled their share of quarterbacks. The odds got stretched again. Just after he snapped his fingers, Walter turned his ocherous eyes toward the nearest bouncer. That's when Sam sucker-punched Walter and knocked him across two tables and a lot of chairs, drinks, and people.

Somebody screamed as the two bouncers reached Sam and grabbed him. But Catcher spun one of the bouncers who hadn't expected to be spun and caught him with a left and right while Sam and the second bouncer traded a few punches 'til trader Sam spotted a weakness and drilled home a left hook.

But the joint hadn't run out of bouncers yet. As more people yelled and screamed and tried to scramble out of harm's way, they got pushed aside by four more Pittsburgh Steelers' rejects.

"Looks like it's the two of us against the world," Sam said to Catcher.

"Three of us," Sabu grinned.

"You better get out of the way, sonny," Sam warned and picked up a chair as the four horsemen knocked Sabu aside and came at Sam and Catcher.

Sam smashed the table across a bouncer's head. He dropped out of the fracas. Then it was Sam and Catcher literally back to back protecting each other and slugging it out with the bouncers and some of the other hired help.

"Just like Alan Ladd and Van Heflin did it in *Shane,*" Sam said.

"I worked in that picture!" Catcher grinned.

"This hard?"

"Hell, no!"

Sabu was the surprise of the night. With a combination of karate and jujitsu, he started tossing people around like sacks of tomatoes. One sack of tomatoes landed smack into the raised disco booth and that stopped the music. The scene still played eerie with the strobes and globes. Sam and Catcher managed to finish off the two finalists in the bouncer contest. Everybody gave the three winners a wide berth as they started to walk.

Sam went over to Sandra, who was still wiggling a little even without the music.

"Oh, hello, Sam," she purred dreamily. "I didn't see you come in."

"And you're not gonna see me go out."

Sam threw a left that hit her on the chin, but he was careful not to break it. She dropped into his arms. He hoisted her over his shoulder, patted her on the lovely curve of her butt, then joined Catcher and Sabu at the door.

"Why did you hit her?" Sabu inquired.

"I don't know," said Sam.

"Can you make it from here?" Catcher asked as they got to the sidewalk.

"Yeah, my car's just down the block. Say, it looks like you lost your date."

"I'll find her."

"I wouldn't go back in there looking for her, pal."

"She'll meet me at the car."

"Say," said Sam, "you're awful good with your deuce of clubs."

"You're not so bad with your fists either. In fact you can fight as good as you can fly."

"Thanks. Uh, why'd you float your stick with mine?"

"I like a man who's good at his job."

"So do I," said Sam and stuck his hand out. They shook.

Sam shifted Sandra a little on his shoulder, and he and Sabu headed for the Plymouth.

CHAPTER
25

Sam dumped Sandra onto the middle of the Plymouth's front seat and motioned for Sabu to get in on the sidewalk side. Sam walked around, got behind the wheel and fired up the engine. Sandra slumped over toward Sabu. He didn't seem to mind a bit.

The three of them—two conscious and one unconscious—drove without speaking for about five minutes until Sabu broke the silence barrier. "Mr. Marlow, where are you going? She doesn't live in this direction."

"No, but she works in this direction."

"We're going to the studio?"

"We're going to the studio."

Sam told the guard at the gate what had happened and what he wanted to do. The guard agreed that it was a good idea. The idea was that they'd take Sleeping Beauty to her permanent dressing room on the lot, put her beddy-bye, call Orlando and tell him to be here at six in the A.M. with his lubricants.

All of the above they did in the above order.

Then Sam instructed Sabu to stay in the outer room of Sandra's dressing room and make sure she didn't do any somnambulating.

"Any what?" Sabu inquired.

"Sleepwalking—or wake-walking. And as for you, Sabu, don't you do any fumadiddling."

"Any what?" Sabu inquired.

"Just keep out of her room, that's what."

Half an hour later Sam turned the key in the door to his apartment. Once again, as he was about to snap on the light, he had that same sinking feeling. In a tenth of a second he decided it wasn't smart to be a target in a well-lit room. He ducked away from the light switch into a dark corner and whipped out the Luger. As he did, he heard a familiar voice.

"It's me, Sam. Bumbera."

Sam shook a little less, walked over and turned on the light, then shut the door. Bumbera was sitting in the overstuffed chair.

"If you're looking for a punching bag, how about trying the YMCA?" Sam suggested.

"About that punch. I . . . I know I was out of line."

"Maybe you were, and maybe you weren't." Sam tugged at his earlobe.

"And I know you coulda ducked it."

"Maybe I could, and maybe I couldn't."

"You forget, I also know the secret of Sam Marlow." Bumbera got up, walked over to Sam and put out his right hand. "Your secret's safe, Sam. At least as far as I'm concerned. And, I'm sorry. OK?"

Sam shook Bumbera's hand and smiled. "Sure, that's a whole lot better than two in the belly. By the way, did you know that's what Brian Donlevy kept saying in a picture called *Beau Geste*? He played Sergeant Markoff and went around threatening to put two or three in everybody's belly. And you didn't come up here just to shake hands."

"That was part of it."

"What's the other part? Say, you're off duty. Want a drink?"

"Hell, yes."

"Bourbon or scotch?"

"Make it scotch."

"OK. And I'll make it two."

Sam poured a couple stiff ones from the bottle of Glenfiddich and passed a drink to Bumbera as they talked.

"They read Flint's will today. That's the other part." Bumbera took a swallow.

"And?"

"Good scotch. And he left practically everything to—"

"Mona Hyland?"

"How did you know?"

"By guess and by God," Sam shrugged. "Well, *she's* been crossed off—as a suspect, I mean. Next question, who's Mona's beneficiary?"

"You figure that's the next suspect?"

"Good as any," said Sam.

"*Not* good. Unless you figure somebody at the Motion Picture Home knocked her off, or at Children's Hospital. She split up what she had about even between them."

"I guess they'll get Flint's money, too, huh? How much is it?"

"Couple a million, give or take some loose change."

"Not bad, even with inflation."

That's when the phone rang.

"Anybody know you're here?" Sam asked Bumbera.

"Nope."

"Then it must be for me." He picked up the phone, took another mouthful of Glenfiddich, swallowed and said, "Sam Marlow." He listened a moment. "OK, OK. Is she all right? Yeah, I'll be right over." Sam hung up.

"Who was that?" Bumbera asked.

"Sabu, the messenger boy. You met him at one of the murders."

"Well, what'd he want?"

"He wanted to tell me that Pantheon Pictures is on fire."

Bumbera adjusted his shoulders. "Big fire or little fire?"

"I don't know," said Sam. He downed the dregs of his drink. "Let's go find out."

Bumbera made good time. He and Sam were at Pantheon in just over ten minutes. There were still a lot of firemen and equipment around, but the fire itself had been, as they say, "knocked down." So had the small wooden bungalow that served as headquarters for the Don Sampson Auction Company. It was one of the older structures on the lot. The timbers still smoldered and occasionally popped and cracked from the combined heat and water.

Sam and Bumbera joined the firefighters and spectators, including Sabu, Josephine Bramer, Fresh Fisher, Don Sampson, and the studio fire chief, Tom Bracken. Just then, Charlie Wentworth, wearing his corduroy Norfolk, a woolen scarf, and a worried look, wandered in from another direction.

"Well, hello there, Charlie," Sam greeted. "You're either up late or early."

"I . . . I don't sleep much these days. I was listening to the radio when the report came in. It's . . . it's . . . did anybody get hurt?"

"No, Charlie," Josephine answered. "Nobody got hurt."

"Well," said Sam, "everybody look busy. Here comes the boss."

Fresh Fisher was already on his way to meet Mellon as he stepped out of his black Mercedes SL-450. So was Josephine. Mellon slammed the door. "I swear to heaven, when things start to go wrong, there's no end to it!"

"I tried to reach you, Mr. Mellon," said Josephine.

"So did I," Fresh Fisher inserted.

"You'd already left the Goldsteins," Josephine continued, "and your car phone—"

"It's on the fritz," Mellon motioned toward the Mercedes. "I got your message when I got home."

"I left one, too," Fresh Fisher appended. "Oh, Major, this is Tom Bracken. He's the studio fire chief."

Bracken gave Mellon a one-finger salute with a touch to his helmet.

"How'd it start?" Mellon asked the chief.

"Bracken here suspects arson," Fisher hastened.

"Arson!"

"Yes, sir," Bracken nodded. "Good thing the alarm was turned in early or it might've spread to those other buildings—maybe to the whole studio." Bracken went back to the fire crew and equipment.

"Who turned in the alarm?" Mellon asked.

Sabu stepped forward, smiled and bowed slightly.

"You again!" Mellon exclaimed. "What do you do, sleep here?!"

"He did tonight," said Sam.

"Marlow, what do you know about all this?"

"Your leading lady went on a binge. Sabu and I brought her here, bunked her down in her dressing room, and I told Sabu to stick around and play sentry. An hour or so later he called and asked if I had any marshmallows. I borrowed some from Bumbera and came over."

"Very funny, Marlow. Is Sandra going to be able to work tomorrow?"

"You mean today? Yeah. I already put in a call to Orlando." Sam walked away toward Mellon's Mercedes.

"Lieutenant Bumbera," Mellon asked, "do you think this fire is connected to Flint and Mona—well, to the murders?"

"I don't know. But it sure as hell could be."

"Look, Fresh," Mellon instructed, "I don't want any mention of arson in any of the papers. Got that? It was an accident—spontaneous combustion, or the wiring, or anything *but* arson. Understand?"

"Sure, Major."

"Well, how about it, Sampson?" Mellon asked. "Is this going to foul up the auction?"

"I don't think so, Mr. Mellon." Sampson pointed to the smoldering rubble. "You can see all our records were destroyed, but, well, we'll work it out."

"That's good. God Almighty—murders, protestors, arson—what the hell else can happen?"

Sam rejoined the group.

"Floods, earthquakes, pestilence."

"Oh, go to hell, Marlow."

"Yes, sir."

Wentworth mustered up enough courage to approach Mellon. "Mr. Mellon, this may not be an appropriate time, but I do want to thank you."

"Huh? What for?"

"Miss Bramer called from your office this afternoon and told me you had decided to keep me on here at Pantheon. I, well, I just . . ."

"Oh, yeah, that. Sure, sure, Charlie. Glad to have you with us."

"Is there anything you'd like me to do, Mr. Mellon?" Josephine asked.

"There's nothing *to* do. We might as well all go home for the night, or what's left of it. Well, good night, everybody."

Mellon started toward his Mercedes. Fisher beat him to it and opened the door. Wentworth and Sampson also walked away and left Sam with Bumbera, Josephine and Sabu.

"Well, Sabu, you better get back to Scheherazade."

Sabu smiled, nodded and melted away into the dead of night. Sam motioned toward the departing Mercedes. "Mellon's phone *is* on the fritz."

Bumbera shook his head.

"Mr. Marlow, you've got a suspicious nature."

Sam Marlow nodded.

"He could've fritzed it himself," Bumbera smiled.

Sam Marlow nodded even more as Josephine Bramer looked at him in disgust. "You think Mr. Mellon would want to burn down his own studio?"

"Maybe *part* of it." Sam's toe lightly touched the scorched auction sign.

"Why?" Josephine demanded.

"Yeah," Sam pulled at his ear lobe. "That is the question. Why? Say, I see you and Mellon drive the same make of automobile."

"I'm going home." Josephine wheeled and walked away.

"Sleep warm, sweetheart," said Sam.

"Well, Sam," Bumbera adjusted his shoulders and looked around. "This one's a lot different than that business with those sapphires. What did they call 'em? The Eyes of Alexander?"

"Yeah, I guess so," Sam twitched. "Well, they can't all be replays of *The Maltese Falcon*."

CHAPTER
26

SAM got to his office late again the next morning. He picked up the *L.A. Times* and the trades from Duchess's desk. She was painting her lips.

" 'Morning, Duchess. Any calls?"

She nodded, kept on painting and said something that Sam couldn't decipher.

"Say again," Sam requested.

Duchess once again repeated the unintelligible message just as unintelligibly and continued to stain the drooping arc of her luscious lower lip.

"Duchess, set the war paint aside for a minute so's I can understand what you're saying."

"I said, Lieutenant Bumbera called about a half hour ago." She resumed her exterior decorating.

"Thanks," said Sam and walked into his office.

The *Times* and the trades downplayed the fire at Pantheon. They could afford to. They had a bigger story. The widow

Flint was contesting her deceased husband's will that left almost all of the spoils to Mona—and now to the Motion Picture Home and Children's Hospital. She had retained a lawyer named Schmidlapp who specialized in such matters and more often won than lost. Sam also noticed that the paper printed a list of Flint's minor beneficiaries. Ten thousand here, five thousand there, and a few who would come into twenty-five hundred. Charlie Wentworth was one of the five-thousand-dollar recipients. Ken, the head guard, got twenty-five hundred and so did Plain Jane Lane. But now that the grieving widow was contesting, it would be a long time before anybody would see anything but courtrooms. Schmidlapp would see to that.

Sam got Bumbera on the phone. "Hello, Bummy, what's playin' at the Roxy?"

"I'll tell you what's playin' at the Roxy. Whoever set that fire didn't have to be there. It was done long distance."

"What do you mean?"

"I mean they found a timing device that touched off the blaze, so it could've been anybody. Did you read about Mrs. Flint's hiring that shyster Schmidlapp?"

"Yeah," said Sam. "You know, Carole Landis was once married to a guy named Schmidlapp. Well, think I'll drift on over to the auction and see what I can see. You call the hospital today?"

"Right. Tim's coming up roses."

"Good. Well, Bummy, don't take any wooden bullets."

"Same to you, shamus."

Sam hung up the phone, tossed down a double Turkey, went to the bathroom, gargled, then walked out to Duchess's office. She was looking into a desk mirror and brushing her tumbling blonde hair.

"Say, Duchess, what time do you finish your morning toilet?"

"Sam, please! Don't say toilet, say tinkles or wee-wee. Toilet don't sound nice."

"OK, Duchess. I'm going."

"Where?"

"To the Mardi Gras."

"Have fun." Then, almost to herself, "Isn't that in St. Louis, or someplace?"

Duchess was still brushing and mumbling to herself as Sam went out the door.

"Mr. Marlow!" Mother barked from the gymnasium's partly open door. "Come in here!"

"Yes, Mother."

Mother sat behind her desk. The pet Pekinese sat on top of it. Nicky was putting a squad of overweight women through a catalog of calisthenics.

"Sign this," Mother said in a voice that could etch glass. "Go ahead and sign it!"

"What is it?"

"It's your new lease. Sign it!" Mother instructed.

"I don't need to sign anything. A simple handshake is good enough."

"Not for me. I don't shake anybody's hand. I did tell you I had to raise your rent seventy dollars, didn't I?"

"On the other hand, I better sign it," said Sam. "This inflation is killing me."

Sam signed Mother's Magna Charta and drove out to Pantheon Pictures.

Less than half an hour later, Sam stood outside Stage 22 and read a notice posted on the door.

DUE TO FIRE OUR RECORDS
HAVE BEEN DESTROYED.
IF YOU MADE A PROXY BID, PLEASE CALL AGAIN—
OR APPEAR IN PERSON TO BID ON ITEM OR ITEMS
OF YOUR CHOICE.
WE APOLOGIZE FOR THIS INCONVENIENCE

Several other people were also reading the notice. Then Sam and most of the people walked into Stage 22 where the auction was in progress. Business had not suffered from the publicity attendant to the recent events at and around Pantheon Pictures. More people than ever were present and the bidding was brisk.

As Sam meandered among the artifacts, the auctioneer went through the sale of several items. Sam paid scant attention as the auctioneer proceeded with his usual routine. Three swords and scabbards from *The Magnificent Musketeers*. The bidding started at thirty dollars and escalated until the auctioneer's gavel and voice vouchsafed, "Sold at three hundred!"

Then the auctioneer went on. "Ladies and gentlemen. For those of you who have just come in, I will repeat that due to the recent fire our records have been destroyed. So we have no record of any proxy bids unless they have been made since the fire.

"The next item is Number 4815 in your catalog, a fabulous twelve-place setting of silverware from the picture *The Thirteenth Guest*. I guess *he* or *she* had to eat with his or her hands. I'd like an opening bid of six hundred dollars."

Sam listened a few seconds, then spotted Josephine Bramer sitting some distance away. He dwarfed the distance until he was leaning over her shoulder. Maybe she perceived his presence and maybe she didn't. But she kept on studying her catalog.

"Who's typing Mellon's memos?" Sam inquired.

"Oh, hello, Sam. There's something I wanted to bid on. Mr. Mellon said I could take a little time off."

"He'll probably make up for it on some weekend. Mind if I sit down?"

"Would it make any difference?"

"Not to me." Sam sat down.

Josephine Bramer seemed nervous. She looked at her catalog, crossed her legs and leaned forward as the auctioneer announced, "Next is Number 4816. Two crosses from a pair of Pantheon Pictures as listed in your catalog. I'd like an opening bid of two hundred and fifty dollars. Do I have an opening bid of two-fifty?"

"Two hundred and fifty." The voice was shy, self-effacing and familiar. Sam recognized that it belonged to Charlie Wentworth, who sat several rows away.

"Three hundred." This voice was also familiar and it belonged to Josephine Bramer, who sat right next to Sam.

"Three hundred," the auctioneer repeated. "Do I have three-fifty? I'm sorry, sir, I already have three hundred. What's that?!"

A heavyset man, maybe fifty-five, rose to his feet, cleared his throat and spoke more clearly. "Three *thousand* dollars."

The auctioneer did his best to take the bid in stride. "Three thousand," he announced. "Do I have another bid?!"

By now Josephine Bramer was trembling visibly. "Three thousand—one hundred," she managed.

"Three thousand one hundred," the auctioneer acknowledged.

"Four thousand," the portly man spoke with calm and confidence.

"Four thousand," the auctioneer sang out. "Any other bids?"

"Four thousand—five hundred," Josephine stammered.

The auctioneer nodded and even before he could repeat the bid the portly man spoke again. "Seven thousand."

"Seven thousand." The auctioneer got it out that time. "Well, well, we have some vigorous bidding here." He looked toward Josephine. "Miss, do I have a counter bid?"

Josephine bit her lip, bent the catalog in her hands, uncrossed her legs and nodded. "Seven thousand—five—hundred." It came out in dribs and drabs.

"Ten thousand," the portly man proffered just as easily as if he were buying a pound of peanuts.

Josephine Bramer blenched. She dropped the catalog, took a handkerchief out of her purse and wiped at her eyes as the auctioneer proceeded. "Ten thousand! Once, twice, three times, and sold to—sir, would you hold up your number?"

The heavyset middle-aged man held up his card.

"Sold to Number R-126!" the auctioneer concluded with a flourish.

Josephine sprang to her feet, bumped against Sam's knees and hurried toward an exit. Sam caught up and grasped her arm. "Hey, Jo, wait a minute."

She whirled. "Leave me alone! Goddammit! Just leave me to hell alone!"

She turned and dashed through the door. Sam thought it best to leave her to hell alone, but he put the arm on a disappointed Charlie Wentworth who was passing by.

"You were a little outta your league, weren't you, Charlie?"

"Yes," Wentworth nodded and sighed. "I thought I'd like to have a memento from one of their pictures, but . . ."

"Yeah," Sam said, "but all of a sudden the price of mementos went right through the roof."

Sam waited his chance, then caught up to the portly middle-aged man who had a package in his hand and a satisfied smile on his face.

"I beg your pardon, sir," Sam said, "I work for this studio and I—"

"Really?" The man smiled wider. "You look more like the Warner Brothers type."

"Yeah," Sam twitched. "I know what you mean. I'm—"

"No need to introduce yourself, Mr. Marlow. You're getting quite a reputation around town. And being a bit of a movie buff myself, I've followed your career with great curiosity and, I must say, even with some vicarious satisfaction. What can I do for you?"

"Answer a couple of questions."

"As Bogart would say, 'Hop to it.' "

"You bought that cross from the John Flint picture *Lucretia*."

"No, from the Mona Hyland picture *Lucretia*."

"I see," Sam nodded and pointed to the package. "How high would you've bid?"

"As high as I had to."

"Why?"

A genuinely emotional look coursed across the man's eyes. "Mona Hyland was someone very special to me."

"You were a friend of hers?"

"I never met her."

"I see. Well, thank you very much, Mr.—"

"Gates. Alan Gates."

CHAPTER
27

"GATES. Alan Gates," Bumbera recited. "Bachelor. Age fifty-two. Occupation: retired millionaire, aluminum siding. Cause of death: gunshot or shots. Motive: robbery— two crosses missing."

Bumbera moved around the paneled library in the tastefully appointed Tudor English hillside home. Also present were Sam Marlow, Horace Hacksaw, and a couple other police officers.

This time the tape outline was marked on the desk where Gates's head, shoulders, and arms fell in a pattern of death. There were dried bloodstains on the leather desk pad.

"Thanks for calling, Bummy." Sam pointed to the desk. "I wonder if he counts as number three?"

"How's that?"

"Just the other day, somebody said that in Hollywood death comes in threes. But Gates wasn't exactly a part of the Hollywood scene."

"Not exactly," Bumbera adjusted his shoulders. "But if the

killer has any more ideas about doing any more killing, they're not gonna work out.''

"What do you mean?"

"I mean this time the murderer was spotted leaving the house. Good description.''

"By the maid?" Sam asked.

"No, by the postman. It's the maid's day off.''

"It always is. Well, who?"

Bumbera looked at his watch. "You'll see any minute now.'' He pointed toward a door to an adjoining room. "First, take a hinge in here.''

"Who found him?''

"A delivery boy from Jurgensen's. Gates had called in an order. When there was no answer at the back door he started around front. Looked in the window and saw . . .'' Bumbera pointed at the desk just before he opened the door to the adjoining room and walked through. Sam followed him.

"What would you call this?'' Bumbera waved his hand around as they entered.

It was a medium-sized room. The only furniture, a swivel chair in the center of the floor. Nothing else—except the walls were literally covered with pictures. Pictures of Mona Hyland. Some blown up to life size. Some even bigger. Mona Hyland in bathing suits. Mona Hyland in costumes. Mona Hyland in publicity glossies. Mona Hyland in posters from her films. Mona Hyland. Mona Hyland. Mona Hyland.

"I guess you'd have to call it—a shrine,'' Sam said.

"Talk about being hung up.'' Bumbera circled the room.

"Yeah, a real fan. You know there was a look that came into his eyes when he mentioned her name. I can see—''

"Lieutenant.'' Hacksaw stood in the doorway between the library and the shrine.

Bumbera walked back into the library and Sam followed.

"She's right outside,'' said Hacksaw.

"Did you tell her anything?''

"You said not to.''

"Bring her in.''

Hacksaw moved toward the opposite door.

"I got a sinking feeling," said Sam, "that I know who you sent for."

Both men remained silent for a moment, then Hacksaw opened the door again and ushered in Josephine Bramer.

"Damn, I wish I was wrong," said Sam, "but I wasn't."

"Hello, Miss Bramer. Thanks for coming." Bumbera stepped from in front of the desk. "You've been here before."

"Why, yes, I . . ." She saw the tape outline on the desk and the bloodstains. Josephine Bramer fainted and fell to the floor like a bushel of spilled beans.

Sam and Bumbera walked over and took a look. Hacksaw never batted an eyebrow or lash.

"Think it's an act?" Bumbera asked.

"If it is, said Sam, "she oughta be in pictures."

Both men helped her to her feet and guided her toward a large leather chair.

"Hey, come on Jo," Sam counseled. "Get a hold of yourself. Here, sit right down here. Atta girl."

"I'm sorry," Josephine said as she looked toward the desk. "But just a little while ago he—"

"Yeah," said Sam, "he was so alive."

"Would you like some water, Miss Bramer?" Bumbera offered.

"No, thanks. I'll be all right."

"Look, ma'am," Bumbera got down to police business. "You, or somebody who looks just like you and drives a car just like yours, were seen leaving here about the time of the murder."

"I said I was here, but—"

"Now you don't have to tell us anything if you don't want to, but if you make a statement—"

"Yes, I know. I'll tell you what happened."

"Shoot," said Bumbera.

Sam looked at the lieutenant, who tried to shrug off his unfortunate wording. Josephine told her story.

"I was terribly upset after the auction when Mr. Gates outbid me. But later I realized that each of us was really bidding on a different item."

"He wanted the cross from Mona's picture," Sam injected.

"Yes, and I wanted the one my father made. It was used in a different picture and had no value to Mr. Gates. But they were being auctioned together."

"So you came over to see him," Bumbera concluded. "Is that it?"

"Yes. I explained to him how much the second cross meant to me—because of my father. Mr. Gates was sympathetic, very understanding. He wanted to give me the cross as a gift."

"So you took it," Hacksaw said and moved a step closer.

"Not exactly. I told him I'd feel much better about it if I could pay him something. He laughed and said, all right, he'd take whatever my opening bid was."

"And did he?" Bumbera asked.

"Yes."

"Did you pay him in cash?"

"Why, no. I don't carry that much money. I wrote him a check for three hundred dollars. He said he'd donate it to charity."

"That's an interesting story, Miss Bramer." Bumbera looked right into her eyes. "But where is it?"

"Where is what?"

"The check for three hundred dollars."

"Well it must be here."

"We found no check."

"Are you sure?"

"Sure, I'm sure," said Bumbera.

"And he had no time to go anyplace and cash it," Hacksaw added, closing his little black notebook as if he were also closing the case on Josephine Bramer.

"Bummy," said Sam, "maybe the delivery boy swiped the check."

"No chance. He never came inside. He went next door and phoned the police. Nobody came inside but us. I'm sorry, Miss Bramer, but there's just too much against you." Bumbera nodded toward the door. "I'm gonna have to take you down to headquarters 'til we do a little more digging. You can call your lawyer or anybody else you want from there."

Bumbera took her by the arm and helped her to her feet. It seemed as if another shock wave were going through her. "Sam, I didn't kill him. I didn't!"

"Sure," said Sam. "Sure you didn't. And is it OK now if I don't leave you to hell alone?"

It was just about six o'clock when Sam got back to his office. Duchess was packing up her possibles. "Oh, hi, Sam. Did you have a nice day?"

"Swell."

"Is there anything you want me to do before I leave?"

"Like what?"

"Oh, I don't know, maybe type an important letter or place a telephone call or file anything, or something like that. You know."

"Yeah, I know. No, nothing, Duchess. Go home, get into your pj's and have pleasant dreams."

"OK, I will. But I don't wear pj's. I find them too inhabiting."

Sam took a couple of hits from the office bottle, smoked a cigarette and went over the case against Josephine Bramer. She had motive. She had opportunity. She was seen leaving the scene. And there was the matter of the check she claimed to have written. The missing check. Pretty tight case against her. But not airtight. Sam still figured Gates's murder was tied to the killings of Flint and Mona. He narrowed down the events and people in his head and decided he was ready to make his next stop.

But first he phoned Bumbera.

CHAPTER
28

THERE were still almost two hours of daylight left when Sam knocked on the door of the tiny bungalow just off the freeway.

"Oh, Mr. Marlow." Charlie Wentworth seemed startled. "I wasn't expecting you."

"Neither were my mother and father. Thought I'd come by for a minute, ask you a favor."

"A favor?" Wentworth stood mumchance at the open door.

"Yeah, Charlie, I'd like to pick your brain, as they say in the business. And you've got a very orderly brain. Can I come in?"

"Uh, oh, excuse me, of course, Mr. Marlow."

Sam stepped inside the Tom Thumb chicken coop as Wentworth closed the door.

"You sure are handy to the freeway."

"Yes, for a time it looked as if they were going to tear the house down."

"You own the place?"

"Oh, no, no, sir, but I've lived here since just after the war."

"WW II?"

Wentworth nodded and smiled. "I'm sorry I have nothing to offer you. Unless you'd like some wine?"

Sam shook his head no and looked around. The place needed paint. The carpeting was threadbare, the furniture hoary and the walls were mostly long wooden planks between cement blocks piled with books, magazines, newspapers, and periodicals.

"You got more books than Pickwick has."

"I do a lot of my research here. You said something about a favor, Mr. Marlow."

"Oh, yeah. But first, I brought you something. A little present."

Sam took a narrow box about two feet long that was sticking out of his trench coat pocket and handed it to Wentworth. "Open it."

Wentworth did. It was Flint's swagger stick.

"You said you'd like a memento."

"I'm deeply grateful." Wentworth seemed like he was. "But are you sure it's all right? I mean—"

"Sure it's all right, Charlie. I see by the paper that Flint left you five Gs."

"Yes. I think that was very generous."

"Oh, I don't know. It adds up to about a hundred and fifty dollars a year for all those years you spent with him. Say, did you know that Lieutenant Bumbera's arrested Josephine Bramer for the murder of Alan Gates?"

"Gates?"

"The high bidder for the crosses."

"He was—murdered?"

"Yeah."

"By Miss Bramer?" Wentworth scratched at his neck just behind his ear. "But why?"

"Same reason Flint and Mona were killed—for the crosses. Now you've got a logical mind, Charlie. I'd like you to go over the evidence with me. Like a research problem. I'm at an impasse and I could use a little help."

Wentworth seemed flattered. He walked over and sat behind his littered desk. "I'll do whatever I can, of course."

"We know now that the killer wanted the crosses."

"Do we know why?"

"We'll table that. We do know the killer had to have access to Pantheon Pictures. And we know the killer had to know something about poisons."

"And about automobiles," Wentworth added.

"Right. But let's take it from the top. When the crosses went on display with all the other stuff, Josephine saw them and had to have them, or one of them. She got to Sampson's records and found out there were a couple of proxy bids already in—Flint's and Mona's. She knew how competitive they were and that they'd drive the price sky high. She poisoned Flint and stole the proxy receipt. She couldn't get to Mona's proxy but took the chance it would be lost in the crash. Even if it wasn't, it wouldn't make any difference because then she set fire to Sampson's books so there'd be no record. Scratch all proxies! Seemed like smooth sailing. That sound logical so far?"

"Well, yes it does. But what about Gates?"

"Ahhh, that's the one thing the killer couldn't foresee. That there'd be some nut, a fanatic fan, who'd recognize one of those crosses as something that once bounced around Mona's bosom, and would have to have it at any price."

"Yes, I see."

"And Josephine was seen leaving Gates's place by the postman, but she also could've been seen by someone else."

"Who?"

"By whoever went in after she left, killed Gates, and stole the check. By whoever killed Flint and Mona Hyland."

"Then you *don't* think it was Miss Bramer."

"Neither do you, Charlie." Sam twitched. "Neither do you."

From the open drawer next to him, Wentworth produced and pointed a Smith and Wesson .45. It was the kind that policemen used to put 9mm holes into bad guys. And Wentworth was pointing it at Sam.

"Know about guns too, huh, Charlie?"

"Yes, Mr. Marlow, I do. I happen to be a crack shot."

"I'll take your word for it."

Sam's left hand was on the Derringer in his trench coat pocket. His other hand on the Luger in the other pocket.

"You won't have to. I'm afraid I have no choice but to demonstrate my marksmanship."

Somehow, suddenly, Wentworth seemed taller and younger and stronger. He seemed like a man who knew exactly what he was doing and exactly how to do it.

"I'll lay you six to an even that that's the gun that killed Gates," said Sam.

"Guns don't kill people," Wentworth grinned. "People do. You win, of course, Mr. Marlow, but still you lose."

"Charlie, before you shoot me, there's something I'm dying to know."

"Why did I want the cross?"

"That's it."

Wentworth smiled. He even laughed a little as he rose, walked over to the shelf, pulled down a fat book and the cross that was hidden behind the book. "It's ironic. The sign at the studio said they were selling 'treasures' from the many Pantheon productions. Little did they know."

Wentworth held on to the cross but put the book down on the desk. "Page 207, Mr. Marlow. Oh, don't pick up the book. Just turn to the page."

Wentworth held the gun in one hand and the cross in the other while Sam let go of the Luger in his pocket and flipped to page 207. There was an illustration of the same cross. But not with the same smooth dull finish it had now. In the illustration it was gleaming gold, ornately and intricately engraved.

"Go ahead. Read the caption."

"It says, 'The Cross of Cellini.' "

"Yes. Benvenuto Cellini. The greatest artist of the Renaissance. This little 'prop' is worth millions, Mr. Marlow. It was commissioned in 1546 by Cellini's patron, Cosimo de' Medici. As you can further read, it disappeared during the war."

"And reappeared in *Lucretia*."

"Yes, but nobody realized it was the lost Cross of Cellini. It was just a small part of the great European junk pile." Wentworth was gathering steam. "After the war, the American studios, including Pantheon, ravaged everything they could from a still bleeding Europe—bought up everything they were able to lay their hands and cash on. *Lucretia* was shot on location. The cross was bought by the property department along with hundreds of other items—after having gone through who knows how many fascist hands. It was dulled down so it wouldn't distract attention from Miss Hyland's . . ."

"Bosom."

"And brought back to the States where it gathered dust until—"

"Good old Charlie spotted it."

"Yes, good old Charlie. Good old subservient, innocuous, two-hundred-dollar-a-week, toss-a-bone-to Charlie."

"Who sounds a little bitter."

"Not anymore, Mr. Marlow," Wentworth smiled. "Not anymore."

"Uh-huh. Probably the polar route to—maybe Sweden?"

"Madagascar—the Malagasy Republic. Where there's no extradition and a rich market. It's getting late."

"I s'pose your bags are already packed."

"Yes. We're traveling very light."

"*We?*" Sam looked toward the partially open bedroom door and sniffed at the air. "I didn't think that was your perfume I smelled. Come on out, sweetheart, and let's have a look-see."

She did. And Sam's eyeballs almost popped out of their caves.

It was Plain Jane Lane. Only it wasn't. It was a thirty-year-old Venus with a body that would stop traffic. She wasn't just a three-alarm fire, she was Dante's Inferno. A gorgeous beauty parlor face featuring playful eyes, glossy red, red lips and high cheeks rouged just right—all framed by flowing fawn-colored hair that settled softly around her shoulders. The sky blue skintight dress accentuated everything a shipwrecked sailor could hope for. Munificent breasts slanting to an elliptic circle of waist and flaring to generously rounded hips supported by splendidly curved twin columns of legs. She looked a little like Hazel Brooks in *Body and Soul.*

"Well, well," said Sam. "As I live and breathe—Calamity Jane has turned into Cinderella. Or is it Cleopatra?"

"It doesn't matter, Mr. Marlow," said Jane Lane, "because you won't be living and breathing very long."

"Uh-huh. Say, Charlie, isn't she a little—combustible for you?"

"Oh, no, Mr. Marlow, *compatible* is the word—and has been for some time."

"Ever since you let her in on your scam to make millions via a little murder." Sam pointed to Jane Lane as she still stood by the bedroom door. "But why the female Jekyll and Hyde act?"

"We don't have enough time for long drawn-out stories, so let's just put it this way. I got tired of men looking at me the way you're looking now—trying to put their dirty hands all over me day and night."

"So you split up into two Janes. The day Jane and the night Jane, that it?"

"Close enough. And now, Mr. Marlow, about your living and breathing."

"I see what you mean." Sam twitched. "One more murder won't make much difference."

"*Two more!*"

That's when Will Catcher stepped from out of the bedroom pointing a .38.

"Say, what is this?" said Sam. "A convention?"

"Charlie, don't move a muscle," Catcher commanded. "Just keep that gun aimed right at Marlow."

"How'd you get in here?!" Wentworth seemed to age a little again. "What're you—"

"I think," said Sam, "that your girlfriend let her boyfriend in the bedroom window. A little double double-cross for the Cross of Cellini. That it, kids?"

"That's it." Catcher smiled his hatchet-blade smile and his narrow green eyes got narrower.

"You see, Charlie," Sam observed, "your two-step is a little rusty." Then to Catcher, "That *was* Jane I got a glimpse of at the disco joint, wasn't it?"

"Yeah, it was. So all we got to do now is scratch one Charlie Wentworth and cross off the man with Bogart's face, then we live happily ever after. You know, Marlow, I liked you. You were good at your job. And now, all good things must come to an end."

They did. But not quite the way Catcher expected.

Wentworth's gun swung over and went off. The slug blew a hole right between Jane Lane's beautiful breasts. Even as she slumped, Catcher fired three shots from the .38. The first two caught Charlie—in the throat and heart. The third one ripped into a bookshelf as Wentworth went down. Sam threw two rounds from the Luger at Catcher, but Catcher ducked back toward the bedroom and the door splintered twice from Sam's shots.

Catcher fired again. The .38 slug ripped into Sam's middle and he dropped onto the worn-out carpet.

Catcher took one look at Jane Lane and knew she was already dead. He snatched the cross off the desk, stepped over Marlow's body and headed out the front door and toward where he'd parked his car.

Sam came to, grabbed at the bloodied front of his coat, got to his feet and staggered after Catcher.

Will Catcher was just getting into his Chevy when Sam came at him with the Luger spurting lead. Catcher dove alongside the Chevy and fired at Sam. Sam ducked and blew both tires out of his side of the Chevy. They blazed away until they were both out of ammunition. Sam even emptied the two shots out of the Derringer. Catcher made a run for it and Sam sprang after him, still leaking blood.

Catcher cut across a narrow street and onto the freeway overpass. He still held the cross in one hand and his empty .38 in the other. For someone who had just bought a bullet, Sam was running like a champion, even gaining on Catcher.

Catcher decided to make his stand right there. He thrust the cross into one pocket, the empty gun into his belt, then turned back and lunged at the onrushing Sam. They were both plenty good with their fists. This was no staged stuntman fight with narrow misses and fake takes. It was bone and gristle with blood and bruises, while below, the freeway traffic—bisected by the middle divider—streaked in opposite directions.

Catcher threw a powerhouse right into Sam's wounded middle and Sam fell to both knees. Catcher pulled out the .38 and knocked Sam across the noodle. Catcher put the gun back in his belt, jumped onto the overpass rail and looked at the traffic below. He picked his target—an International Harvester semi hauling a long tank and doing fifty-five, approaching from the north. Catcher bent both knees and waited. Sam came to and saw what Catcher had in mind.

"Will, don't! Don't try it!"

"So long, play-actor," Catcher cried and dropped fifteen feet straight down.

Catcher slammed onto the tail end of the tanker, teetered, then lost his balance and almost went over the side. But he grabbed a rung, pulled himself back on top and started crawling toward the front of the tanker in the direction of the cab and the driver, who was unaware that he had taken a passenger aboard.

Sam got a good look at the semi. Then, still oozing blood, he ran back toward Wentworth's bungalow as fast as he could.

Bumbera had just pulled up and was opening the door of his car when Sam got there.

"Don't get out!" Sam hollered. "I'm getting in." Sam did and asked, "Where the hell you been? You were supposed to be here half an hour ago."

"I had a goddamn flat tire. Sam, for Christ's sake, you're bleeding!"

"Yeah, yeah, just enough. Get on the freeway and head south."

Bumbera took off fast. "What happened in there?"

"Two dead bodies—and there's liable to be a lot more dead

bodies on that freeway." Sam wiped away some of the blood. "Damn, I thought I'd get outta this without one."

"One what? Bullet?"

"No. Car chase." Sam pulled something out of his pocket. "Look what he did to my gold watch." The .38 slug had gone all the way through and shattered the watch.

"Better *it* should stop running than you."

"Amen, brother."

Bumbera burned rubber and turned onto the on ramp while Sam gave him an abbreviated version of the Wentworth-Plain Jane-Catcher love story capped by the Cross of Cellini and Catcher's getaway.

By now Catcher had crawled the length of the shiny stainless steel tanker. He swung onto the right side of the cab, managed to open the cab door and just about startled the overweight driver out of his pants as he shoved the .38 against the driver's ribs and said, "Get out!"

"Mister, you're outta your goddamn mind!! Do you know what—"

"Out! I want this rig!"

"You can have it!!"

The driver slowed as much as he could and opened the door. Catcher slid behind the wheel, pushed the driver out onto the freeway and hit the accelerator. The driver landed on his feet but not for long. He staggered, stumbled then toppled against the freeway divider as a Cadillac Seville swerved and barely avoided hitting him. Other approaching cars and trucks also swerved, honked their horns, hollered and waved their fists at the hapless fellow until Bumbera hit his siren, pulled over and motioned toward the back seat. "Get in."

The driver did and as he slammed the door shut, Bumbera pulled away again into the traffic, siren still screaming. "You're the driver, huh?" Bumbera asked.

"Yeah." The driver tried to catch his breath while he rubbed at the mosaic of scrapes and bruises all over his thick body. Sam turned back and asked, "Are you OK?"

That's when the driver's dapple grey eyes bulged as they first saw Sam's face.

"Jesus Christ. What is this? A bad dream or am I already dead?!" To Bumbera, "Who is this guy? Is he Bogart or what?"

"Settle for 'or what,' " Sam said. "And are you hauling what I think you're hauling?"

"I was. He is now. And I don't think he knows it, but he might just as well be sitting on dynamite."

"What is it?" Bumbera asked.

"Acetone," the driver answered. "Three thousand gallons— and if she goes, *oatmeal!*"

"Bummy, you better get on that radio. Tell the cops to give him a wide berth and have 'em chase away as much traffic as they can."

Bumbera got on the radio and relayed instructions.

"Can I get off at the next exit?" the driver asked.

"No. You're sitting pretty," Sam said.

"Yeah. So was Hiroshima."

"There he is!" Sam pointed. "About six or seven cars ahead."

By now a couple Highway Patrol cars and motorcycles were on the scene. Bumbera grabbed the mike again. "This is Bumbera. This is Lieutenant Bumbera. Do not approach tanker. I repeat, do not approach tanker. And keep all traffic away. Divert all traffic from tanker. Tanker is carrying highly volatile cargo."

"You're not just whistling 'Dixie.' " the driver piped.

"Get alongside him," Sam said to Bumbera.

"What?!" the driver shrilled. "Don't do it! I tell you that guy's nuts!" Then he whispered, "And so are the both of you." He buried his head between his hands.

The Highway Patrol had pretty much speared away the traffic. Bumbera, doing over seventy, raced ahead between the divider and the tanker. He caught up to the tail end of the tanker and shot faster toward the cab as Sam rolled down his window. Bumbera switched off the siren.

The car and cab were neck and neck as Sam leaned out of the window and hollered up at Catcher. "Will! Will!! Pull over! Listen to me!" He pointed back toward the tanker. "Explosives! Dynamite!!"

That's as much as Sam got out. Catcher smiled that deadly smile and steered the tanker toward the left, grinding the truck's heavy tire against the car as Sam ducked in fast. Again Catcher swerved and scudded against the car now sandwiched between the divider and the tanker.

Catcher pulled the cross out of his pocket and set it on his lap. It caught the setting sun and glinted, reflecting its pattern on the ceiling of the cab just above Catcher's head.

Catcher twisted the wheel again and the truck's twirling tire ground against metal. But Bumbera held her steady, though he slowed to let the tanker pull ahead into the clear, but Catcher wheeled hard left and then right so the tail of the tanker whiplashed and knocked the front fender off the police car.

The impact and the severe swaying motion caused Catcher to lose control for a moment. The tanker swerved toward the divider and the sidewall of the front tire ripped along a high rough cement ridge. It had the effect of a can opener. The front tire blew. The cab careened crazily at seventy miles an hour and Catcher—looking like a man who just rose from hell with his hair on fire—fought for control. The front tire skidded and bounced off as a curtain of dust poured down from under the fender onto the steel tire rim that sparked and scarred across the cement highway. Catcher turned the wheel and hit the brakes in a desperate attempt to slacken speed, but the cab and tanker jackknifed with a thunderous impact that set off the explosion.

Three thousand gallons of liquid dynamite detonated in every direction—in every color.

The cab door blew off and with it the Cross of Cellini— twenty feet into the air, across the divider and into the oncoming traffic that was weaving crazily because of the explosion.

The cross bounced onto and off the windshield of a car and

landed on the freeway directly in the path of a huge cement truck that was trying to stop but couldn't. The massive truck tires rolled over it once, twice, again, then again, smashing and squashing as they finally screeched to a stop, scraping the cross along with them.

Bumbera had stopped just far enough away from the tanker so the explosion only shattered all the windows of what was left of his car. The truck driver had passed out on the floorboard of the back seat. Both Sam and Bumbera were still conscious, but both were conspicuously shaky.

"You know something?" said Bumbera. "Before I met a guy named Sam Marlow, I was a carefree fellow."

"Yeah," sighed Sam, "so was I."

Fifteen minutes later the Highway Patrol was diverting traffic as Sam and Bumbera made their way across the freeway. Sam picked up the flat, patternless, tire-treaded plate of gold and turned it in his hand.

"Looks like the Renaissance fell victim to the freeway."

The sun was setting.

CHAPTER
29

S<small>AM</small> had spent a couple days in the hospital with time out for Mona's funeral. The doctor told him the pocket watch had probably saved his life. Will Catcher was a good shot. He was a good lot of things, and a few bad. And now, like the driver said, he was—oatmeal.

Sam thought about Will Catcher's last words just before leaping onto the truck, "So long, play-actor!" Did Catcher know he was repeating Douglas Fairbanks, Jr.'s final salutation to Ronald Colman in *The Prisoner of Zenda?* As Fairbanks stood poised to dive into the castle's moat, he looked back, flashed that familiar flaunting smile and said, "Farewell, play-actor!" Well, maybe Catcher knew and maybe he didn't. It didn't make much difference. It was just one of those things that skittered across Sam Marlow's movie mind.

In his pajamas, Sam leaned against the headboard of his bed and glanced at the trade papers. Both *The Hollywood Reporter* and *Variety* bannered the same story: "MELLON

SELLS INTEREST IN PANTHEON PICTURES—End Of A Dynasty."

Sam tossed the papers aside and dialed his office. Duchess answered. "Sam Marlow's office. He's absent at the present. May I take a message?"

"Duchess, this is Sam."

"Oh, how are we feeling this morning?"

"We're feeling in the pink, but we're not coming in today."

"But I'm already in."

"I know that. Why don't you take the day off and have a long weekend."

"Gee, Sam, that sounds terrific. Mother went up to San Francisco on some business, so Mr. Kalamavrakinopoulos came over and was going to show me some exercises."

"I'll bet."

"On what?"

"Never mind. As they say in the business, have a good weekend, Duchess."

She giggled. Sam figured Nicky was already showing her some exercises.

"See you Monday, Sam. Oooohh, Mr. Kalamavrakinopoulos . . ."

He hung up. As soon as he did, the phone rang again.

"Sam Marlow."

"Sam, this is Josephine. Did I thank you enough times?"

"Too many times. Say, how do you like your new boss?"

Oh, I'm not staying on very long. I'm going into the husband-and-kids business. Adam's getting a divorce and we're going to get married. Sam, about you and me . . ."

"We'll always have the night of the soft shoulders. We lost it for a while, but we got it back again."

"Yes, we did. Sam, my new boss would like to talk to you. May I put him on?"

"Sure."

After a click and a slight pause, a familiar but harried voice came through. "Mr. Marlow."

"Hello, Sabu. How do you like show business?"

"I'm, I'm not sure."

"Say, why didn't you tell me you were a son of a shah?"

"Well, I thought I could learn more incognito. You see, I thought it would be fun to run a studio."

"That's what Orson Welles said in *Citizen Kane*—he thought it would be fun to run a newspaper. He found out it wasn't."

"And so am I, Mr. Marlow. Sandra Kent has disappeared again. She's been missing for two days. It's costing us a fortune. If you are well enough by now—if you can find her and bring her in today, or even Monday—would five thousand dollars be agreeable?"

"It would, Sabu. I'll see what I can do."

As Sam hung up, Sandra Kent came in carrying a breakfast tray. She wore one of Sam's shirts with only one button buttoned. It didn't conceal very much—especially the fact that she wore nothing underneath.

"How do you like your eggs, Sam?"

"Over easy."

"I thought so." Sandra smiled.

"You know," Sam reflected, "I never did get that windshield with the bullet hole fixed."

"So?"

"So, on second thought . . ." Sam twitched.

"On second thought, what?"

"I'm not very hungry—for eggs."

"That's funny. Neither am I."

She set the tray on a chair, unbuttoned the one button and let the shirt drop from her naked body onto the bedroom floor. She stood there shimmering in the morning light. There wasn't a grown man in America who wouldn't've given his right eye to be in Sam's pajamas.

She leaned down and kissed him. She put her arms around him and pressed that soft, warm, wavy body right where it would do the most good.

Maybe she *was* doomed. Maybe they were both doomed. But not right now. Not this weekend.

Ed Barrow

THE MONDAY PASTA CLUB

60 easy pasta recipes
for every occasion

Ed Barrow

KYLE BOOKS

CONTENTS

WELCOME TO THE CLUB

It's my 12th birthday. The smell of recently blown-out candles hangs in the air. I am surrounded by cards and a mountain of wrapping paper. Paula and Steve (known to me as Mum and Dad) have just unwittingly submitted themselves to a year of culinary experimentation, because first among my presents is a shiny new pasta machine. Fresh out of the box in all its glory, it will be used to create some questionable meals with, let's say, 'mixed results'. Nonetheless, my passion for pasta is born.

Fast-forward ten years and I rediscover the rather less shiny piece of kit at the back of a kitchen cupboard. With a little more knowledge, though I must admit about the same confidence as my 12-year-old self, I blow off the cobwebs and start to make pasta again.

However, handmade pasta is only half the story... most of the time it's barely the introduction. I mostly use dried, shop-bought pasta and it is loved all the same. Because, for me, pasta is a genesis. The beginning of something which, with a dash of flavour and creativity, becomes something very special indeed.

The Monday Pasta Club has been the start of something incredibly special for me. It began in 2020 on Instagram as an expression of my love for the thing I enjoyed cooking the most. There I was, day after day, making dish after dish. And the club was my way of sharing them. The traditions, the techniques, the 'Italian way' and of course recipes featuring none of the above – scrapping the rules and allowing myself creative freedom. Going off-piste. Thinking 'Oh how the Italians would hate this...'.

To my surprise, people started to make the recipes and post how much they enjoyed them. Every Monday at 5pm a new list of ingredients and instructions pieced together in my own kitchen was shared with the world. I hope I never tire of hearing that someone has also discovered the delights of pasta by recreating something they found on The Monday Pasta Club.

That's why I have written this book. It's a new means of sharing my passion for the versatility of an ingredient that is miraculously created when you mix flour with eggs or water.

No other ingredient captivates me quite like pasta. It has a magical quality. It's humble, quietly lurking in the background of so many meals that simply couldn't exist without it. It can also be transformed into a quick and easy, and yet delicious, meal using just a few key ingredients. Think olive oil, garlic, tomato and basil!

I wanted to share my journey of reading and learning about pasta, the experimentation and the time well spent. Through this collection of recipes, I hope you too can fall in love with the joy that only a simple bowl of pasta can provide. In that spirit, it is worth pointing out that pasta is not just for Mondays. It is for:

• **Heart-warming suppers for one on a cold winter's evening.**

• **A simple meal that packs a punch shared with a loved one.**

• **Impressing friends at a Friday evening dinner party.**

• **Slow Sunday afternoon labours of love.**

But you probably knew that already.

My pasta dishes are divided into four chapters for good reason. As you make your way through the book, you will see that the recipes increase in the quantity of ingredients, the number of steps and the time needed to create them. This way, you can choose a dish that suits you and the occasion. From a quick and easy bowl of spaghetti to rich, slow-cooked ragùs and fresh simple salads, you're sure to find a dish that suits you and the moment.

It is my belief that books like this should be a guide, not a set of rules to slavishly follow. The recipes have been developed to work as they are. But they can be adapted, depending on what you may already have in the refrigerator or your kitchen cupboard, swapping out one vegetable for another or reaching for spaghetti instead of fettuccine. All the recipes in this book have been written to work with dried pasta, but you could use fresh pasta – shop-bought or homemade – as well, just double the weight of the pasta. Make these dishes your own or take them as they are.

Tips to get you started

Every time I cook pasta at home there are a few key things I do to make the most of my time in the kitchen. You may already be familiar with these – if so, skip this bit and jump head first into the rest of the book. For those looking for some small tweaks that make a big difference, read on.

The art of al dente

Al dente, literally meaning 'to the tooth' in Italian, is the slight bite that the pasta retains when it is drained a minute or so before it is cooked all the way through. In the simplest terms if the packet says 'cook in boiling water for 9 minutes' then stop at 8 minutes.

You'll notice that in many of these recipes the final few steps involve draining your pasta, adding it to a pan and combining with the sauce, bringing them together over some heat. The pasta will reach its full cooking time with this last dance in the pan.

Pasta cooked al dente retains more of its natural starch, and this allows it to combine with the sauce, thickening it and coating the pasta shapes. In essence, with this technique, pasta and sauce become one, improving the overall texture and mouthfeel of the finished dish.

Al dente is more of an art than a science. The shape and thickness of the pasta, the brand you use, and the intensity at which your water boils will all play a part in how quickly your pasta will cook. Beyond taking a minute or so off the timing given in the instructions on the packet, I would recommend regularly trying the pasta as you go. When it is tender but very slightly firm in the centre when you bite into it, then you've got al dente. It shouldn't feel hard or chalky.

Liquid gold

You may be familiar with the idea of keeping back some of the cooking water to use in a recipe. The reason for this is that when it is cooked pasta releases starch into the water creating what is sometimes referred to as 'liquid gold'. This is key to creating a great bowl of pasta. It emulsifies fats, cheeses and other ingredients that have been used in your sauce, while thinning it to the right consistency. It also helps with coating your pasta.

To create the best liquid gold, you need to generously salt your cooking water. Don't be afraid of putting a generous teaspoon of salt into the pan. When you think you've added too much, add a little more. Well-seasoned water will bring out the best in your pasta. Don't worry, not all of this salt ends up in the final dish. I recommend you taste and season as you go, and most definitely before serving.

When it comes to the pan itself, I recommend something large enough to allow a good rolling boil without it splashing over the hob, and to cook your pasta uncovered.

To chop or not to chop

As you work your way through the recipes in this book you will see that the ingredients will sometimes need to be, among other things, 'roughly chopped', 'finely grated (shredded)' or 'very finely sliced'. Tempting as it may be to ignore these little instructions, they are there for a reason, I promise! This is because the cooking time of, say, an onion that is roughly chopped will be different to that of one that has been finely sliced.

It is not absolutely crucial to follow the instructions to the letter in every recipe, but if you do have the time to prepare your ingredients in the ways I have indicated, the end result will be better. I would definitely recommend you follow the guidance most closely for Chapter 1 where cooking time is 10–15 minutes.

Taste, taste, taste

This tip is what I like to call 'the chef's privilege'. You get to eat as you cook. I like to combine this with a glass of wine, but that is not mandatory.

By trying your food as you prepare it you can make small tweaks to seasoning that will make all the difference when you sit down to eat. Doing this regularly will also train your tastebuds to understand how different flavours interact when added – perhaps adding some lemon for acidity or a touch more salt and pepper to balance out the dish. There is no hard-and-fast rule here; adjust to your own preference.

Recipe key

Each of the four chapters in this book has a selection of vegetarian, fish and meat recipes, denoted using these symbols:

Service please!

The recipes are written to serve two generously; you should find there are a couple of extra spoonfuls left in the pan so you can go back in for seconds, which is just how I like to serve pasta myself. All of dishes can be halved, doubled and adapted depending on how many people are going to be gathered round the table.

I hope you enjoy using this book as much as I have loved creating it. 12-year-old Ed would be blown away to think that one day his recipes might end up in here, so I encourage you to take a leaf out his book and create something for those you love, no matter how much or how little experience you have. Welcome to the club.

With love,

Ed x

Proud founder of The Monday Pasta Club

 Vegetarian recipes

 Fish recipes

 Meat recipes

KNOW YOUR PASTA SHAPE

The shapes used throughout these
60 recipes are purely suggestions. Certain
shapes do lend themselves to certain
sauces better: larger, thicker shapes such
as pappardelle or rigatoni partner well with
meaty, robust sauces and ragùs, whereas
smaller, thinner ones like fregola and
tagliolini pair with creamy, lighter sauces
and broths. That said, I don't believe there
are hard-and-fast rules when it comes to
the world of cooking. If there is a shape
you personally prefer or one that you've
already got in the cupboard, then go for it.

Anelli

Small hoop-shaped pasta traditionally served in soups and broths. My recipe uses these little hoops in a more British than Italian way (see page 60). Any other very small pasta shapes, such as ditalini or stelline, will also work well in soups.

Bucatini

A long pasta shape, like a thicker version of spaghetti with a very small hole running through the middle of the pasta. It is most traditionally used in bucatini all'amatriciana, one of the four classic Roman pasta dishes (see page 41).

Cannelloni

One of the largest pasta shapes you can get, these large cylindrical tubes are traditionally filled, layered and then baked until golden and bubbling. My recipe follows this method but uses leeks and Gorgonzola rather than the traditional spinach and ricotta filling (see page 135).

Casarecce

A short, twisted pasta shape originating from Sicily. It is extremely versatile, pairing perfectly with cheesy, creamy or even meaty sauces that are held within the curves of the pasta. Other twisted shapes like gemelli or fusilli would be good substitutes.

Cavatelli

Little shells that are similar to gnocchi in appearance. Usually made from a semolina and water dough, this small, firm little pasta shape works well with robust, chunky ingredients and sauces, such as my Cavatelli with Cavolo Nero and Bacon (page 42).

Conchigliette

A variation of conchiglie, commonly known as 'shells' or 'seashells', conchigliette is the smallest version of this pasta type. It is well suited to thicker sauces such as puttanesca, thanks to its ability to hold chunky ingredients inside the shell shape.

Fettuccine

Most popular in Roman cuisine, this long, flat pasta pairs well with thick, creamy sauces or ragù. The flat shape gives a soft, almost silky, mouthfeel. It is very similar to tagliatelle, though tagliatelle is ever so slightly wider and rolled a little thinner. These two shapes can be used interchangeably.

Fregola

A traditional Sardinian shape, this pasta is somewhere between a grain and a pasta in appearance. The very small little rounds have a distinct nutty flavour. Fregola is rolled, sun dried and often toasted to a mix of yellow, gold and brown shades. Pearl or Israeli couscous can easily be substituted.

Fusilli lunghi

A variation of the well-known fusilli shape. The elongated, corkscrew shape means that ingredients in a sauce – such as the crab meat in my Crab, Lime and Crispy Chilli dish (page 64) – can blend and fold within the twists of the pasta.

Garganelli

A traditional hand-rolled pasta with a tubular shape and deep ridges that make it an excellent vessel for heavy sauces. It is often served with a rich ragù, such as Slow -cooked Squid and Preserved Lemon (page 150). Penne is a good store-cupboard staple that can be swapped for garganelli.

Gemelli

With the appearance of two small strings of pasta intertwined, this shape gives the pasta its name, which is the Italian word for twins. The shape is in fact made from one long piece of pasta, folded back up on itself and twisted together. It is traditionally paired with salads, like in my Goat's Cheese and Caramelized Red Onion Salad (page 92).

Gnocchi Sardi

Small, ridged pasta from Sardinia made with a semolina and water dough, and also known as malloreddus. The semolina gives a distinct firm and bouncy texture, similar to orecchiette and trofie.

Lasagne

The well-known, very large pasta sheets that are layered up, usually with béchamel sauce and meat ragù.

Linguine

A long pasta shape, similar to spaghetti but wider and flatter. Usually around 4mm in width, linguine is traditionally served with sauces such as pesto, or paired with fish and seafood, such as my King Prawn and Aleppo Chilli Linguine (page 33).

Macaroni

Small pasta tubes made with durum wheat, and famous for being baked with a béchamel sauce and topped with plenty of cheese. The shape is sometimes shorter and curved and known as elbow macaroni.

Mafalde

A long, ribboned pasta shape, mafalde is also called reginette, meaning 'little queens', in honour of Princess Mafalda of Savoy. Mafalde is one of the sturdiest, thickest pasta shapes with ruffled edges, perfect for clinging to sauce.

Orecchiette

A pasta typical of Puglia, in southern Italy. It is named for its shape, which resembles a small ear, and allows them to be filled with sauce. Other small, semolina-based pasta – such as cavatelli or trofie – are good substitutes for the same texture.

Orzo

A short-cut pasta shape, resembling the shape of rice grains. Orzo is one of the most versatile pasta shapes, working perfectly in pasta salads, or used as you would risotto rice to create creamy, luxurious bowls of pasta.

Paccheri

A short, wide, tube shape ideal for chunky sauces. Conchiglioni (big shells) is another oversized pasta shape that could be used instead of paccheri.

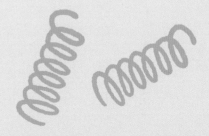

Pappardelle

Long, flat, wide ribbons of pasta, originating from Tuscany. Its slightly rough surface makes it ideal for tossing with thick, hearty sauces that can stand up to its size, such as my Beef Shin and Merlot Ragù (page 158).

Penne

A store-cupboard classic, with a cylindrical shape and ends cut at an angle. Penne is usually made from wheat flour and is very versatile. It is usually paired with thick, hearty, tomato-based sauces.

Pici

A long, thick pasta that almost resembles oversized spaghetti. It originates from Tuscany and is made of semolina and water, resulting in a firm pasta with a nice amount of bite.

Rigatoni

Wide tubular pasta with deep ridges, making it one of the best shapes to pair with coarse, textured sauces. The chunky ingredients in recipes such as my Crispy Sausage, Romano Pepper and Chilli Rigatoni (page 111) balance the robust textures of the sauce with the equally robust, bulky pasta.

Spaghetti

An extremely popular and well-used pasta in the UK and Italy. The long thin strands give a delicate feel, pairing well with lighter, creamier sauces, or even a simple olive oil and chilli dressing. Spaghetti can also be paired with thicker sauces, such as a tomato based ragù like Bolognese.

Tagliatelle

Originating from Emilia-Romagna in Italy, tagliatelle are long, flat ribbons that are similar in shape to fettuccine. Traditionally about 6mm wide, they have a silky, soft texture. When cooked al dente the surface of tagliatelle will cling to a sauce.

Tagliolini

Very similar to tagliatelle, but only 2–3mm wide. Tagliolini works well with delicate sauces and ingredients, such as my Asparagus, Pecorino and Lemon Tagliolini (page 87). Capellini and angel hair both work well as substitutes as they are also super thin, delicate and long.

Trofie

A short, thin, twisted pasta from Liguria, northern Italy. Trofie is hand-rolled, noticeable as all the pieces will have a slightly different shape and length. It is commonly made from off-cuts when making other pasta.

How to choose your pasta

Not all pasta is made equal. The quality of shop-bought, dried pasta can vary significantly. The use of high-quality flour, superior production methods and a prolonged drying time can make all the difference when it comes to the different pastas you can find on the shelves. Spending just a little more on a premium brand can really elevate your cooking.

My personal favourite, and the one I use the most is Garofalo, an Italian pasta-making company established in 1789 on the slopes of the Gulf of Naples in the town of Gragnano, known as the homeland of Italian pasta. Not only does Garofalo offer a wide range of pasta types, but also a huge variety of shapes: from the most traditional to the more unusual, less well-known ones I use in many of my recipes.

Garofalo use robust durum wheat flour and local spring water, and form pasta shapes through a bronze die, giving their pasta a rough, porous surface that sauces stick beautifully to. The Pasta di Gragnano PGI certification also guarantees an exceptional texture and flavour that comes through clearly when I use Garofalo in my cooking.

READY IN 10–15 MINUTES

Tomato Butter Penne

150g (5½oz) penne
40g (1½oz) salted butter
1 large garlic clove, finely
   chopped
200g (7oz) cherry
   tomatoes, halved
handful of fresh basil,
   leaves separated and
   stalks finely chopped
salt and pepper

In the height of summer when tomatoes are at their best this is my go-to pasta sauce. Using the best-quality tomatoes you can find will result in an incredibly sweet and wonderful sauce. This is enriched with butter and finished with plenty of fresh basil.

Put the penne in a large pan of boiling well-salted water. Cook until al dente, using the timing on the packet instructions as your guide.

Meanwhile, add the butter to another pan and place over a medium heat. Once melted, add the garlic and fry for 1 minute until fragrant. Then add the tomatoes and the finely chopped basil stalks. Season generously with salt and pepper. Use a potato masher to break down the tomatoes and release their juices. Turn up the heat to high and let the tomatoes cook down and bubble away for 5 minutes, stirring often to ensure they don't stick to the pan.

Once the tomatoes have broken down and softened, remove from the heat and either use a stick blender in the pan or transfer the tomatoes to a food processor and blend until completely smooth. Taste for seasoning and adjust as needed.

Drain the pasta and return it to the pan. Roughly tear most of the basil leaves. Pour the sauce into the pan with the pasta and add the torn basil leaves. Toss together until everything is combined then divide between 2 bowls and top with the remaining basil leaves.

Pistachio and Parsley Pesto

150g (5½oz) spaghetti
30g (1oz) pine nuts
90g (3¼oz) shelled, salted
   pistachio nuts
large handful of fresh
   flat-leaf parsley
45g (1¾oz) finely grated
   (shredded) Parmesan
   cheese, plus extra to
   serve
80ml (2¾fl oz) extra virgin
   olive oil, plus extra to
   serve
salt and pepper

Pistachio nuts and parsley are a winning combination for a super-fresh, earthy-tasting pesto, a slightly lighter version of the classic *pesto genovese*.

Put the spaghetti in a large pan of boiling well-salted water. Cook until al dente, using the timing on the packet instructions as your guide.

Meanwhile, toast the pine nuts and pistachios in a small dry frying pan (skillet) over a medium heat until lightly golden all over. Remove from the pan and set aside to cool.

Tip the toasted pine nuts and pistachios into a large pestle and mortar or a food processor, along with the parsley and Parmesan. Pour in the olive oil and season well with salt and pepper. Grind or blitz together until everything is smooth. If the pesto is looking a little too thick, add a small splash of water to loosen it slightly.

Drain the pasta, reserving a little of the cooking water. Return the pasta to the pan then add the pesto and a little splash of the reserved cooking water. Toss or stir over a medium heat for a minute or two until the pesto and pasta water emulsify and coat the pasta. Divide between 2 bowls then top with a drizzle of oil and a little extra Parmesan.

Brown Butter and Sage Pappardelle

150g (5½oz) pappardelle
60g (2¼oz) salted butter
20 sage leaves
freshly grated (ground)
nutmeg
40g (1½oz) finely grated
(shredded) Parmesan
cheese
salt and pepper

Five ingredients are all that are needed for this deep, flavourful dish. The nutty brown butter and earthy-flavoured sage make for a perfect autumn pasta sauce, finished of course with a generous sprinkling of Parmesan on top.

Put the pappardelle in a large pan of boiling well-salted water. Cook until al dente, using the timing on the packet instructions as your guide.

Meanwhile, add the butter to a large frying pan (skillet) and place over a medium heat. Once the butter is melted and bubbling add the sage leaves. Fry for 2–3 minutes until the milk solids in the butter start to turn a dark golden-brown colour. The aroma should start to become nutty and almost caramelized. Remove the pan from the heat once it reaches this stage. Take out half the sage leaves and set aside for the garnish.

Drain the pasta and add to the sage butter. Season well with salt and pepper and add a little grated (ground) nutmeg. Toss everything together until well combined then divide between 2 bowls. Top each one with a mound of Parmesan and garnish with the reserved sage leaves.

Porcini Mushroom Spaghetti

150g (5½oz) spaghetti
20g (¾oz) dried porcini mushrooms, very finely chopped
olive oil, for frying
200g (7oz) baby chestnut (cremini) mushrooms, thinly sliced
50ml (1¾fl oz) dry white wine
60ml (4 tablespoons) single (light) cream
40g (1½oz) finely grated (shredded) Parmesan cheese, plus extra to garnish
salt and pepper

This is a really simple dish with an incredible depth and earthiness from the dried porcini mushrooms. Simply rehydrate them in boiling water to create a mouthwatering bowl of pasta.

Put the spaghetti in a large pan of boiling well-salted water. Cook until al dente, using the timing on the packet instructions as your guide.

Meanwhile, rehydrate the dried porcini. Add them to a small bowl with 2 tablespoons of boiling water. Mix well and set aside.

To make the sauce, add a large splash of oil to a large frying pan (skillet) and place over a high heat. Once hot, add the chestnut mushrooms and fry for 4–5 minutes until they are brown and caramelized all over – the better the caramelization the more the flavour will be intensified.

Add the white wine and turn down the heat to medium. Let the wine bubble for a minute to evaporate off the alcohol and gently scrape the base of the pan to incorporate any caramelized bits stuck to the bottom. Then add the cream and rehydrated porcini mushrooms along with the soaking water. Stir in the Parmesan and season with salt and pepper. Turn down the heat to low and stir well. Leave to simmer until the spaghetti has finished cooking.

Drain the pasta, reserving a little of the cooking water. Add the pasta to the sauce with a little splash of the reserved cooking water. Toss for a minute or two until the sauce thickens, becomes glossy and coats the spaghetti. Divide between 2 bowls and garnish with extra Parmesan and a couple of grinds of pepper.

Shaved Asparagus, Wensleydale and Watercress Pasta Salad

150g (5½oz) conchigliette
8 asparagus spears, shaved lengthways with a mandolin or swivel-head peeler
2 tablespoons extra virgin olive oil
½ tablespoon Dijon mustard
1 lemon, zested then halved for squeezing
2 large handfuls of watercress
70g (2½oz) Wensleydale cheese, crumbled
salt and pepper

Here is a light, summery pasta salad to serve as the perfect side for a barbecued main dish or to enjoy as a quick dinner on a sunny evening. Wensleydale cheese provides a smooth, subtle nuttiness that balances the strong pepperiness of the watercress.

Put the conchigliette in a large pan of boiling well-salted water. Cook until al dente, using the timing on the packet instructions as your guide.

One minute before the end of the pasta's cooking time, add the shaved asparagus to the pan and cook for 1 minute until tender. Drain the contents of the pan then immediately run under cold water. This will keep the asparagus a bright vibrant green and cool down the pasta. Drain thoroughly.

Meanwhile, add the olive oil to a large salad bowl. Next, add the mustard, lemon zest and a small squeeze of the juice. Season generously with salt and pepper. Whisk together until combined then add in the cooled drained pasta and asparagus shavings. Top with the watercress and two-thirds of the crumbled Wensleydale. Gently toss together using salad tongs or a large spoon. Divide between 2 bowls and top with the remaining cheese.

Anchovy and Caper Spaghetti

f

150g (5½oz) spaghetti
50g (1¾oz) salted butter
8 anchovies in oil, drained
and roughly chopped
1 tablespoon capers, finely
chopped
small handful of fresh
flat-leaf parsley, very
finely chopped
1 lemon, halved, for
squeezing
salt and pepper

A beautifully simple bowl of spaghetti is achieved with an anchovy and caper butter sauce. Getting your hands on the best-quality anchovies will elevate the flavours of this dish to the next level.

Put the spaghetti in a large pan of boiling well-salted water. Cook until al dente, using the timing on the packet instructions as your guide.

Meanwhile, make the sauce. Add the butter to a large frying pan (skillet) and place over a low heat to melt. Once melted, add the anchovies and capers. Stir together then gently cook in the butter for the remaining cooking time of the spaghetti, keeping the heat very low to ensure the butter doesn't burn and the anchovies gently melt into the butter.

Drain the pasta, reserving some of the cooking water. Add the spaghetti to the frying pan along with a small splash of pasta water. Add the chopped parsley and a good squeeze of lemon juice. Season well with pepper then turn up the heat to high and toss the contents of the pan. After a minute or so the butter, lemon and pasta water should emulsify to form a sauce that coats the spaghetti. Once this has been achieved, divide between 2 bowls.

King Prawn and Aleppo Chilli Linguine

f

150g (5½oz) linguine
40g (1½oz) salted butter
3 teaspoons dried Aleppo
   chilli flakes (pul biber)
3 garlic cloves, finely sliced
165g (5¾oz) uncooked
   peeled king prawns
   (jumbo shrimp)
1 lemon, halved, for
   squeezing
salt and pepper

Flakes of sun-dried Aleppo chillies (known as pul biber) have a savoury, fruity and mild heat that pairs perfectly with sweet plump king prawns (jumbo shrimp). A big squeeze of lemon is added just before serving to balance the dish.

Put the linguine in a large pan of boiling well-salted water. Cook until al dente, using the timing on the packet instructions as your guide.

Meanwhile, put the butter in a large frying pan (skillet) and place over a low heat. Once melted, stir in the chilli flakes and garlic. Leave to gently infuse into the butter for 5 minutes, keeping the heat low heat to ensure the garlic does not burn.

Next, add the prawns (shrimp) to the pan. Gently cook, stirring, over a medium–low heat for about 3 minutes or until they turn just pink on both sides. Do not overcook, otherwise the prawns will become tough and bouncy – keep the heat low and gentle.

Drain the pasta and add to the pan with prawns. Add a good squeeze of lemon juice then season well with salt and pepper. Toss over the heat for a minute or two until fully combined then divide between 2 bowls.

Tuna, Chilli and Samphire Spaghetti

f

150g (5½oz) spaghetti
olive oil, for frying
1 large red chilli, deseeded
  and finely chopped
2 garlic cloves, finely sliced
90g (3¼oz) samphire
1 can high-quality tuna in
  brine (approx. 100g/3½oz
  drained weight)
1 lemon, zested then
  halved for squeezing
salt and pepper

Using the best-quality canned tuna you can find will help create the best-tasting bowl of pasta, so have a look in your local deli or food store for premium line-caught tuna. The salty tang of fresh samphire is perfect here but when it is out of season you can use asparagus or a dark leafy green such as spinach.

Put the spaghetti in a large pan of boiling well-salted water. Cook until al dente, using the timing on the packet instructions as your guide.

Meanwhile, make the sauce. Pour a generous glug of oil into a large frying pan (skillet). Add the chilli and garlic then place the pan over a low heat. Let them gently fry for about 5 minutes, ensuring the garlic doesn't burn.

For the final 3 minutes of the spaghetti's cooking time, add the samphire to the boiling water and continue to cook until both are al dente. Drain, reserving a little of the cooking water.

Add the spaghetti and samphire to the pan with the chilli and garlic, along with a small splash of the cooking water, the drained tuna and a good squeeze of lemon juice. Season well with salt and pepper. Toss gently over the heat for 2 minutes or so until everything is well combined.

Taste to check the seasoning then divide between 2 bowls and garnish with lemon zest.

Smoked Salmon and Leek Tagliatelle

f

150g (5½oz) tagliatelle
olive oil, for frying
1 leek, trimmed and thinly
  sliced
1 fat garlic clove, finely
  chopped
4 heaped tablespoons
  crème fraîche or soured
  cream
zest of 1 lemon
80g (2¾oz) smoked
  salmon, roughly chopped
salt and pepper

Here is a flavour-packed sauce created with sweet leeks, garlic and crème fraîche then finished with the salty, mild tang of smoked salmon.

Put the tagliatelle in a large pan of boiling well-salted water. Cook until al dente, using the timing on the packet instructions as your guide.

Meanwhile, make the sauce by adding a splash of oil to a large frying pan (skillet) and placing over a medium–low heat. Add the sliced leek and fry for 5 minutes until well softened and translucent. Add the garlic, cook for a further minute, then stir through the crème fraîche and lemon zest. Leave to gently simmer until the tagliatelle is cooked.

Drain the pasta, reserving some of the cooking water. Add the pasta to the simmering sauce, then the smoked salmon. Season well with pepper and a small pinch of salt. Add a small splash of the cooking water and toss over the heat for a minute or so until everything is well combined, the tagliatelle is coated and the smoked salmon has turned opaque. Divide between 2 bowls and grind over a little extra pepper.

Smoky Spaghetti Vongole

F

150g (5½oz) spaghetti
olive oil, for frying
2 garlic cloves, finely sliced
1 generous tablespoon
   chipotle chilli paste
500g (1lb 2oz) fresh clams,
   shells scrubbed (discard
   any that do not close
   when tapped on the work
   surface)
80ml (2¾fl oz) dry white
   wine
large handful of fresh
   flat-leaf parsley, roughly
   chopped
salt and pepper

This one is a twist on the classic spaghetti alle vongole that originates from Naples. A good spoonful of chipotle chilli paste adds a mouthwatering touch of heat to the dish.

Put the spaghetti in a large pan of boiling well-salted water. Cook until al dente, using the timing on the packet instructions as your guide.

Meanwhile, make the sauce by pouring a generous glug of oil into a large lidded pan. Place over a medium–low heat, add the garlic and fry for 3–4 minutes until sizzling and fragrant. Then add the chipotle chilli paste, clams and white wine. Season well with salt and pepper then place the lid on the pan. Steam the clams for 8–10 minutes until they are fully opened. Be careful not to have the heat too high; you are looking to gently steam the clams rather than boil them, which will result in them becoming tough.

Drain the pasta and add to the pan with the cooked clams. Sprinkle over the parsley and toss everything together before dividing between 2 bowls and drizzling with a little extra olive oil.

Bucatini all'Amatriciana

150g (5½oz) bucatini

120g (4¼oz) guanciale, skin removed and cut into 2cm (¾in) cubes

2 teaspoons dried chilli flakes

400g (14oz) canned chopped tomatoes

8 basil leaves

50g (1¾oz) finely grated (shredded) Pecorino cheese, to serve

salt and pepper

This is a classic Italian dish, originating from the town of Amatrice in Lazio, north of Rome. Fatty pieces of guanciale (cured pork cheek) are rendered down, releasing the fat that makes up the base of the sauce. Pancetta can be substituted if you cannot find guanciale.

Put the bucatini in a large pan of boiling well-salted water. Cook until al dente, using the timing on the packet instructions as your guide.

Meanwhile, make the sauce. Put the guanciale in a large, heavy-bottomed frying pan (skillet). Place over a medium heat and fry for about 6 minutes. The fat should start to render out of the meat. The guanciale will fry in the melted fat and start to darken and crisp up. Once the guanciale is well browned, add the chilli flakes and chopped tomatoes. Mix well and season with a little salt and a generous amount of pepper. Let the sauce simmer over a medium–low heat until the bucatini is cooked.

Drain the pasta and add it to the sauce along with the basil leaves. Toss everything together over the heat for a minute or two until combined. Check for seasoning then divide between 2 bowls and sprinkle over the Pecorino.

Cavatelli with Cavolo Nero and Bacon

M

150g (5½oz) cavatelli
olive oil, for frying
6 thick-cut smoked streaky
  bacon rashers (strips),
  chopped into thick
  lardons, or 120g (4¼oz)
  smoked lardons
40g (1½oz) salted butter
1 red chilli, deseeded and
  finely chopped
150g (5½oz) cavolo nero,
  leaves stripped from the
  stem and roughly
  chopped into 5cm (2in)
  pieces
60g (2¼oz) finely grated
  (shredded) Parmesan
  cheese, plus extra to
  serve
salt and pepper

This makes a well-balanced meal, perfect as a mid-week dinner. It provides big flavours from smoky, salty bacon lardons and a pleasant bitterness from the iron-rich cavolo nero.

Put the cavatelli in a large pan of boiling well-salted water. Cook until al dente, using the timing on the packet instructions as your guide.

Meanwhile, place a large frying pan (skillet) over a high heat. Add a small splash of oil and the bacon lardons. Fry for 3–4 minutes until golden brown and crispy. Once crisp, remove from the pan using a slotted spoon and set aside, leaving the fat from the bacon in the pan.

Turn down the heat to low and add the butter. Once melted and foaming, add the chilli and fry for 2 minutes. Add the cavolo nero and a splash of water from the cooking pasta. Let the cavolo nero steam and cook down for a couple of minutes until it is tender and the water has evaporated from the pan.

Drain the pasta, reserving some of the cooking water. Add the drained pasta to the pan with the cavolo nero. Return the fried lardons and add a small splash of the cooking water. Sprinkle over the Parmesan and season well with salt and pepper. Let the cheese melt into the top of the pasta for 1 minute before tossing or stirring vigorously to emulsify the water, cheese and butter. Add a little more of the cooking water to loosen the sauce if needed. Divide between 2 bowls and finish with a little extra Parmesan and pepper.

Pancetta and Gruyère Orecchiette

M

150g (5½oz) orecchiette
100g (3½oz) diced pancetta
2 egg yolks
80g (2¾oz) finely grated (shredded) Gruyère cheese, plus extra to serve
leaves from a few fresh thyme sprigs
salt and pepper

Salty pancetta alongside the creamy smoothness of egg yolks and Gruyère make for a winning combination in this dish. This is the perfect bowl for when you're needing something comforting and quick to help you get through that mid-week slump.

Put the orecchiette in a large pan of boiling well-salted water. Cook until al dente, using the timing on the packet instructions as your guide.

Add the pancetta to a cold frying pan (skillet) and place the pan over a medium heat. Cook for 5 minutes, to allow the fat to render out of the pancetta. After 5 minutes, once the pancetta starts to turn golden brown, remove from the pan using a slotted spoon (reserve the rendered fat) and set aside to cool.

Put the egg yolks, Gruyère and thyme in a small bowl with a generous seasoning of pepper and a small pinch of salt. Add the cooled pancetta and the rendered fat and mix well. Whisk in a small splash of the water from the cooking pasta to warm the egg yolk mixture.

Drain the pasta, reserving some of the cooking water. Return the pasta to the pan along with the warmed egg yolk mixture. Add a generous splash of the cooking water then toss and stir everything together over a low heat for a minute or so. The cheese, egg yolk and pancetta fat will emulsify with the pasta water, creating a rich and shiny sauce that coats the orecchiette. Divide between 2 bowls and finish with a little extra Gruyère.

Prosciutto and Pea Tagliatelle

150g (5½oz) tagliatelle
8 slices of prosciutto, roughly sliced into thin strips
3 egg yolks
60g (2¼oz) finely grated (shredded) Pecorino Romano cheese, plus extra to serve
zest of ½ lemon
100g (3½oz) frozen petits pois

A classic pairing of prosciutto and peas, finished in the classic carbonara-style egg yolk sauce. The addition of a small grating of lemon zest balances the creamy sauce, along with a generous sprinkle of tangy Pecorino Romano just before serving.

Put the tagliatelle in a large pan of boiling well-salted water. Cook until al dente, using the timing on the packet instructions as your guide.

Meanwhile, add the prosciutto to a small cold frying pan (skillet) and place the pan over a medium–low heat. Gently fry for about 4 minutes until some of the prosciutto fat has rendered out and the meat is starting to turn a light golden brown in places. Remove from the pan and set aside.

While the prosciutto is frying, put the egg yolks, Pecorino Romano and lemon zest in a small bowl. Season well with pepper and a small pinch of salt then mix together. Whisk in a small splash of water from the cooking pasta and mix well to warm the egg yolk mixture.

For the final 2 minutes of the tagliatelle's cooking time, add the frozen peas to the boiling water and continue to cook until the pasta is al dente. Drain, reserving a little of the cooking water. Return the drained tagliatelle and peas to the pan along with the warmed egg yolk mixture and the cooked prosciutto. Toss well over the a medium heat for a minute, adding a little splash of the cooking water to loosen the sauce until it coats the tagliatelle. Divide between 2 bowls and finish with a generous grating of Pecorino over the top.

Tuscan Sausage Paccheri

M

150g (5½oz) paccheri
olive oil, for frying
4 good-quality pork
    sausages, skins removed
6 sun-dried tomatoes, finely
    chopped
2 garlic cloves, finely sliced
5 tablespoons double
    (heavy) cream
125g (4½oz) baby spinach
    leaves
salt and pepper

It takes only a handful of ingredients to make this creamy, rich bowl of pasta. Using sausage meat in the ragù means there is already real flavour and depth to the base of this sauce.

Put the paccheri in a large pan of boiling well-salted water. Cook until al dente, using the timing on the packet instructions as your guide.

Meanwhile, make the sauce. Pour a generous glug of oil into a large frying pan (skillet). Place over a high heat and then add the sausage meat to the pan. Use a wooden spoon to break up the meat into small bite-size chunks then fry roughly 5 minutes until golden brown and the meat starts to develop a dark golden crust and become crisp. After about 5 minutes turn down the heat to medium–low and add the sun-dried tomatoes and garlic. Fry for 1 minute until fragrant then add the cream. Season well with salt and pepper and stir everything together. Leave to gently simmer while the pasta finishes cooking.

Drain the pasta, reserving some of the cooking water. Add the paccheri to the sauce, along with a splash of the cooking water. Add the baby spinach and toss everything together over the heat for a minute or two until the sauce coats the pasta and the spinach has wilted. If the sauce is looking a little thick, loosen it with another splash of the cooking water until it has a good consistency. Divide between 2 bowls.

READY IN 15–30 MINUTES

TWO

Balsamic Roasted Tomato Spaghetti

♥

250g (9oz) cherry tomatoes
1 small red onion, roughly
  chopped
40ml (scant 3 tablespoons)
  balsamic vinegar
olive oil, for roasting
100ml (3½fl oz) passata
  (strained tomatoes)
½ tablespoon honey
1 tablespoon dried oregano
150g (5½oz) spaghetti
salt and pepper
Parmesan, to serve

The intense sharpness of balsamic vinegar cuts through the sweetness of the cherry tomatoes which are roasted hot and fast until blistered and softened. They are then blended to a smooth sauce and tossed with spaghetti.

Preheat the oven to 220°C (200°C fan), 425°F, Gas Mark 7 and put a large pan of well-salted water on to boil.

Put the tomatoes and onion in a large roasting tin (roasting pan). Pour over the balsamic vinegar along with a large glug of oil. Season well with salt and pepper then roast for 20 minutes until the skins have blistered and burst open.

Remove the tomatoes from the oven. Place roughly three-quarters of them into a large pan, setting the rest aside. Add the passata (strained tomatoes), honey and oregano. Place over a low heat and gently simmer while you cook the pasta.

Add the spaghetti to the pan of boiling water and cook until al dente, using the timing on the packet instructions as your guide.

After the sauce has simmered for 10 minutes, transfer it to a food processor or blender and blend until completely smooth. Taste for seasoning, adjust as needed, pour the sauce back into the pan over a low heat and bring back to a simmer.

Drain the spaghetti, reserving a little of the cooking water. Add the spaghetti to the pan with the sauce, along with a small splash of reserved pasta water, and toss over the heat for a minute or so until well combined. Divide between 2 bowls and garnish with the reserved whole roasted tomatoes, and a grating of Parmesan.

Braised Courgette, Mint and Mascarpone Paccheri

40g (1½oz) salted butter
2 large garlic cloves, finely
 sliced
2 courgettes (zucchini),
 sliced into 1cm (½in)
 rounds
60ml (4 tablespoons) dry
 white wine
1 lemon, zested then
 halved for squeezing
1 tablespoon dried mint
150g (5½oz) paccheri
125g (4½oz) mascarpone
 cheese
handful of fresh mint
 leaves, finely chopped
salt and pepper

Slowly softening the courgettes (zucchini), breaking them down and cooking them in white wine, creates a super-flavourful base for this sauce. It is then enriched with mascarpone and finished with fresh mint to lift the whole dish. This recipe is perfect for the summer when courgettes are at their best.

Put a large pan of well-salted water on to boil for the pasta.

Add the butter to a large frying pan (skillet) and place over a medium heat. Once the butter has melted, add the garlic and fry for 1 minute until fragrant. Then add the courgettes (zucchini), wine, most of the lemon zest and the dried mint. Season well with salt and pepper then leave to cook for 15 minutes over a low heat, stirring regularly to break down and soften the courgettes.

After 15 minutes, add the paccheri to the boiling water and cook until al dente using the timing on the packet instructions as your guide.

Once the courgettes are very soft and cooked down, add the mascarpone and stir well to melt it in. Add a good squeeze of lemon juice and check the seasoning.

Drain the paccheri, reserving a little of the cooking water. Add the drained pasta to the sauce along with a splash of the cooking water and roughly 1 tablespoon of the finely chopped fresh mint. Turn up the heat to medium and toss over the heat for a minute or two until the sauce coats the pasta and the courgettes break down, mixing with the pasta. Add a little more cooking water to loosen the sauce if needed. Divide between 2 bowls and garnish with the remaining lemon zest and fresh mint.

Marsala Mushroom Penne with Brown Butter Pangrattato

♥

50g (1¾oz) salted butter
2 slices of stale white bread, blitzed into fine breadcrumbs
leaves from a few sprigs of fresh thyme
150g (5½oz) penne
200g (7oz) mixed mushrooms (enoki, shiitake, chestnut and oyster all work well), roughly torn into large pieces
2 garlic cloves, finely sliced
60ml (4 tablespoons) dry Marsala
60g (2¼oz) finely grated (shredded) Parmesan cheese
1 lemon, halved, for squeezing
salt and pepper

This one is a super-luxurious dish using Marsala wine to cook the mushrooms. This combination provides a rich umami flavour, giving an intense base for the sauce. The earthy and nutty mushrooms pair perfectly with the caramelized brown butter in the pangrattato (breadcrumbs).

Put a large pan of well-salted water on to boil for the pasta.

First make the pangrattato. Add half the butter to a frying pan (skillet), place over a medium heat and, once melted, let it foam then the bubbles will settle and disappear and the colour will start to darken slightly. At this point add the breadcrumbs and toss or stir constantly for 3–4 minutes until the breadcrumbs are nicely golden brown in colour and crispy. Remove from the pan, stir through the thyme leaves and set aside.

Add the penne to the pan of boiling water and cook until al dente using the timing on the packet instructions as your guide.

Meanwhile, add the remaining butter to the pan used for the pangrattato. Add the mushrooms and fry over a medium heat for 5 minutes until they have softened and started to take on some colour. Then add the garlic and fry for a further minute before adding the Marsala. Let the wine bubble away over a high heat until it has reduced in quantity by about half. Turn off the heat while waiting for the pasta to finish cooking.

Once cooked, drain the penne, reserving some of the cooking water. Add the pasta to the pan with mushrooms along with a splash of the cooking water. Sprinkle over the

grated (shredded) Parmesan and leave to melt into the
top of the pasta for 30 seconds. Once it has started to melt,
vigorously toss or stir together over a medium heat. Add a
little more cooking water until everything is well combined
and the sauce has a good consistency. Add a squeeze
of lemon juice and season with salt and pepper to taste.
Divide between 2 bowls and top with a generous sprinkling
of the pangrattato.

Shredded Sprout Orecchiette

40g (1½oz) salted butter
olive oil, for frying
1 small onion, finely
  chopped
2 garlic cloves, finely
  chopped
200g (7oz) Brussels
  sprouts, trimmed then
  finely shredded as thinly
  as possible
freshly grated (ground)
  nutmeg
1 teaspoon dried chilli
  flakes
150g (5½oz) orecchiette
100ml (3½fl oz) double
  (heavy) cream
6 sage leaves, finely
  shredded
50g (1¾oz) finely grated
  (shredded) Parmesan
  cheese, plus extra to
  serve
salt and pepper

These are Brussels sprouts but with a difference. First, they are finely shredded and sautéed in plenty of butter flavoured with nutmeg and sage, then they are combined with orecchiette, double (heavy) cream and plenty of Parmesan.

Put a large pan of well-salted water on to boil for the pasta.

Add the butter to a large frying pan (skillet) along with a glug of oil and place over a medium heat. Once the butter is melted and starts to foam, add the onion and fry for 4 minutes until softened. Then add the garlic and fry for a further minute before adding the shredded sprouts. Season well with salt and pepper and a little grated (ground) nutmeg and add the chilli flakes. Continue to fry gently for 10 minutes until the sprouts have started to soften.

After the sprouts have been cooking for 10 minutes, add the orecchiette to the pan of boiling water and cook until al dente, using the timing on the packet instructions as your guide.

Meanwhile, add the cream and sage to the sprouts, followed by the Parmesan. Mix well and gently simmer over a low heat while the pasta finishes cooking.

Drain the orecchiette, reserving some of the cooking water. Add the pasta to the sprouts pan followed by a splash of the cooking water. Toss together over the heat until well combined and the sauce coats the orecchiette. Add a little more cooking water to loosen the consistency of the sauce if needed. Taste for seasoning then divide between 2 bowls and top with extra Parmesan.

Anelli Hoops
on Toast

♥

olive oil, for frying
1 small white onion, finely
  chopped
2 garlic cloves, finely sliced
5 large plum tomatoes,
  quartered
pinch of sugar
2 teaspoons red wine
  vinegar
150g (5½oz) anelli
2 slices of sourdough
butter, for spreading
30g (1oz) finely grated
  (shredded) Parmesan
  cheese
fresh basil leaves, torn
salt and pepper

For me, this is an after-school classic that holds so many memories – the ultimate comfort food. This is my version: a simple pomodoro sauce mixed with the little pasta hoops, served on toasted sourdough with fresh basil and Parmesan.

Put a large pan of well-salted water on to boil for the pasta.

First make the sauce. Add a glug of oil to a large frying pan (skillet) and place over a medium heat. Add the onion and fry for 5 minutes until soft and translucent. Add the garlic and fry for a further minute before adding the tomatoes, sugar and red wine vinegar. Add a small splash of water and season well with salt and pepper. Stir together, turn down the heat to low and leave to simmer.

Add the anelli to the pan of boiling water and cook until al dente, using the timing on the packet instructions as your guide.

Once the pasta has 5 minutes remaining of its cooking time, transfer the tomato and onion mixture to a food processor or blender. Blend until completely smooth then return it to the pan. Check for seasoning and adjust as needed. Place over a low heat and bring to a gentle simmer.

Toast the sourdough and spread generously with butter before putting it on plates.

Drain the anelli and add to the pan with the sauce. Toss over the heat for 30 seconds before spooning over the toast. Top with the Parmesan and torn basil leaves.

Chilli and Tarragon Tagliolini with Pan-fried Red Mullet

F

olive oil, for frying
1 large garlic clove, finely sliced
1 red chilli, deseeded and finely chopped
3 tablespoons tomato purée (paste)
80ml (2¾fl oz) double (heavy) cream
150g (5½oz) tagliolini
4 red mullet or red snapper fillets, skin on and deboned
small handful of fresh tarragon, finely chopped
small handful of fresh flat-leaf parsley, finely chopped
1 lemon, halved, for squeezing
salt and pepper

This is a super-elegant, impressive-looking dish that is surprisingly simple to make. Soft, sweet red mullet is paired with a warming chilli and cream sauce freshened up by stirring fresh herbs through it.

Put a large pan of well-salted water on to boil for the pasta.

Pour a generous splash of oil into a large frying pan (skillet) and place over a medium–low heat. Add the garlic and chilli and fry for 3 minutes until sizzling and fragrant. Then add the tomato purée (paste) and cream and season well with salt and pepper. Whisk together until combined then turn off the heat and set aside.

Add the tagliolini to the pan of boiling water and cook until al dente, using the timing on the packet instructions as your guide.

Meanwhile, place a separate frying pan over a medium–high heat. Season each fish fillet with salt and pepper and rub a little oil over both sides. Once the pan is hot, place the fillets in the frying pan, skin-side down, and fry for 3 minutes or until the skin starts to turn golden and become a little crisp on the edges. Flip the fillets and fry for a further minute. Remove from the pan and leave to rest for a few moments while the pasta finishes cooking.

Drain the tagliolini, reserving a little of the cooking water. Place the sauce back over a medium heat. Add the drained pasta and a good splash of the cooking water. Add the tarragon and parsley along with a good squeeze of lemon. Toss over the heat for a minute or two until well combined and the sauce coats the pasta. Divide between 2 bowls and top with the fish fillets.

Crab, Lime and Crispy Chilli Fusilli Lunghi

f

35g (1¼oz) salted butter
½ fennel bulb, finely sliced
1 large garlic clove, finely sliced
½ red chilli, deseeded and finely chopped
150g (5½oz) fusilli lunghi
100g (3½oz) mixed white and brown crab meat
1 lime, zested then halved for squeezing
2 tablespoons finely chopped fresh flat-leaf parsley
crispy chilli oil, to serve
salt and pepper

Crab is a classic choice to pair with pasta but this dish shakes up that combination a little with the addition of lime zest and a good squeeze of the juice. For a final flourish, pour some punchy crispy chilli oil over the pasta before serving.

Put a large pan of well-salted water on to boil for the pasta.

Add the butter to a large frying pan (skillet) and place over a medium–low heat. Once the butter melts and is foaming, add the fennel and fry for 4 minutes until softened. Then add the garlic and chilli and fry for a further 2 minutes until fragrant.

Add the fusilli lunghi to the pan of boiling water and cook until al dente, using the packet instructions as your guide.

Meanwhile, add the crab meat to the frying pan and mix together. Season with salt and pepper and add the lime zest followed by a little splash of water from the cooking pasta to loosen the crab meat to a sauce consistency. Turn down the heat to low and gently simmer until the pasta is cooked.

Drain the fusilli lunghi and add to the pan with the sauce. Add a good squeeze of the lime juice followed by the chopped parsley. Toss together over the heat for a minute until well combined. Divide between 2 bowls and garnish with a spoonful of crispy chilli oil.

King Prawn and Preserved Lemon Orzo

f

olive oil, for frying
2 garlic cloves, finely sliced
1 teaspoon dried chilli
   flakes
2 tablespoons tomato
   purée (paste)
400g (14oz) canned
   chopped tomatoes
½ preserved lemon, very
   finely chopped
150g (5½oz) orzo
165g (5¾oz) uncooked
   peeled king prawns
   (jumbo shrimp)
30g (1oz) salted butter
small handful of fresh
   flat-leaf parsley, finely
   chopped
salt and pepper

Preserved lemon brings a much more subtle, less sour citrus element to the dish. A deeper, more complex flavour profile which pairs perfectly with king prawns (jumbo shrimp), giving their sweetness a chance to shine.

Put a large pan of well-salted water on to boil for the pasta.

Add a drizzle of oil to a large frying pan (skillet) and fry the garlic and chilli flakes over a medium–low heat for 3 minutes until sizzling and fragrant.

Add the tomato purée (paste), chopped tomatoes and preserved lemon. Season with salt and pepper and stir together until all combined. Leave to simmer over a medium–low heat, stirring regularly.

While the sauce is simmering, add the orzo to the pan of boiling water and cook until al dente, using the timing on the packet instructions as your guide.

Once the orzo has about 3 minutes remaining of its cooking time, add the king prawns (jumbo shrimp) and butter. Turn down the heat to low and gently stir together, letting this bubble away gently for 2–3 minutes until the prawns just turn pink, being careful not to overcook them or boil them in the sauce.

Drain the orzo then add to the pan with the sauce along with the freshly chopped parsley. Stir together then divide between 2 bowls.

Hot-smoked Salmon, Fennel and Mascarpone Rigatoni

f

olive oil, for frying
40g (1½oz) salted butter
1 large banana shallot,
   finely chopped
½ fennel bulb, very finely
   chopped
150g (5½oz) rigatoni
1 tablespoon capers,
   roughly chopped
50ml (1¾fl oz) dry white
   wine
125g (4½oz) mascarpone
   cheese
2 fillets of hot-smoked
   salmon, broken up into
   large flakes
zest of 1 lemon
small handful of fresh dill
   fronds, very finely
   chopped
salt and pepper

Fennel and smoked salmon make a wonderful pairing in this dish. The subtle aniseed flavour of the fennel, gently cooked down in butter, works perfectly alongside the distinct smokiness of the salmon.

Put a large pan of well-salted water on to boil for the pasta.

Heat a large splash of oil with the butter in a large frying pan (skillet) over a medium–low heat. Once hot, add the shallot and fennel and cook down for about 10 minutes, stirring regularly until well softened and translucent.

Add the rigatoni to the pan of boiling water and cook until al dente, using the timing on the packet instructions as your guide.

Meanwhile, add the capers and wine to the sweated-down vegetables. Turn up the heat to high and let the wine bubble rapidly for a minute or so to evaporate the alcohol. Add the mascarpone and season well with pepper and a little salt. Whisk together until combined and then leave to gently simmer over a low heat.

Once the rigatoni is cooked, drain, reserving some of the cooking water. Add the rigatoni and a small splash of the cooking water to the pan with the sauce. Add most of the flaked smoked salmon, the lemon zest and a good sprinkling of dill. Toss over the heat for a minute or two until the sauce thickens and coats the pasta, adding a little more of the reserved water if needed to loosen the sauce. Divide between 2 bowls and top with the remaining salmon.

Saffron Mussel Tagliatelle

f

large pinch of saffron
strands
olive oil, for frying
1 large banana shallot,
finely chopped
1 fat garlic clove, finely
sliced
150g (5½oz) tagliatelle
600g (1lb 5oz) mussels,
shells cleaned and
debearded (discard any
that do not close when
tapped on the work
surface)
100ml (3½fl oz) dry white
wine
80ml (2¾fl oz) single (light)
cream
3 tablespoons finely
chopped chives
salt and pepper

The delicate flavour of mussels needs an equally delicate
sauce to match. This dish has exactly that. Saffron has
a deep, complex but also very gentle flavour, which is
delicious alongside sweet mussels and fresh chives.

Put a large pan of well-salted water on to boil for the pasta.
Put the saffron into a small bowl and add 3 tablespoons
of boiling water to bloom the strands.

Meanwhile, add a generous glug of oil to a large lidded
pan. Place over a medium–low heat then add the shallot
and garlic. Stir well and fry for 4 minutes until softened.

Add the tagliatelle to the pan of boiling water and cook
until al dente, using the timing on the packet instructions
as your guide.

Meanwhile, add the mussels along with the wine to the
shallot and garlic. Mix well and place a lid on top. Cook
over a medium–low heat, stirring occasionally. Make sure
not to cook the mussels too fast and high as this will cause
them to become tough and bouncy. Once the mussels
have just about opened, add the cream and bloomed
saffron along with its soaking liquid. Mix well and turn
the heat off until the tagliatelle has finished cooking.

Drain the pasta and add to the pan with the mussels
and cream mixture. Add the chives and season well with
pepper and a little salt to taste. Mix well together over the
heat for 1 minute then divide between 2 bowls.

Chorizo and Sun-dried Tomato Fregola with Pan-fried Sea Bass

f

olive oil, for frying
1 small white onion, finely chopped
100g (3½oz) chorizo, cut into roughly 2cm (¾in) cubes
60g (2¼oz) sun-dried tomatoes, roughly chopped into small bite-size pieces
2 tablespoons tomato purée (paste)
200g (7oz) cherry tomatoes, halved
150g (5½oz) fregola
2 sea bass fillets, skin on and deboned
1 lemon, halved, for squeezing
10 coriander leaves
salt and pepper

A perfect summer evening pasta dish. The fregola is served in a gentle sweet but smoky sauce made of the fresh cherry tomatoes and the distinct smokiness from the chorizo. This all goes perfectly with the soft flaky crispy skinned sea bass.

Put a large pan of well-salted water on to boil for the pasta.

Start by making the sauce. Heat a large glug of oil in a large frying pan (skillet) over a medium heat. Add the onion and fry for 4 minutes until it starts to soften and turn translucent. Add the chorizo and fry for a further 2 minutes to render some of the oil out of the chorizo. Add the sun-dried tomatoes, tomato purée (paste) and cherry tomatoes. Season well with salt and pepper then stir together. Turn the heat down to medium–low and gently simmer while you cook the pasta.

Add the fregola to the pan of boiling water and cook until al dente, using the timing on the packet instructions as your guide.

Meanwhile, drizzle the sea bass fillets with a little oil and season well with salt and pepper. Place another frying pan over a high heat then, once hot, add the sea bass fillets. Cook, skin-side down, for about 4 minutes or until the skin is starting to turn golden brown. Flip and cook, flesh- side down, for a further minute. Remove and leave to rest while you finish the pasta.

Drain the fregola and add to the pan with the sauce along with a good squeeze of lemon juice. Toss or stir over the heat until well combined and check for seasoning. Divide between 2 bowls then top each one with a sea bass fillet and a few coriander leaves.

Crispy Prosciutto, Oyster Mushroom and Gruyère Tagliatelle

M

8 slices of prosciutto
150g (5½oz) tagliatelle
200g (7oz) oyster
    mushrooms, roughly torn
    with any tough stems
    removed
40g (1½oz) salted butter
1 large banana shallot,
    finely chopped
1 large garlic clove, finely
    sliced
50ml (1¾fl oz) dry white
    wine
80g (2¾oz) finely grated
    (shredded) Gruyère
    cheese
small handful of fresh
    flat-leaf parsley, finely
    chopped
salt and pepper

Simply by placing the prosciutto slices under the grill (broiler) until crisp, you achieve a salty crunch that contrasts perfectly with the soft, velvety texture of the oyster mushrooms.

Put a large pan of well-salted water on to boil for the pasta.

Meanwhile, make the crispy prosciutto. Preheat the grill (broiler) to medium. Lay the prosciutto slices on a baking tray (baking sheet). Grill for about 2–3 minutes until they start to crisp up and the white parts are turning a light golden brown. Once crisp, remove from the tray, place on a sheet of paper towel and set aside.

Add the tagliatelle to the pan of boiling water and cook until al dente, using the timing on the packet instructions as your guide.

Put the oyster mushrooms in a dry frying pan (skillet) over a high heat. Fry for a couple of minutes until they are softened and well browned. Remove from the pan and set aside. Turn down the heat to medium then add the butter, shallot and garlic to the pan. Cook for 4–5 minutes until softened. Add the wine, let it bubble for a minute to evaporate the alcohol, then return the mushrooms to the pan and stir everything together.

Once the tagliatelle is cooked, drain it, reserving some of the cooking water. Add the pasta to the sauce along with a generous splash of the cooking water. Sprinkle in the Gruyère and season with salt and pepper. Leave the pan untouched for 30 seconds until the cheese starts to melt into the top of the pasta. At this point, add the chopped parsley then immediately toss over the heat for a minute until the cheese, wine and cooking water emulsify into a light sauce that coats the pasta. Divide between 2 bowls then top with the crispy prosciutto broken into small pieces.

Fennel, Sausage and Harissa Mafalde

1 tablespoon fennel seeds
olive oil, for frying
4 good-quality pork
    sausages, skins removed
30g (1oz) salted butter
1 small white onion, finely
    chopped
1 fat garlic clove, finely
    chopped
3 tablespoons harissa
1 tablespoon dried oregano
1 tablespoon tomato purée
    (paste)
400g (14oz) canned
    chopped tomatoes
150g (5½oz) mafalde
large handful of fresh basil
    leaves, torn
salt and pepper

Richly spiced and warming harissa pairs perfectly with the sweet, subtle aniseed flavour that comes from fennel.

Put a large pan of well-salted water on to boil for the pasta.

Add the fennel seeds to a separate large pan and dry-fry them for 2 minutes over a medium heat until fragrant and slightly darker in colour. Then add a good splash of oil followed by the sausages. Use a wooden spoon to break down the sausages into bite-size chunks. Brown the meat well for about 4 minutes without constantly stirring and moving it around the pan. This will ensure a better browning, resulting in a more complex-tasting sauce. Once the meat is well browned, remove from the pan using a slotted spoon and set aside, keeping the oil in the pan.

Add the mafalde to the pan of boiling water and cook until al dente, using the timing on the packet instructions as your guide.

Meanwhile, make the sauce. Add the butter and onion to the pan used to cook the sausages and fry for 4 minutes until starting to soften. Add the garlic, harissa and dried oregano then cook for a further minute, stirring well. Then add the tomato purée (paste) and canned tomatoes followed by the cooked sausage. Season well with salt and pepper and simmer gently until the pasta is cooked.

Drain the mafalde, reserving a little of the cooking water. Add the pasta to the sauce with a generous splash of the cooking water. Toss everything over the heat for a minute or two, adding a little more cooking water if needed to create a glossy sauce that coats the pasta. Divide between 2 bowls and scatter over the basil leaves.

Pancetta, Courgette and Lemon Trofie

M

120g (4¼oz) diced pancetta
150g (5½oz) trofie
40g (1½oz) salted butter
2 courgettes (zucchini),
  sliced diagonally into
  1cm (½in) rounds
2 fat garlic cloves, finely
  sliced
small handful of fresh mint
  leaves, finely chopped,
  plus extra to serve
1 lemon, zested then
  halved for squeezing
100g (3½oz) mascarpone
  cheese
finely grated (shredded)
  Parmesan cheese
salt and pepper

Fresh lemon zest and finely chopped mint in this pasta sauce lift the whole dish, providing a perfect foil to the fatty and rich pancetta. A mixture of green and yellow courgettes (zucchini) is nice if you can find them. The result is a well-balanced bowl of pasta.

Put a large pan of well-salted water on to boil for the pasta.

Add the pancetta to a cold frying pan (skillet) and place over a medium–high heat. Fry for about 5 minutes, turning occasionally to ensure the pancetta is well browned on all sides and starting to crisp. Remove from the pan using a slotted spoon, leaving the fat in the pan.

Add the trofie to the pan of boiling water and cook until al dente, following the timing on the packet instructions as your guide.

Meanwhile, add the butter to the pan with the pancetta fat and place over a medium heat. Add the courgettes (zucchini) and fry for about 3 minutes until they start to soften and become lightly caramelized. Add the garlic, chopped mint and lemon zest and fry for a further minute before adding the mascarpone. Add a little splash of the pasta cooking water and a good squeeze of lemon. Mix until the mascarpone melts into a sauce. Season well with salt and pepper then turn down the heat to low and gently simmer until the pasta is cooked.

Drain the trofie, reserving a little of the cooking water. Add the drained pasta and a splash of its cooking water to the pan with the sauce. Toss over the heat for a minute or two until you have a glossy sauce that coats the pasta. Divide between 2 bowls and top with the Parmesan and mint.

Sausage, Kale and Chilli Rigatoni

M

olive oil, for frying
4 good-quality pork
   sausages, skins removed
1 small white onion, finely
   diced
150g (5½oz) rigatoni
2 garlic cloves, finely sliced
1 red chilli, deseeded and
   finely chopped
1 teaspoon dried chilli
   flakes, plus extra to serve
2 tablespoons tomato
   purée (paste)
150g (5½oz) curly kale
   leaves, stripped from the
   stem and shredded
75ml (5 tablespoons)
   double (heavy) cream
salt and pepper

Rich meaty pork has a real affinity for the pleasantly tangy flavour of iron-rich kale, while red chilli delivers warmth to make this a truly comforting pasta dish.

Put a large pan of well-salted water on to boil for the pasta.

Heat a splash of oil in another large pan over a high heat. Once the oil is hot, add the sausages and use a wooden spoon to break them into bite-size chunks. Leave the meat to brown well for 5 minutes or so without stirring and moving it around the pan. This will ensure a caramelized crust develops, creating a tastier and more complex flavour. Once the meat is well browned, remove it from the pan using a slotted spoon. Add the onion to the pan with a good glug of oil. Turn down the heat to medium–low and fry for about 5 minutes until softened.

Add the rigatoni to the pan of boiling water and cook until al dente, guided by the timing on the packet instructions.

Add the garlic, fresh chilli and dried chilli flakes to the softened onion and cook for a further minute. Stir in the tomato purée (paste) and kale along with a large splash of the pasta cooking water. Let the kale cook down until it starts to wilt. Add the cream then return the sausages to the pan and season with salt and pepper. Allow to gently simmer while the pasta finishes cooking.

Drain the rigatoni, reserving a little of the cooking water. Add the pasta to the sauce and toss together over the heat for a minute or two, adding a splash of cooking water if needed to loosen the sauce to a consistency that coats the pasta. Divide between 2 bowls and top with a pinch of chilli flakes.

THREE

READY IN 30 MINUTES – 1 HOUR

Asparagus, Pecorino and Lemon Tagliolini

35g (1¼oz) salted butter
½ leek, trimmed and finely
  sliced
2 small garlic cloves, finely
  sliced
leaves from a few fresh
  thyme sprigs
60ml (4 tablespoons) dry
  white wine
120ml (4fl oz) crème fraîche
  or soured cream
2 teaspoons Dijon mustard
freshly grated (ground)
  nutmeg
150g (5½oz) taglioini
1 bunch of asparagus,
  tough ends trimmed
60g (2¼oz) finely grated
  Pecorino Romano
  cheese, plus extra to
  serve
1 lemon, halved, for
  squeezing
salt and pepper

This dish has gently sautéed leeks as its base, lightly flavoured with mustard and nutmeg, finished with tangy Pecorino Romano and topped with tender asparagus. Perfect for an evening meal in summer, when asparagus is at its best.

Add the butter to a large frying pan (skillet) and place over a low heat. Once melted, add the leek, garlic and thyme leaves and gently fry over a low heat for about 20 minutes, stirring regularly, by which time the leek should be completely soft and translucent.

Put a large pan of well-salted water on to boil for the pasta.

Meanwhile, add the wine to the softened leeks and turn up the heat to high. Boil the wine for a minute or two to evaporate the alcohol. Add the crème fraîche, Dijon mustard and a little grated (ground) nutmeg. Turn down the heat to low and stir together until combined. Leave to gently simmer while cooking the pasta.

Add the tagliolini to the pan of boiling water and cook until al dente, using the timing on the packet instructions as your guide. Add the asparagus to the pan for the final 4 minutes until just tender.

Drain the tagliolini and asparagus, reserving a little of the cooking water.

Continued overleaf...   Ready in 30 minutes–1 hour

Add the pasta to the pan with the sauce, keeping the asparagus to one side while you finish the sauce.

Sprinkle the Pecorino Romano over the tagliatelle in the pan and squeeze over a little lemon juice and a generous splash of the cooking water. Season well with salt and pepper and let the cheese melt into the top of the tagliolini for 30 seconds. Toss vigorously together over the heat for a minute or two until the sauce is emulsified and coats the pasta. Add a little more of the pasta cooking water to loosen the sauce if needed to give it a good creamy consistency. Divide between 2 bowls and top with the asparagus, followed by a little extra Pecorino.

Burnt Aubergine Rigatoni

1 large aubergine
  (eggplant)
extra virgin olive oil, for
  cooking and drizzling
1 small red onion, finely
  sliced
1 red (bell) pepper, finely
  sliced
1 large garlic clove, finely
  sliced
½ teaspoon dried chilli
  flakes
small handful of fresh basil,
  stalks and leaves
  separated
1 tablespoon tomato purée
  (paste)
200g (7oz) passata
  (strained tomatoes)
½ tablespoon red wine
  vinegar
1 teaspoon granulated
  sugar
150g (5½oz) rigatoni
salt and pepper

Inspired by the traditional Sicilian dish pasta alla Norma, in this version aubergine (eggplant) is roasted and charred before being added to the sauce. By burning the whole aubergine its flesh is steamed and softened while its flavour is intensified, giving a subtle smokiness to the sauce.

Preheat the oven to 220°C (200°C fan), 425°F, Gas Mark 7. Place the aubergine (eggplant) on a baking tray (baking sheet), drizzle with a little oil and spread it over the skin of the aubergine. Bake for 25 minutes: the skin should be wrinkled and charred while the flesh will be completely soft. Remove from the oven, slice in half lengthways and set aside to cool.

Add a generous glug of oil to a large lidded pan. Place over a medium–low heat and add the onion and (bell) pepper. Fry for about 5 minutes until they start to soften. Add the garlic and fry for a further minute before adding the chilli flakes. Finely chop the stalks of the basil and add them to the pan. Mix well then stir in the tomato purée (paste), passata (strained tomatoes), vinegar and sugar. Season generously with salt and pepper then turn down the heat to low and leave to gently simmer, stirring occasionally.

Put a large pan of well-salted water on to boil for the pasta.

Continued overleaf...   Ready in 30 minutes–1 hour

Remove the soft flesh of the aubergine using a spoon and roughly chop. Add to the pan with the sauce and mix well. Cover with the lid and continue to gently simmer while you cook the pasta.

Add the rigatoni to the pan of boiling water and cook until al dente, using the timing on the packet instructions as your guide.

Drain the rigatoni then add it to the pan with sauce. Toss over the heat for a minute or two until the sauce coats the pasta.

Divide between 2 bowls then finish with a good drizzle of extra virgin olive oil and garnish with the basil leaves.

Goat's Cheese and Caramelized Red Onion Gemelli Salad

olive oil, for frying
2 red onions, finely sliced
leaves from a few fresh
  thyme sprigs
leaves from a few fresh
  rosemary sprigs
2 tablespoons balsamic
  vinegar
½ tablespoon light brown
  sugar
50g (1¾oz) pine nuts
150g (5½oz) gemelli
300ml (10fl oz) extra virgin
  olive oil
juice of 1 lemon
1 teaspoon Dijon mustard
2 large handfuls of
  watercress
40g (1½oz) soft fresh goat's
  cheese, frozen
salt and pepper

Jammy, caramelized onions form the basis of this dish, their sweetness offset by a lemon vinaigrette and peppery watercress. The whole dish is finished with a generous grating of goat's cheese. This is a pasta salad, but not as you know it!

First make the caramelized red onions. Add a generous drizzle of oil to a medium pan, place over a low heat then add the red onions, thyme and rosemary. Season well with salt and pepper and cook gently for 15 minutes.

Meanwhile, put a large pan of well-salted water on to boil for the pasta.

Add the vinegar and sugar to the onions, turn up the heat to medium–high and cook for a further 5 minutes until the onions have become sticky and caramelized. Set aside.

Toast the pine nuts in a small dry frying pan (skillet) over a medium heat until golden brown on all sides. Remove from the pan and set aside.

Add the gemelli to the pan of boiling water and cook until al dente, using the timing on the packet instructions as your guide.

Drain the pasta then cool it for a few seconds under cold running water. Transfer it to a large bowl.

Add the olive oil, lemon juice and Dijon mustard to the bowl along with the caramelized red onions. Add the toasted pine nuts and mix together to cool the onions slightly. Then add the watercress and quickly but gently toss together. Divide between 2 bowls and grate (shred) the frozen goat's cheese over the top.

Caramelized Shallot Tagliatelle

60g (2¼oz) salted butter
olive oil, for frying
8 banana shallots, thinly sliced lengthways
1 large garlic clove, finely chopped
1 tablespoon light brown sugar
2 teaspoons red wine vinegar
1 bay leaf
150g (5½oz) tagliatelle
60ml (4 tablespoons) dry white wine
leaves from 6 fresh thyme sprigs
70g (2½oz) finely grated Parmesan cheese, plus extra to serve
½ lemon, for squeezing
salt and pepper

Cooking shallots slowly and very gently gives them time to sweeten and caramelize, which works wonderfully here. Thyme adds woody, earthy notes and a good squeeze of lemon at the end lightens the dish: a perfect balance of flavours.

Add 30g (1oz) of the butter and a generous drizzle of oil to a large pan and place over a very low heat until melted. Add the shallots, garlic, sugar, vinegar and bay leaf. Cook very gently for 30 minutes, stirring occasionally to make sure the contents don't stick to the pan. After this time the shallots should be extremely soft and caramelized, and pale gold in colour.

Meanwhile, put a large pan of well-salted water on to boil for the pasta.

After the shallots have cooked for 30 minutes, add the tagliatelle to the pan of boiling water and cook until al dente, using the timing on the packet instructions as your guide.

Meanwhile, turn up the heat to medium–high under the shallots, remove the bay leaf and pour in the wine. Stir well, letting the wine bubble for a minute or so to evaporate the alcohol. Deglaze the pan by gently scraping the bottom of the plan to release any caramelized bits then add the remaining butter and most of the thyme leaves. Season well with salt and pepper.

Continued overleaf...   Ready in 30 minutes–1 hour

Drain the tagliatelle, reserving a little of the cooking water then add the pasta to the pan of caramelized shallots. Sprinkle over the Parmesan, a large splash of cooking water and a good squeeze of lemon. Let the cheese melt into the top of the pasta for 30 seconds before tossing everything together over the heat for a minute, adding a little more water if needed to loosen the consistency. Once everything is incorporated and the sauce is shiny and coats the pasta, taste for seasoning and adjust as needed.

Divide between 2 bowls and garnish with a little extra Parmesan and thyme leaves.

Creamed Spinach Penne with Flaked Almond Pangrattato

50g (1¾oz) salted butter

olive oil, for frying

2 slices of stale white bread, blitzed into fine breadcrumbs

40g (1½oz) flaked (slivered) almonds

leaves from a few fresh thyme sprigs

2 garlic cloves, finely sliced

260g (9½oz) spinach leaves

80ml (2¾fl oz) dry white wine

zest of 1 lemon

100ml (3½fl oz) single (light) cream

freshly grated (ground) nutmeg

150g (5½oz) penne

salt and pepper

This recipe uses the classic side dish of creamed spinach as a luxurious sauce. Finished with a mixture of golden and nutty brown butter breadcrumbs and flaked (slivered) almonds.

First make the pangrattato. Add 25g (1oz) of the butter and a little splash of olive oil to a frying pan (skillet) and place over a medium heat. When the butter has melted and is foaming, cook for 2 minutes until its colour starts to darken very slightly. Once you start to see the colour change, add the breadcrumbs, flaked (slivered) almonds and thyme leaves. Season with salt and pepper and fry for 3–4 minutes, stirring constantly until the breadcrumbs become golden brown and crispy and the almonds are a little golden. Remove from the pan and set aside.

Put a large pan of well-salted water on to boil for the pasta.

Meanwhile, make the creamed spinach. Add the remaining butter to a large lidded pan and place over a medium–low heat. Once melted, add the garlic and fry for about 2 minutes until sizzling and fragrant. Add the spinach leaves followed by the wine and let the spinach wilt down. After a couple of minutes, once the spinach is fully wilted, add the lemon zest, cream and a little grated (ground) nutmeg. Season well with salt and pepper then turn down the heat to low and cover with a lid. Simmer very gently for 15 minutes.

Continued overleaf...   Ready in 30 minutes–1 hour

Add the penne to the pan of boiling water and cook until al dente, using the timing on the packet instructions as your guide.

Drain the pasta, reserving a little of the cooking water. Add the pasta to the pan of creamed spinach followed by a splash of cooking water. Toss over the heat for a minute or two until everything is well combined and the sauce coats the pasta. Divide between 2 bowls and top with a few spoonfuls of the pangrattato.

Salmon, Tenderstem Broccoli and Chilli Orzo Traybake

f

olive oil, for frying
1 small white onion, finely sliced
2 garlic cloves, finely chopped
1 red chilli, deseeded, finely chopped
150g (5½oz) orzo
330ml (11½fl oz) fish stock
zest and juice of 1 lemon
180g (6¼oz) tenderstem broccoli, halved lengthways then each cut into 3
95ml (3¼fl oz) double cream
2 salmon fillets
pinch of dried chilli flakes
small handful of freshly chopped dill fronds
salt and pepper

This traybake is perfect for an easy, simple dinner that doesn't scrimp on flavour. The orzo is baked in fish stock with plenty of chilli and garlic running through it. Served with tenderstem broccoli and salmon fillets, it makes for a very healthy bowl of pasta. If you want to reduce the serving size then ensure the tray used to bake the dish is small enough for the orzo to be covered by the stock.

Preheat the oven to 200°C (180°C fan), 400°F, Gas Mark 6.

Add a generous splash of oil to a frying pan (skillet) and place over a medium heat. Once hot, add the onion and fry for 4 minutes until softened slightly. Then add the garlic and fresh chilli and fry for a further 2 minutes.

Transfer the fried onion, garlic and chilli to a small deep oven tray (pan) or baking dish. Add the orzo and fish stock, squeeze in the lemon juice and season well with salt and pepper. Gently mix everything together before covering the tray with foil to seal. Bake for 15 minutes.

After 15 minutes, remove the tray from the oven and take off the foil. Stir the cream and tenderstem broccoli into the orzo until well combined. Season the salmon fillets with salt and pepper, the chilli flakes and the lemon zest.

Gently place the salmon fillets on top of the orzo. Re-cover the tray with the foil and return it to the oven for a further 14 minutes.

Remove from the oven after 15 minutes; the salmon will be cooked through and the broccoli tender but with a slight bite. Lift the salmon fillets off the orzo and set aside. Add the dill and stir everything together before spooning into 2 bowls. Top each one with a salmon fillet.

Sardine and Burnt Lemon Casarecce

F

200g (7oz) cherry
  tomatoes, halved
2 lemons, halved
olive oil, for cooking
1 small white onion, finely
  chopped
2 garlic cloves, finely sliced
½ teaspoon dried chilli
  flakes
1 tablespoon capers,
  roughly chopped
2 tablespoons tomato
  purée (paste)
1 teaspoon granulated
  sugar
95g (3¼oz) good-quality
  sardines in oil
150g (5½oz) casarecce
small handful of fresh
  flat-leaf parsley, finely
  chopped
salt and pepper

Roasting lemons mellows out their sharpness, which works perfectly in savoury recipes like this one. The lemon paired with the intense saltiness of the sardines makes for a beautiful dish.

Preheat the oven to 200°C (180°C fan), 400°F, Gas Mark 6.

Arrange the cherry tomatoes and lemon halves cut-side down on a roasting tray (roasting pan). Drizzle generously with oil and season well with salt and pepper. Roast for 20 minutes until the tomatoes are starting to blister and soften. Remove from the oven and set aside.

Put a large pan of well-salted water on to boil for the pasta.

Meanwhile, add a generous splash of oil to a large frying pan (skillet) and place over a medium heat. Add the onion and fry for 5 minutes until softened and translucent. Then add the garlic and fry for a further minute before adding the chilli flakes, capers, tomato purée (paste) and sugar. Mix well then turn the heat to low and leave to simmer gently.

Add the casarecce to the boiling water and cook until al dente, using the timing on the packet instructions as your guide.

Continued overleaf...   Ready in 30 minutes–1 hour

Transfer the cooled roasted tomatoes to a blender or food processor and blitz until smooth. Tip into the pan with the onion mixture and squeeze in the juice from 1 of the roasted lemons. Add the sardines and a little of the oil from the can. Stir well to break down the sardines. Let the sauce gently simmer until the pasta is cooked.

Drain the casarecce then add it to the pan with the sauce. Toss or stir well over the heat for a minute before dividing between 2 bowls. Sprinkle with parsley and serve with the remaining roasted lemon halves on the side for squeezing.

Za'atar Salmon with Caramelized Onion and Feta Orzo

olive oil, for frying
1 white onion, finely sliced
1 tablespoon white wine
   vinegar
1 tablespoon dark brown
   sugar
1 garlic clove, finely
   chopped
2 teaspoons dried
   rosemary
2 tablespoons runny honey
2 tablespoons za'atar
2 salmon fillets
150g (5½oz) orzo
30g (1oz) salted butter
small handful of fresh
   flat-leaf parsley, finely
   chopped
80g (2¾oz) feta cheese
salt and pepper

This is a more experimental, untraditional pasta dish using the Middle Eastern condiment za'atar, honey and Greek feta cheese. The za'atar and honey glaze over the salmon gives an aromatic sweetness to the fish, which, along with salty feta and sweet caramelized onions means this pasta dish delivers every flavour profile you could want.

Add a large splash of oil to a large frying pan (skillet) and place over a low heat. Add the onions and allow to cook down for 20 minutes, stirring occasionally until they are very soft. (At this stage you are not trying to get much colour on the onions, just for them to soften and become sweeter in flavour.)

Preheat the oven to 200°C (180°C fan), 400°F, Gas Mark 6.

Turn up the heat under the onions to medium–high and add the vinegar and sugar. Stir over the heat for 5 minutes until the sugar has dissolved and the onions are shiny and sticky. Add the garlic and dried rosemary. Turn off the heat and set the pan aside.

Put a large pan of well-salted water on to boil for the pasta.

Meanwhile, add the honey and za'atar to a small bowl along with a small glug of oil. Season with salt and pepper and mix well. Brush half of this glaze over the salmon fillets using a pastry brush or spoon. Roast in the oven for 12–14 minutes, depending upon the size of your fillets.

Continued overleaf...   Ready in 30 minutes–1 hour

Add the orzo to the pan of boiling water and cook until al dente, using the timing on the packet instructions as your guide.

Add the remaining half of the za'atar and honey glaze to the pan with the onions, along with the butter and parsley. Mix well and place the pan over a low heat.

Drain the orzo and add to the pan with the onion mixture. Toss together for a minute then divide between 2 bowls. Top with the salmon fillet and then crumble over the feta.

Rosé Roasted Tomato and Mussel Linguine

f

200g (7oz) plum tomatoes, quartered
2 garlic cloves, finely sliced
½ tablespoon dried oregano
6 anchovies in oil, drained
a few fresh tarragon sprigs, finely chopped, plus extra to garnish
80ml (2¾fl oz) dry rosé wine
150g (5½oz) linguine
600g (1lb 5oz) fresh mussels, cleaned and debearded (discard any that do not close when tapped on the work surface)
1 lemon, halved, for squeezing
salt and pepper

A tomato sauce made by roasting plum tomatoes in rosé wine. The dry fruitiness of the rosé pairs perfectly with the sweet plump mussels, finished with a good squeeze of lemon for balance.

Preheat the oven to 190°C (170°C fan), 375°F, Gas Mark 5.

Put the tomatoes, garlic, dried oregano, anchovies and tarragon in a large roasting tin (roasting pan). Mix well and season with salt and pepper. Pour the rosé wine into the tin and roast for 25 minutes.

When the tomatoes are nearing the end of their cooking time, put a large pan of well-salted water on to boil for the pasta. Once boiling, add the linguine and cook until al dente, using the timing on the packet instructions as your guide.

After 25 minutes, remove the tomatoes from the oven and transfer to a large lidded frying pan (skillet). Place over a medium–low heat and bring to a gentle simmer. Once simmering, add the mussels and toss together. Leave the mussels to cook for about 6 minutes until you see the first few start to open. Ensure the heat is not too high; you don't want the mussels to boil and become tough. A gentle simmer is best.

Drain the linguine and add to the pan with the sauce and mussels. Squeeze over the lemon juice then toss everything together over the heat for a minute or two until the last few mussels open. Divide between 2 bowls and garnish with a little extra fresh tarragon.

Crispy Sausage, Romano Pepper and Chilli Rigatoni

3 red Romano (long bell) peppers
olive oil, for frying
4 good-quality pork sausages, skins removed
150g (5½oz) rigatoni
1 large banana shallot, finely chopped
1 large garlic clove, finely chopped
1 red chilli, deseeded and finely chopped
2 teaspoons fennel seeds
1 tablespoon smoked paprika
2 tablespoons tomato purée (paste)
100ml (3½fl oz) double (heavy) cream
50g (1¾oz) finely grated (shredded) Parmesan cheese
crispy chilli oil, to finish
salt and pepper

Charring Romano (long bell) peppers brings out their sweetness, creating the soft and slightly smoky ribbons that run through this dish. Combined with chilli, herbs and caramelized pork and finished with crispy chilli oil, this bowl of pasta really packs a punch.

Preheat the oven to 220°C (200°C fan), 425°F, Gas Mark 7.

Put the whole (bell) peppers on a baking tray (baking sheet) and roast for about 20 minutes or until the skins are blackened. Remove from the oven and leave until they are cool enough to touch.

While the peppers are cooling, put a large pan of well-salted water on to boil for the pasta.

Heat a generous splash of oil in a large pan over a high heat. When the oil is hot, add the sausages and use a wooden spoon to break up the sausages into bite-size chunks. Leave the meat to brown well for 6 minutes without stirring or moving it around the pan. This will ensure a caramelized crust develops, providing a deeper flavour. Once the meat is well browned, remove it from the pan using a slotted spoon and set aside.

Add the rigatoni to the pan of boiling water and cook until al dente, using the timing on the packet instructions as your guide.

Add the shallot and garlic to the pan used to cook the sausages, along with a splash of oil. Fry over a medium–low heat for about 5 minutes until softened, then add the chilli, fennel seeds, paprika and tomato purée (paste).

Continued overleaf...   Ready in 30 minutes–1 hour   **111**

Return the browned sausage meat to the pan along with the cream and bring to a gentle simmer.

Use your fingers to remove the blackened skins from the peppers and take out the seeds. Slice the flesh into long thin strips then add to the pan with the sauce. Season well with salt and pepper.

Drain the rigatoni, reserving a little of the cooking water. Add the drained pasta to the pan with the sauce along with the Parmesan. Toss everything together over the heat for a minute or two, adding a splash of the cooking water if needed to loosen the sauce to a consistency that coats the pasta. Once everything is combined and the sauce is thick and glossy, check for seasoning. Divide between 2 bowls and garnish with crispy chilli oil to taste.

Roasted Spring Onion, Prosciutto and Walnut Gremolata Gnocchi Sardi

5 large spring onions
(scallions), halved
lengthways
olive oil, for cooking
150g (5½oz) gnocchi sardi
40g (1½oz) salted butter
1 large garlic clove, finely
chopped
50g (1¾oz) grated
(shredded) Gruyère
cheese
6 slices of prosciutto
salt and pepper

For the gremolata
40g (1½oz) walnuts
large handful of fresh
flat-leaf parsley, finely
chopped
1 teaspoon dried chilli
flakes
60ml (4 tablespoons) extra
virgin olive oil
1 lemon, zested then
halved for squeezing

Roasting the spring onions (scallions) softens and sweetens their flavour. They work perfectly with salty prosciutto with a walnut gremolata spooned over the top to finish.

Preheat the oven to 200°C (180°C fan), 400°F, Gas Mark 6.

First make the gremolata. Put the walnuts in a small dry frying pan (skillet) and place over a medium heat. Toast gently for 3–4 minutes until they are slightly darkened in colour and give off their nutty aroma. Remove from the pan and very finely chop into small pieces. Transfer to a small bowl and add the parsley, chilli flakes and olive oil. Add a squeeze of lemon (reserving the lemon zest) and season well with salt and pepper. Mix well or, for a smoother texture, you can grind everything together using a pestle and mortar. Set aside.

Lay the halved spring onions (scallions) on a baking tray (baking sheet) and drizzle generously with oil. Add the lemon zest then season with salt and pepper. Roast for 15 minutes.

Put a large pan of well-salted water on to boil for the pasta.

Once the spring onions have softened, remove the tray from the oven and lower the temperature to 180°C (160°C fan), 350°F, Gas Mark 4. Transfer half the onions to a chopping board and roughly chop into small pieces. Return the rest to the oven to continue roasting for a further 10 minutes while you cook the pasta.

Continued overleaf...   Ready in 30 minutes–1 hour

Put the gnocchi sardi into the pan of boiling water and cook until al dente, using the timing on the packet instructions as your guide.

Meanwhile, add the butter and a drizzle of oil to a large frying pan (skillet). Place over a medium–low heat and, once the butter has melted, add the garlic and chopped spring onions. Fry for 3 minutes until sizzling and fragrant. Season well with salt and pepper then turn off the heat until the pasta has finished cooking.

Drain the gnocchi sardi, reserving a little of the cooking water. Add the pasta to the pan with the garlic and spring onions. Turn the heat to medium–high, sprinkle in the cheese and add a splash of the cooking water. Leave the cheese to melt into the top of the pasta then toss over a medium heat for a minute or two until everything is well combined. Divide between 2 bowls. Top with the reserved roasted spring onions, then the prosciutto slices, followed by a couple of spoonfuls of the gremolata.

Pork and 'Njuda Meatballs with Bucatini

M

olive oil, for frying
1 white onion, finely
  chopped
1 garlic clove, finely
  chopped
100ml (3½fl oz) red wine
400g (14oz) canned
  chopped tomatoes
1 tablespoon red wine
  vinegar
1 teaspoon granulated
  sugar
150g (5½oz) bucatini
small handful of fresh basil
  leaves
finely grated (shredded)
  Parmesan cheese, to
  finish
salt and pepper

For the meatballs
200g (7oz) minced (ground)
  pork
50g (1¾oz) 'nduja
1 tablespoon dried
  rosemary
1 teaspoon dried chilli
  flakes
1 tablespoon smoked
  paprika
40g (1½oz) soft white
  breadcrumbs

The Italian spicy sausage 'njuda is the perfect addition to this dish. It brings aromatic flavour as well as a nice warm kick to the meatballs, which are gently simmered in a red wine sauce.

First make the meatballs. Put all the ingredients into a bowl. Season well with salt and pepper then mix with your hands until well combined. Divide into 8 small balls, weighing roughly 30g (1oz) each. Place in the refrigerator while you make the sauce.

Add a good glug of oil to a large lidded pan and place over a medium heat. Add the onion and fry for 5 minutes until softened before adding the garlic and frying for a further minute. Pour in the wine followed by the chopped tomatoes, vinegar and sugar. Season with salt and pepper then turn down the heat to low. Put the lid on the pan and leave to gently simmer while you fry the meatballs.

Put a large pan of well-salted water on to boil for the pasta.

Drizzle a good amount of oil into a large frying pan (skillet) and place over a medium–high heat. Once the pan is hot, add the meatballs and fry for about 3 minutes without disturbing, to gain a good golden caramelization on the meat before turning and browning the other sides. Once cooked, add the meatballs to the sauce along with any cooking juices. Cover the pan with the lid and simmer for 15 minutes over a medium–low heat until the meatballs are cooked through, turning them occasionally.

Meanwhile, add the bucatini to the pan of boiling water and cook until al dente, using the timing on the packet instructions as your guide.

Drain the pasta and add to the pan with the sauce, along with the torn basil. Gently stir until everything is combined. Divide between 2 bowls and top with Parmesan.

Pea, Mascarpone and Crispy Ham Hock Orzo

olive oil, for frying
100g (3½oz) cooked,
 shredded ham hock
40g (1½oz) salted butter
1 small white onion, finely
 chopped
½ leek, finely sliced
1 large garlic clove, finely
 chopped
60ml (4 tablespoons) dry
 white wine
120g (4¼oz) mascarpone
1 teaspoon dried mint
150g (5½oz) frozen petits
 pois
40g (1½oz) finely grated
 (shredded) Parmesan
 cheese, plus extra to
 serve
150g (5½oz) orzo
small handful of fresh mint
 leaves, finely chopped
salt and pepper

Gently sautéed onion and leek form the basis of this super-creamy sauce. Sweet petits pois are then added and blended with mascarpone to create a rich, vibrant sauce. Shards of salty crisp ham provide a pleasing finishing touch.

Add a splash of oil to a small frying pan (skillet) and place over a medium heat. Add the ham hock and fry for about 4 minutes until it starts to crisp up and turn golden brown in places. Remove from the pan and set aside.

Meanwhile, make the sauce. Add the butter and a generous splash of oil to a large saucepan. Add the onion and leek then cook gently for about 10 minutes over a medium–low heat until well softened and translucent.

Put a large pan of well-salted water on to boil for the pasta.

Finish the sauce by adding the garlic to the onion and leek mixture before pouring in the wine and turning up the heat to high. Allow the wine to bubble and the alcohol to evaporate for a minute before adding the mascarpone, dried mint and 100g (3½oz) of the peas. Turn down the heat to medium and simmer for 5 minutes until the mascarpone has melted and the peas have cooked.

Add the Parmesan and season well with salt and pepper. Stir together before transferring to a food processor or blender and blend until completely smooth. Pour back into the pan and taste for seasoning. Leave on low to simmer gently while you cook the pasta.

Continued overleaf...   Ready in 30 minutes–1 hour

Cook the orzo in the pan of boiling water until al dente, using the timing on the packet instructions as your guide.

Drain the pasta and add to the pan with the sauce. Add the chopped mint and the remaining peas. Toss or stir well over the heat for a minute or two until well combined and the peas have just cooked. Taste for seasoning then divide between 2 bowls and top with the crispy ham hock and a little more Parmesan.

Pancetta, Pork and Fennel Fettuccine

100g (3½oz) diced pancetta
220g (8oz) good-quality
    minced (ground) pork
olive oil, for frying
1 white onion, finely sliced
1 fennel bulb, finely sliced
2 fat garlic cloves, finely
    chopped
leaves from 4 fresh thyme
    sprigs
2 teaspoons fennel seeds
1 bay leaf
60ml (4 tablespoons) dry
    white wine
40ml (scant 3 tablespoons)
    full-fat (whole) milk
freshly grated (ground)
    nutmeg
150g (5½oz) fettuccine
80ml (2¾fl oz) crème
    fraîche or soured cream
35g (1¼oz) finely grated
    (shredded) Parmesan
    cheese, plus extra
    shavings to serve
salt and pepper

The aniseed notes of fennel work perfectly with rich, fatty pork which is then flavoured with white wine and nutmeg. The sauce has crème fraîche (or soured cream) and Parmesan stirred through, resulting in a creamy, indulgent ragù.

Add the pancetta to a large heavy-bottomed pan or casserole and place over a medium heat. Fry for 5 minutes – the fat content will melt out of the meat as the pan heats up – until the cubes are golden brown and starting to crisp. Remove the pancetta using a slotted spoon, leaving the rendered fat in the pan. Set aside.

Brown the pork in the pan in 2 batches to ensure it does not overcrowd the pan. Leave it undisturbed for about 4–5 minutes to get a good dark-golden crust before stirring and turning to brown the other sides. Remove from the pan and set aside.

Add a drizzle of oil to the pan and turn down the heat to low. Add the onion and sliced fennel and fry for 5 minutes until starting to soften. Add the garlic, thyme, fennel seeds and bay leaf. Season well with salt and pepper. Pour in the wine and turn up the heat to high. Let it bubble away for 1 minute before returning the pancetta and pork to the pan. Turn down the heat to very low, add the milk and a little grated (ground) nutmeg then leave the ragù to gently simmer and bubble away for about 25 minutes.

Continued overleaf...   Ready in 30 minutes–1 hour   **121**

Put a large pan of well-salted water on to boil for the pasta. Once the ragù has only 10 minutes remaining cooking time, add the fettuccine to the pan of boiling water and cook until al dente using the timing on the packet instructions as your guide.

Drain the fettuccine, reserving a little of the cooking water. Add the crème fraîche to the ragù followed by the pasta and Parmesan. Add a little splash of the cooking water and toss or stir over the heat for a minute or two until everything is combined and the sauce coats the fettuccine. Divide between 2 bowls and top with extra Parmesan.

Pesto Chicken and Tenderstem Broccoli Orzo Salad

2 chicken supremes, skin on
olive oil, for frying
1 tablespoon dried basil
1 lemon, zested then halved for squeezing into the pesto
140g (5oz) tenderstem broccoli, each stem cut in half
150g (5½oz) orzo
salt and pepper

For the pesto
large handful of fresh basil, plus extra to garnish
1 large garlic clove, peeled but left whole
40g (1½oz) finely grated (shredded) Parmesan cheese, plus extra to serve
50ml (1¾fl oz) extra virgin olive oil
40g (1½oz) pine nuts

For me, this is the perfect dish for a summer evening. Crispy-skinned chicken is paired with a fresh and light salad of tenderstem broccoli and pesto.

Preheat the oven to 200°C (180°C fan), 400°F, Gas Mark 6.

To cook the chicken, season each supreme well with salt and pepper and drizzle with a little oil. Place a heavy-bottomed frying pan (skillet) over a high heat. Once hot, add the chicken, skin-side down. Leave undisturbed to fry for 5 minutes or until the skin has gained a good caramelized crust. Do not be tempted to move the chicken around the pan while it is cooking; once the skin has crisped it will self-release from the pan. Turn the supremes and cook for a further 2 minutes on the other side. Transfer to an ovenproof dish, sprinkle with the dried basil and lemon zest. Place in the centre of the oven for about 20 minutes or until cooked through and the juices run clear. Once cooked, set aside to rest.

Put a large pan of well-salted water on to boil for the pasta.

Meanwhile, add the tenderstem broccoli to the pan used to fry the chicken, and drizzle with a little more oil. Cook over a high heat for 3 minutes on each side until they start to char a little. Halfway through the cooking, add a small splash of water so that the tenderstem steams and cooks until tender. Once cooked, transfer to a large mixing bowl.

Add the orzo to the pan of boiling water and cook until al dente, using the timing on the packet instructions as your guide.

Make the pesto. Add the basil, garlic, Parmesan, extra virgin olive oil and half the pine nuts to a blender (or you can use a pestle and mortar). Blend until smooth, adding a little more oil if needed to loosen to a pesto consistency. Season with salt and pepper, add a squeeze of lemon juice to taste and blend again. Add two-thirds of the pesto to the bowl with the broccoli and mix well.

Drain the orzo and cool under cold running water to room temperature. Add the cooled orzo to the bowl with the broccoli and pesto. Mix well and check for seasoning.

Spoon the pasta and broccoli into 2 bowls or a large serving dish. Slice the chicken supremes and lay across the top. Finish with the remaining pesto, extra basil leaves, the remaining pine nuts and a little more Parmesan.

Roasted San Marzano Tomatoes with Burrata Trofie

6 large San Marzano
   tomatoes, halved
   lengthways
4 garlic cloves, skin left on
1 white onion, peeled and
   quartered
1 red chilli, halved
   lengthways and
   deseeded
1 bay leaf
medium handful of fresh
   basil, leaves and stalks
   separated
1 tablespoon dried thyme
1 tablespoon dried
   rosemary
olive oil, for roasting
150g (5½oz) trofie
1 tablespoon balsamic
   vinegar
½ tablespoon honey
150g (5¼oz) ball of burrata
extra virgin olive oil, to
   serve
salt and pepper

This recipe produces a totally luxurious tomato sauce. The flavour of beautifully sweet San Marzano tomatoes is intensified by very gently cooking them in the oven. The dish is finished with creamy burrata just before serving.

Preheat the oven to 160°C (140°C fan), 325°F, Gas Mark 3.

Place the tomatoes, cut side up, in a single layer in an ovenproof dish. Scatter the garlic cloves, onion, chilli, bay, basil stalks, dried thyme and rosemary evenly over the top. Drizzle generously with oil then put the dish in the centre of the oven and cook for 1 hour.

After 50 minutes, put a large pan of well-salted water on to boil for the pasta. Once boiling, add the trofie and cook until al dente, using the timing on the packet instructions as your guide.

Once the tomatoes have cooked for an hour, remove them from the oven. Lift out 4 of the halves and set aside. Squeeze the flesh out of the garlic clove skins then add the contents of the oven tray to a food processor or blender. Add the vinegar and honey, season well with salt and pepper and blend until smooth. Pour the sauce into a small pan and place over a low heat. Check for seasoning and adjust as needed.

When the trofie is cooked, drain then return it to the pan. Pour in the sauce and a handful of torn basil leaves. Mix over the heat for a moment or two then transfer to a serving plate, top with the reserved tomato halves and place the burrata in the middle. Add a drizzle of extra virgin olive oil and serve, easing the burrata open into pieces.

Butternut Squash and Pecorino Pici

1 small butternut squash, halved, fibres and seeds removed
olive oil, for roasting
leaves from a few fresh rosemary sprigs, finely chopped
6 sage leaves, roughly chopped
4 garlic cloves, skin left on
40g (1½oz) salted butter
1 banana shallot, finely chopped
½ tablespoon cumin seeds
1 teaspoon ground (powdered) cinnamon
leaves from a few fresh thyme sprigs
60ml (4 tablespoons) single (light) cream
freshly grated (ground) nutmeg
80g (2¾oz) finely grated (shredded) Pecorino Romano cheese
1 lemon, halved, for squeezing
150g (5½oz) pici
salt and pepper

Here, sweet mellow squash is roasted with plenty of garlic and sage. It is then blended until smooth and mixed with a lightly spiced shallot cream to make the perfect silky sauce. I have paired it with tangy Pecorino cheese, which complements the sauce perfectly.

Preheat the oven to 190°C (170°C fan), 375°F, Gas Mark 5.

Place the halved butternut squash on a large baking tray (baking sheet), drizzle over a generous glug of oil and season well with salt and pepper. Scatter the rosemary, sage and garlic cloves over the squash then bake in the oven for 1 hour until the flesh is completely tender. Then remove the squash from the oven and set aside.

Put a large pan of well-salted water on to boil for the pasta. Meanwhile, add the butter to a large pan and place over a medium–low heat. Add the shallot and cook for 5 minutes until softened. Then add the cumin seeds, cinnamon, thyme, cream, a little grated (ground) nutmeg and half the Pecorino Romano. Stir together then turn off the heat.

Scoop out the cooked flesh from the skin of the squash and squeeze the cooked garlic from its skin. Transfer both to a food processor or blender. Add the shallot and cream mixture along with a squeeze of lemon juice. Blend together until super smooth. Return to the pan and bring to a gentle simmer while you cook the pasta.

Cook the pici in the pan of boiling water until al dente, guided by the timing on the packet instructions. Drain, reserving a little cooking water. Add the pasta and a splash of reserved cooking water to the sauce. Toss over the heat for a minute or two until the sauce coats the pasta. Divide between 2 bowls then top with the remaining cheese.

Roasted Leek and Gorgonzola Cannelloni

2 leeks, trimmed and thinly sliced
2 garlic cloves, finely chopped
2 banana shallots, thinly sliced
olive oil, for roasting
1 tablespoon dried thyme
1 tablespoon dried parsley
30g (1oz) salted butter
30g (1oz) plain (all-purpose) flour
300ml (10fl oz) full-fat (whole) milk
freshly grated (ground) nutmeg
50g (1¾oz) finely grated (shredded) Parmesan cheese
100g (3½oz) baby spinach leaves
75g (3¾oz) Gorgonzola cheese
100g (3½oz) full-fat cream cheese
small handful of fresh flat-leaf parsley, finely chopped
zest of 1 lemon
10 cannelloni tubes

Blue cheese paired with sweet roasted leeks make a winning combination in this baked pasta dish. Filled tubes of pasta baked in a thick cheesy béchamel finished with a super-crispy panko and thyme topping.

Preheat the oven to 180°C (160°C fan), 350°F, Gas Mark 4.

Put the leeks, garlic and shallots in a small deep-sided ovenproof dish. Season with salt and pepper then drizzle over a generous glug of oil. Sprinkle over the dried thyme and parsley and mix everything together. Place in the centre of the oven and cook for 30 minutes until the leeks are completely soft.

Meanwhile, make the béchamel sauce. Add the butter to a medium pan and place over a medium heat. Once melted, add the flour. Whisk together then cook for 2 minutes to cook out the raw flour taste. Slowly add the milk in stages, whisking as you go to avoid lumps. Bring to a simmer until it thickens to the consistency of thick pouring cream. Season with salt and pepper, add a little grated (ground) nutmeg and the Parmesan. Whisk until the cheese has melted then turn off the heat and set aside.

Once the leek and shallot mixture has cooked for 30 minutes, remove from the oven. Mix well to break up the leeks and combine everything. Set aside to cool a little.

Wilt the spinach in another pan with a little splash of oil and season with salt and pepper. After a couple of minutes and once cooked down, remove from the pan and remove any of the excess moisture. To do this, squeeze it through a clean tea towel (dish towel). Remove from the towel and finely chop then transfer to a large bowl.

Continued overleaf...　　　　　Ready in 1 hour+　　**135**

75g (3¾oz) panko
  breadcrumbs
leaves from a few fresh
  thyme sprigs
salt and pepper

Once the leek and shallot mixture has cooled, add it to the bowl, along with half the Gorgonzola, the cream cheese, chopped parsley and lemon zest. Season generously with salt and pepper then mix together well. Fill a disposable piping (pastry) bag with this mixture.

Turn up the oven temperature to 200°C (180°C fan), 400°F, Gas Mark 6.

Pour just under half the béchamel sauce into an ovenproof dish. Cut the end off the piping bag and fill each cannelloni tube. Place them, side by side, in the dish, on top of the béchamel to make a single layer that completely covers the base of the dish. Then pour the remaining béchamel evenly over the cannelloni. Sprinkle with the breadcrumbs and thyme leaves and finally dot the remaining Gorgonzola over the top. Bake for 30–35 minutes until the top is golden brown, the béchamel is bubbling and the breadcrumbs are crispy. Leave to rest for 5 minutes before serving.

Slow-roasted Tomato, Mozzarella and Basil Oil Pasta Salad

300g (10oz) mixed tomatoes (different sizes and colours work well in this dish), halved widthways

5 garlic cloves, skin left on

olive oil, for roasting

1 tablespoon dried basil

1 tablespoon dried thyme

2 tablespoons balsamic vinegar

150g (5½oz) gnocchi sardi

1 tablespoon red wine vinegar

1 small banana shallot, very finely chopped

100g (3½oz) Kalamata olives, pitted and halved

125g (4½oz) ball of buffalo mozzarella, torn into bite-size chunks

salt and pepper

For the basil oil

2 large handfuls of fresh basil, plus extra leaves to garnish

60ml (4 tablespoons) extra virgin olive oil

This pasta salad packs a punch. If you make this during the summer, when tomatoes are at their ripe best, it really takes the dish to another level. Here, the tomatoes are slowly roasted to intensify their flavour and sweetness, and served with the classic flavour pairing of buffalo mozzarella and basil.

Preheat the oven to 160°C (140°C fan), 325°F, Gas Mark 3.

Place the tomatoes on a large baking tray (baking sheet) lined with baking (parchment) paper. Season generously with salt and pepper. Drizzle over a good glug of oil then add the dried herbs and balsamic vinegar. Mix the tomatoes to ensure they are evenly coated in the seasonings and oil. Arrange evenly, cut-side up, on the tray then place in the oven for 45 minutes. After this time, add the garlic cloves to the tray then roast for a further 45 minutes, until the tomatoes are well roasted and a lot of the moisture has evaporated.

After the tomatoes have been cooking for an hour, make the basil oil. First blanch the fresh basil. Bring a pan of water to the boil and have a bowl of ice-cold water ready. Add the basil to the boiling water and cook for 20 seconds. Remove from the pan and immediately plunge into the ice-cold water. Mix in the cold water for 1 minute, before squeezing out any excess liquid. Transfer to a food processor or blender and add the oil. Blend for 2 minutes until fully incorporated. Pour through a fine sieve (strainer) to remove any large bits of basil that may have not blended then set aside.

Continued overleaf...   Ready in 1 hour+

Put a large pan of well-salted water on to boil for the pasta. Cook the gnocchi sardi until al dente, using the timing on the packet instructions as your guide. Drain and cool under cold running water.

Transfer the cooled pasta to a large salad bowl. Add half the basil oil, the vinegar, shallot and olives. Season with a little salt and generously with pepper then mix well.

Remove the tomatoes from the oven and leave to cool slightly for about 5 minutes. Add the tomatoes to the bowl with the pasta and squeeze out the cooked garlic flesh from the skins. Toss gently together until everything is incorporated. Then top with the torn mozzarella, drizzle with the remaining basil oil and garnish with extra basil leaves.

Kalamata and Aubergine Ragù with Whole Roasted Sea Bass

F

olive oil, for frying and roasting

1 aubergine (eggplant), diced into 1cm (½in) cubes

35g (1¼oz) salted butter

1 small white onion, very finely chopped

1 celery stick, very finely diced

2 garlic cloves, finely chopped

medium handful of fresh basil, stalks and leaves separated

150g (5½oz) Kalamata olives, pitted and halved

1 tablespoon capers, roughly chopped

2 tablespoons tomato purée (paste)

400g (14oz) canned plum tomatoes

1 tablespoon red wine vinegar

1 teaspoon granulated sugar

150g (5½oz) linguine

salt and pepper

A gentle simmer for an hour transforms the flavours of this sauce. The powerful saltiness of the olives and capers is mellowed out, cooked down with the sweet soft flesh of aubergine (eggplant). Served alongside whole roasted sea bass, it makes a decadent pasta dish. A medium sea bass is enough for two people.

Preheat the oven to 170°C (150°C fan), 340°F, Gas Mark 3½.

First make the ragù. Heat a generous splash of oil in a large pan over a high heat. Add the aubergine (eggplant) and fry for about 3 minutes, without stirring or moving around, before frying the other sides until it has gained a good golden brown colour on all sides. Turn down the heat to medium–low and add the butter to the pan. Add the onion and celery and cook down gently for 10 minutes until they have really softened and become translucent.

Add the garlic and fry for a further minute. Finely chop the basil stalks then add to the pan. Add the olives, capers and tomato purée (paste). Mix well and cook for about 5 minutes, stirring regularly. Add the canned tomatoes, vinegar and sugar. Season well with salt and pepper then add 100ml (3½fl oz) of water. Stir well then add the contents of the pan to an ovenproof dish. Cover the dish with a lid or with foil and bake for 30 minutes, stirring halfway through.

After 30 minutes, turn up the temperature to 200°C (180°C fan), 400°F, Gas Mark 6, leaving the sauce in the oven to continue cooking.

For the sea bass
1 medium sea bass, gutted
   and scaled
zest and juice of 1 lemon
large rosemary sprig

Sit the sea bass on a piece of foil and place in a roasting tin (roasting pan). Score the upper side of the skin four times. Drizzle with a generous splash of oil and sprinkle with lemon zest, squeeze over the juice and season well with salt and pepper. Using your fingers, massage this over the skin, then place the rosemary inside the cavity. Roast for 20–25 minutes or until just cooked through; the exact timing will depend on the size of the fish. To check it is cooked, gently press the thickest part of the flesh with the back of a spoon. If cooked, the flesh should start to gently break up and flake away.

While the fish is cooking, put a large pan of well-salted water on to boil for the pasta. When the fish has 10 minutes left, add the linguine to the pan of boiling water and cook until al dente, using the timing on the packet instructions as your guide.

Drain the linguine then return it to the pan. Remove the sauce from the oven and pour it into the pan with the pasta. Tear up the fresh basil leaves then toss or stir everything together. Divide between 2 bowls or pile onto a large serving platter with the sea bass on top.

French Onion and Anchovy Spaghetti with Gruyère Pangrattato

F

50g (1¾oz) salted butter
1 large white onion, finely
   sliced
leaves from a few fresh
   thyme sprigs
½ tablespoon soft brown
   sugar
80g (2¾oz) finely grated
   (shredded) Gruyère
   cheese
2 slices of stale white
   bread, blitzed into fine
   breadcrumbs
1 garlic clove, finely
   chopped
4 anchovy fillets in oil,
   drained and roughly
   chopped
½ teaspoon dried chilli
   flakes
1 tablespoon tomato purée
   (paste)
½ tablespoon plain (all-
   purpose) flour
100ml (3½fl oz) dark beef
   stock
1 tablespoon
   Worcestershire sauce
150g (5½oz) spaghetti

This recipe is based on French onion soup. Jammy, sweet onions make the base of the dish, combined with salty anchovies. The Gruyère pangrattato is inspired by the cheesy crouton that is usually found bubbling away on top of the classic French dish.

Start by caramelizing the onion. Put half the butter in a large pan, place over a low heat and leave to melt. Add the onion to the pan along with the thyme leaves and sugar. Season well with salt and pepper and stir in. Cook gently over a low heat for 20 minutes until the onion has softened and become translucent. Be sure to keep the heat low to gently cook it; you are not looking to gain colour at this stage, just to soften and sweeten it.

While the onion cooks, make the pangrattato. Preheat the grill (broiler) to high. Sprinkle the grated (shredded) Gruyère evenly over a baking tray (baking sheet) lined with baking paper. Place under the grill for about 4–5 minutes until the cheese melts and starts to bubble vigorously. After a couple of minutes, once the bubbling stops, the cheese will start to darken slightly. Watch it carefully as it will quickly go from golden brown to black and taste burnt. Once it turns a light golden brown, remove the tray from the grill and set aside to cool.

Meanwhile, add the remaining butter to a small frying pan (skillet) and place over a medium heat to melt. Add the breadcrumbs and mix well. Fry for about 4 minutes until the breadcrumbs become golden brown and crisp. Tip into a small bowl.

Continued overleaf...   Ready in 1 hour+   **145**

small handful of fresh
  flat-leaf parsley, finely
  chopped
salt and pepper

Once the Gruyère has cooled, transfer from the paper to a chopping board. Finely chop the cheese into fairly small crumbs and add to the breadcrumbs. Mix well and set aside.

Put a large pan of well-salted water on to boil for the pasta.

Once the onion has been cooking for 20 minutes, stir in the garlic, anchovies and chilli flakes. Cook for a further couple of minutes before turning up the heat to medium–high and adding the tomato purée (paste) and flour. Mix well and fry for 2 minutes until sizzling and fragrant. Add the beef stock, a little at a time, stirring well between additions to ensure the flour does not form lumps. Once all the stock is incorporated, taste and check for seasoning. Gently simmer over a low heat for a further 20 minutes, stirring regularly. By the end of this time the stock should have reduced a little and thickened and created a thick glossy sauce with the caramelized onions.

After the sauce has simmered for 10 minutes, add the spaghetti to the pan of boiling water and cook until al dente, using the timing on the packet instructions as your guide.

Meanwhile, add the chopped parsley to the pangrattato and mix well.

Drain the spaghetti and add to the sauce. Toss well over the heat for a minute before dividing between 2 bowls. Top with a couple of spoonfuls of the pangrattato.

Roasted Puttanesca Sauce with Pan-fried Cod

f

olive oil, for frying
2 large garlic cloves, finely chopped
1 red chilli, deseeded and finely chopped
3 anchovy fillets in oil, drained and finely chopped
1½ tablespoons capers, roughly chopped
75g (3¾oz) black olives, pitted and halved
1 tablespoon dried oregano
400g (14oz) canned chopped tomatoes
100g (3½oz) cherry tomatoes, halved
1 tablespoon red wine vinegar
1 teaspoon granulated sugar
150g (5½oz) spaghetti
small handful of fresh basil leaves, torn
salt and pepper

For the cod
2 cod loins, skinned and deboned
40g (1½oz) salted butter
1 lemon, zested then halved for squeezing

The flavours of puttanesca sauce – chilli, anchovies, capers, garlic, olives, tomato and olive oil – lend themselves perfectly to fish. This version slowly roasts the sauce in the oven, intensifying the flavours and giving the ingredients time to blend. Serve it with a perfectly cooked piece of cod.

Preheat the oven to 170°C (150°C fan), 340°F, Gas Mark 3½.

First make the puttanesca sauce. Add a very generous glug of oil to a large pan and place over a medium–low heat. Add the garlic and chilli and fry for 3 minutes until sizzling and fragrant. Stir in the anchovies, capers, olives and oregano. Mix well and fry for a further 2 minutes. Add the canned and fresh tomatoes, the vinegar and sugar. Season well with salt and pepper and bring to a simmer. Once simmering, transfer to a lidded ovenproof dish. Transfer to the oven and roast for 45 minutes, stirring halfway through.

After the sauce has been cooking for 35 minutes, put a large pan of well-salted water on to boil for the pasta. Once the water is boiling, add the spaghetti and cook until al dente, using the timing on the packet instructions as your guide.

Meanwhile, heat a generous drizzle of oil in a frying pan (skillet) over a medium–high heat. Season the cod with salt and pepper. Once the pan is hot, add the fish and cook for 4–5 minutes on one side until starting to become golden brown and a crust starts to form. After 5 minutes flip the fish over and turn down the heat to medium–low.

Continued overleaf...   Ready in 1 hour+   **147**

Add the butter and lemon zest. Baste the loins with butter by constantly spooning it over the fish for a further 3 minutes until it is just cooked through. Remove from the pan and leave to rest while you finish the dish.

Drain the spaghetti and return it to the pan.

Remove the puttanesca sauce from the oven then pour it into the pasta pan. Add the torn basil and toss or stir everything together over the heat for 1 minute. Divide between 2 bowls, top with the cod and squeeze some lemon juice over the fish.

Slow-cooked Squid and Preserved Lemon Tagliatelle

F

olive oil, for frying and drizzling
1 small white onion, finely chopped
1 red chilli, deseeded and finely chopped
½ teaspoon dried chilli flakes
1 large garlic clove, finely chopped
2 tablespoons tomato purée (paste)
220g (8oz) cherry tomatoes, halved
100ml (3½fl oz) passata (strained tomatoes)
80ml (2¾fl oz) dry white wine
1 tablespoon red wine vinegar
1 teaspoon granulated sugar
½ preserved lemon, very finely chopped
350g (12oz) fresh squid tubes, cleaned and sliced into 1cm (½in) rings
150g (5½oz) tagliatelle
small handful of fresh flat-leaf parsley, finely chopped
zest of 1 lemon
salt and pepper

Squid is slow-cooked until tender in a warming tomato sauce flavoured with sweet yet tangy preserved lemon.

Add a generous glug of oil to a large lidded pan. Place over a medium–low heat and add the onion, chilli and chilli flakes. Fry for about 5 minutes until softened and fragrant. Add the garlic and fry for a further minute before adding the tomato purée (paste), cherry tomatoes, passata, wine, vinegar, sugar and preserved lemon. Season well with salt and pepper. Mix well then add the squid, making sure it is submerged. Cover the pan with the lid then very gently simmer over a very low heat for 1 hour. Keep the heat down as low as it will go: you should see the occasional bubble rise to the surface of the sauce but no more than that. After an hour the squid should be very tender and can be cut with a spoon.

When the squid has been cooking for 40 minutes, put a large pan of well-salted water on to boil for the pasta. Once the water is boiling, add the tagliatelle and cook until al dente using the timing on the packet instructions as your guide.

Drain the pasta and add to the pan with the sauce. Add the chopped parsley and lemon zest and mix well until everything is combined. Divide between 2 bowls and drizzle extra virgin olive oil over the top.

Lemon and Thyme Roast Chicken with Spring Vegetable Fregola

80g (2¾oz) salted butter, at room temperature

zest and juice of 2 lemons

leaves from a few fresh thyme sprigs

1 tablespoon dried oregano

1 whole free-range chicken, weighing about 1.5kg (3lb 5oz)

olive oil, for frying

1 small white onion, finely chopped

2 garlic cloves, finely chopped

80ml (2¾fl oz) dry white wine

300ml (10fl oz) chicken stock

large handful of fresh flat-leaf parsley, finely chopped

150g (5½oz) fregola

120g (4¼oz) asparagus spears, tough ends removed then each cut on the diagonal into 3

100g (3½oz) sugar snap peas

100g (3½oz) petits pois

salt and pepper

This is for those spring and summer days that are just too hot for a full roast dinner. It is a much lighter, fresher way to serve roast chicken, flavoured with lemon and thyme butter. The fregola is pan-cooked in white wine and garlic then added to the roasting chicken to soak up all its tasty juices. Serve with crunchy green spring vegetables.

Preheat the oven to 200°C (180°C fan), 400°F, Gas Mark 6.

Mix the butter, lemon zest and juice, the thyme and oregano together in a small bowl. Season generously with pepper and a little salt. Sit the chicken breast-side up in a large, deep-sided roasting tin (roasting pan). Using the back of a metal spoon, loosen the skin at the neck end of the bird from the carcass. You will then be able to push the flavoured butter beneath the skin to entirely cover the top of the chicken. This keeps it succulent and gives the meat delectable flavour as it cooks. Put the juiced lemon halves into the cavity for extra flavour. Transfer to the oven and roast for 1 hour.

Meanwhile, add a generous glug of oil to a large pan and place over a medium heat. Add the onion and fry for about 5 minutes until softened and translucent. Then add the garlic and fry for a further minute. Pour in the white wine and let it simmer for a few minutes to evaporate the alcohol before adding the chicken stock and parsley. Season well with salt and pepper. Add the fregola and stir together before turning off the heat and setting the pan aside.

Continued overleaf...   Ready in 1 hour+

After the chicken has roasted for an hour, remove from the oven. Add the fregola and onion mixture to the tin so that it surrounds the chicken. Return to the oven to roast for a further 10 minutes then again remove the tin from the oven and add the asparagus, sugar snaps and petits pois. Gently stir the vegetables into the fregola then place the tin back in the oven for a final 10 minutes until the vegetables are tender and the juices from the chicken run clear.

Cover the tin with foil and leave to rest in a warm place for 10 minutes before carving the chicken into portions (there will be leftovers, which are perfect for my Chicken and Oyster Mushroom Broth, see opposite). Serve on top of the fregola and spring vegetables.

Chicken and Oyster Mushroom Broth

1 whole roasted chicken
    carcass (see page 153),
    or 1kg (2lb 4oz) roasted
    chicken wings
1 carrot, quartered
1 celery stick, quartered
1 onion, quartered
2 leeks, trimmed and cut
    into 2.5cm (1in) chunks
3 garlic cloves, peeled but
    left whole
4 fresh thyme sprigs
2 bay leaves
4 black peppercorns
1 whole clove
1½ tablespoons dark soy
    sauce
120g (4¼oz) anelli
50g (1¾oz) salted butter
200g (7oz) oyster
    mushrooms, roughly torn
1 lemon, halved, for
    squeezing
small handful of fresh
    flat-leaf parsley, roughly
    chopped
crème fraîche or soured
    cream, to serve
salt and pepper

The perfect recipe for using up the leftovers of a roast chicken. For this dish it's really worth spending a little extra time and effort making your own chicken stock, then reducing it down to a super-flavourful, warming broth. To increase the serving quantity, simply increase the amount of water for making the stock and add more chicken bones or a second chicken carcass.

First make the broth. Put the chicken carcass (or wings) in a large pan that accommodates the carcass snugly. Carefully fill with enough cold water to cover the chicken by about 2.5cm (1in). Add the carrot, celery, onion, half the chopped leeks, 2 of the garlic cloves, the thyme, bay leaves, peppercorns and clove to the pan. Place over the lowest heat possible and very gently simmer for 2 hours. The broth should not boil; you should see the occasional bubble rise to the surface but no more than that. Skim off any scum as it forms.

After 2 hours, drain the broth through a sieve (strainer) into another large pan. Remove the chicken carcass and set aside to cool.

Place the pan over a high heat and add the soy sauce. Boil over a very high heat for about 20 minutes or until the broth has reduced by about half – this reduction will significantly intensify its flavour.

Pick off the remaining chicken meat from the carcass. Set aside.

Continued overleaf...   Ready in 1 hour+   **155**

Once the broth has reduced by half, turn down the heat to medium and add the anelli. Cook until al dente, using the timing on the packet instructions as your guide.

Meanwhile, cook the mushrooms. Add the butter to a frying pan (skillet) and place over a medium heat. Once melted and foaming, add the mushrooms and the remaining leek. Fry for about 6 minutes until softened. Finely chop the remaining garlic clove and add to the pan along with a generous squeeze of lemon juice and some salt and pepper. Stir together then turn off the heat and set aside until the pasta is cooked.

Once the anelli is al dente stir the chicken meat into the broth. Divide between 2 bowls and spoon over the fried mushroom and leek mixture. Finish with a sprinkle of chopped parsley and a spoonful of crème fraîche.

Beef Shin and Merlot Ragù

M

2 tablespoons plain
(all-purpose) flour
olive oil, for frying
250g (9oz) beef shin, cut
into 5cm (2in) pieces
1 white onion, finely
chopped
1 large carrot, finely
chopped
1 celery stick, finely
chopped
1 large garlic clove
3 anchovy fillets in oil,
drained and roughly
chopped
3 tablespoons tomato
purée (paste)
150ml (5fl oz) Merlot, or
other medium-bodied red
wine
1 bay leaf
leaves from 2 fresh thyme
sprigs
400g (14oz) canned
chopped tomatoes
200ml (7fl oz) beef stock
1 tablespoon brown sugar
150g (5½oz) pappardelle
Parmesan cheese, finely
grated (shredded), to
finish
salt and pepper

This recipe is a true labour of love: a super-indulgent ragù of very gently cooked beef shin in red wine. The longer it cooks, the better the end result as the meat has time to break down, soften and enrich the sauce with its flavours. A slow cooker works perfectly for this ragù.

Preheat the oven to 170°C (150°C fan), 340°F, Gas Mark 3½.

Put the flour in a shallow bowl and season well with salt and pepper. Heat a large splash of oil in a large heavy-bottomed frying pan (skillet) over a medium–high heat. Add the beef shin to the bowl and gently toss until coated with flour on all sides. Shake off any excess then add a handful of the beef to the hot oil, being careful not to overcrowd the pan. Fry until the meat is a dark golden-brown colour and caramelized all over; it takes about 6–8 minutes to ensure caramelization. Leave undisturbed for several minutes to gain a good colour before turning the pieces to brown the other sides. Remove the meat from the pan once browned and add to a large, lidded casserole dish. Repeat with the rest of the pieces.

Turn down the heat under the pan to medium–low. Add a generous splash of oil followed by the onion, carrot and celery. Fry gently for about 5 minutes or until well softened and the onion has become translucent.

Add the garlic and anchovies and fry for a further minute before adding the tomato purée (paste) and frying for a final minute before pouring in the red wine to deglaze the pan, scraping the base to release any extra caramelized bits stuck to it.

Pour the red wine and onion mixture into the casserole dish. Add the herbs, tomatoes, beef stock and sugar. Season well with salt and pepper. Cover with the lid and transfer to the oven to cook for at least 3 hours or until the meat is completely falling apart and soft.

Once the ragù is cooked, put a large pan of well-salted water on to boil for the pasta. Add the pappardelle to the boiling water and cook until al dente, using the timing on the packet instructions as your guide. Drain and add to the cooked ragù. Mix well then taste to check for seasoning. Divide between 2 bowls and finish with Parmesan just before serving.

Lamb and Rosemary Ragù with Pangrattato

100g (3½oz) pancetta lardons

olive oil, for frying

350g (12oz) lamb shoulder, cut into 1cm (½in) pieces

1 large carrot, finely chopped

1 white onion, finely chopped

2 red (bell) peppers, finely sliced

2 fat garlic cloves, finely chopped

5 anchovy fillets in oil, drained and roughly chopped

leaves from 6 fresh rosemary sprigs, finely chopped

1 bay leaf

2 tablespoons tomato purée (paste)

1 tablespoon balsamic vinegar

400g (14oz) canned chopped tomatoes

120g (4¼oz) plum tomatoes, quartered

150g (5½oz) pappardelle

40g (1½oz) salted butter

Here is another indulgent slow-cooked ragù. Super savoury, rich in herbs and sweet with red (bell) pepper, this one is finished with a rosemary pangrattato for a salty, crunchy contrast.

Preheat the oven to 170°C (150°C fan), 340°F, Gas Mark 3½.

Add the pancetta and a small splash of oil to a large frying pan (skillet) and place over a medium–high heat. Fry for 5 minutes or until the pancetta has caramelized and is nicely browned all over. Remove from pan using a slotted spoon and place in a large lidded casserole, leaving the fat in the pan.

Season the lamb all over with salt and pepper. Add half the meat to the frying pan and cook undisturbed for 4 minutes over a high heat on one side before turning the pieces to gain a dark-brown caramelization on all sides. Use a slotted spoon to transfer the pieces to the dish with the pancetta and then repeat with the rest of the lamb.

Once all the lamb is browned, turn down the heat to medium and add a generous glug of oil to the pan. Add the carrot, onion and (bell) peppers, fry for 5 minutes until everything starts to soften. Add the garlic, anchovies, half the chopped rosemary and the bay leaf. Cook for a further 2 minutes then add the tomato purée (paste), vinegar and all the tomatoes. Stir well then season generously with salt and pepper. Cover the casserole with the lid and transfer to the oven. Cook for 3 hours or until the lamb is completely soft and easily pulled apart with a spoon.

Continued overleaf...

Ready in 1 hour+   **161**

½ tablespoon dried
  rosemary
2 slices of stale white
  bread, blitzed into fine
  breadcrumbs
salt and pepper

When the ragù has 20 minutes remaining of its cooking time, put a large pan of well-salted water on to boil for the pasta.

Meanwhile, make the pangrattato. Add the butter to a frying pan and place over a medium heat. Once melted, add the dried rosemary and the remaining half of the fresh rosemary. Then add the breadcrumbs and mix well. Leave to fry for about 5 minutes, frequently tossing or stirring to ensure it doesn't burn. Once fried, the breadcrumbs should be crisp and golden brown. Remove from the pan and set aside.

Add the pappardelle to the pan of boiling water and cook until al dente using the timing on the packet instructions as your guide.

Drain the pasta and add it to the casserole. Mix well for a minute or two, breaking up the lamb shoulder. Taste for seasoning then divide between 2 bowls and top with the pangrattato.

Pancetta, Spinach and Taleggio Lasagne

200g (7oz) diced pancetta

70g (2½oz) salted butter

1 small white onion, finely chopped

1 leek, trimmed and finely sliced

2 garlic cloves, finely chopped

60ml (4 tablespoons) dry white wine

500g (1lb 2oz) baby spinach leaves

zest of 1 lemon

handful of freshly chopped flat-leaf parsley, plus extra to finish

40g (1½oz) plain (all-purpose) flour

350ml (12fl oz) full-fat (whole) milk

60g (2¼oz) finely grated (shredded) Parmesan cheese

150g (5½oz) Taleggio cheese, half of it cut into small dice

freshly grated (ground) nutmeg

2 egg yolks

9 lasagne sheets

oil, for greasing

salt and pepper

This is a lasagne but with a twist. It switches out the tradional ragù for a mix of spinach and leeks studded with plenty of salty pancetta. This is layered with lasagne sheets and finished with a béchamel enriched with egg yolks and flavoured with creamy Taleggio cheese.

Start by adding the pancetta to a large frying pan (skillet). Place over a high heat and let the fat start to render. Fry for about 5 minutes until the pancetta starts to develop good caramelization, turning and mixing often to ensure all sides are coloured golden brown. Remove the pancetta from the pan, using a slotted spoon, and set aside.

Add 30g (1oz) of the butter to the pan along with the onion and leek. Gently sweat them down for about 15 minutes over a low heat until well softened. Add the garlic and fry for a further 2 minutes. Turn up the heat to high and add the wine. Allow it bubble for 2 minutes before adding the spinach, lemon zest and parsley. Season well with salt and pepper then return the pancetta to the pan and turn down the heat to medium–low. Stir for a few minutes until the spinach has fully wilted and everything is well combined. Turn off the heat and set the pan aside while you make the béchamel.

Add the remaining 40g (1½oz) of butter to a medium pan and place over a medium heat to melt. Once foaming, add the flour and mix together. Stir over the heat for 2 minutes to cook out the raw flour taste. Add the milk a little at a time, whisking between each addition to ensure there are no lumps.

Continued overleaf...   Ready in 1 hour+

Once all the milk is incorporated, add half the Parmesan, the diced Taleggio and a little grated (ground) nutmeg. Whisk over the heat until the cheeses have melted. Season well with salt and pepper and, once the béchamel has thickened to the consistency of thick double (heavy) cream, turn off the heat and stir in the egg yolks. Set aside.

Preheat the oven to 200°C (180°C fan), 400°F, Gas Mark 6. Put a pan of well-salted water on to boil for the pasta. Once boiling, cook the lasagne sheets for 4 minutes until partially cooked. Drain then cool them under cold running water to stop the cooking.

To assemble the lasagne, lightly oil the bottom of a small casserole or ovenproof dish that will accommodate the size of the lasagne sheets. Lay 3 sheets in the dish, side by side and slightly overlapping, to create the first layer of pasta. Spread about a third of the pancetta and spinach mixture evenly over the lasagne. Pour in a third of the béchamel, then repeat the process twice until you have created three layers of each component. Sprinkle with the remaining Parmesan and tear the remaining Taleggio over the top. Transfer to the centre of the oven and bake for 30 minutes, until the surface is golden brown and bubbling hot. Sprinkle over the remaining chopped parsley and allow to rest for 10 minutes before serving.

Venetian Duck Ragù with Crispy Skin Pangrattato

olive oil, for frying
2 duck legs, skin on
2 banana shallots, finely
   diced
1 large garlic clove, finely
   chopped
1 bay leaf
leaves from a few fresh
   rosemary sprigs, finely
   chopped
2 teaspoons ground
   (powdered) cinnamon
1½ tablespoons tomato
   purée (paste)
125ml (4fl oz) white wine
400g (14oz) canned
   chopped tomatoes
1 teaspoon granulated
   sugar
50ml (1¾fl oz) full-fat
   (whole) milk
50g (1¾oz) salted butter
100g (3½oz) fresh
   breadcrumbs
150g (5½oz) paccheri
small handful of fresh
   flat-leaf parsley, finely
   chopped
salt and pepper

This rich duck ragù is a traditional dish from the Veneto, the region around Venice. It is flavoured with cinnamon and white wine, which give it an extremely warming, winter feel. Serving it with a crunchy pangrattato, made using the skin of the duck leg, creates a pleasing contrast to the soft meat.

Preheat the oven to 170°C (150°C fan), 340°F, Gas Mark 3½.

Start by adding a splash of oil to a large frying pan (skillet). Put the duck legs in the cold pan and place over a medium heat. Cook for 5 minutes, leaving it undisturbed. The fat will render out of the duck then the skin will start to crisp up and become golden brown. Once well browned, turn over the legs and fry for a further 3 minutes. Lift them from the pan and set aside.

Fry the shallots in the same frying pan for 5 minutes over a medium–low heat until softened and translucent. Add the garlic and continue to cook for 2 minutes. Add the bay leaf, rosemary, cinnamon and tomato purée (paste) then mix well and again cook for 2 minutes. Pour in the wine then turn up the heat to high and let it bubble fast for a final 2 minutes to evaporate off the alcohol. Add the tomatoes, sugar and milk. Season well with salt and pepper then transfer the contents of the pan into a small ovenproof dish. Pull away and reserve the skin from the duck legs, then place the legs into the dish along with the sauce – ensure they are as fully submerged in the sauce as possible. Cover with a lid or foil and put in the oven for 3 hours.

Continued overleaf...

While the ragù slowly cooks, make the pangrattato. Very finely chop the duck skin and add to a clean, dry frying pan. Place over a medium heat and fry for about 3 minutes until it starts to darken in colour. Add the butter and, once melted and foaming, add the breadcrumbs and season with salt and pepper. Fry for roughly 3 minutes, mixing frequently until the crumbs are crispy and golden brown. Remove from the pan and set aside.

Once the duck has been cooking for 2½ hours, put a pan of well-salted water on to boil for the pasta.

Remove the duck from the oven once it has only 15 minutes remaining of the cooking time. Use two forks to remove the meat from the bones and shred it. Add the shredded meat back into the sauce and mix well. Cover the dish and return it to the oven while you cook the pasta.

Add the paccheri to the pan of boiling water and cook until al dente, using the timing on the packet instructions as your guide.

Drain the pasta and return it to the pan. Add the ragù to the pan and mix well until everything is combined. Divide between 2 bowls.

To finish, add the chopped parsley to the pangrattato and sprinkle over the ragù before serving.

Bacon, Chestnut and Thyme Macaroni Cheese

200ml (7fl oz) full-fat (whole) milk

75ml (5 tablespoons) single (light) cream

180g (6¼oz) cooked whole chestnuts

2 garlic cloves, peeled but left whole

1 bay leaf

8 smoked streaky bacon rashers (strips), chopped into lardons

olive oil, for frying

leaves from a few fresh thyme sprigs

50g (1¾oz) salted butter

50g (1¾oz) plain (all-purpose) flour

freshly grated (ground) nutmeg

80g (2¾oz) grated (shredded) mature Cheddar cheese

120g (4¼oz) ready-grated (shredded) mozzarella cheese

1 tablespoon Dijon mustard

For an ultra-comforting mac 'n' cheese, here chestnuts bring a sweet, butteriness to the classic béchamel sauce, taking the flavour to another level. The sauce is then mixed with crispy bacon lardons and a mix of Cheddar and mozzarella cheese.

Start by infusing the milk for the sauce. Add the milk and cream to a small pan along with the chestnuts, garlic and bay leaf. Season well with salt and pepper then place over a low heat. Very gently simmer for 20 minutes over a very low heat to infuse the milk.

After 20 minutes pour the milk and cream mixture through a sieve (strainer) into a jug. Remove the chestnuts from the sieve and set aside.

Preheat the oven to 200°C (180°C fan), 400°F, Gas Mark 6. Put a large pan of well-salted water on to boil for the pasta.

Meanwhile, fry the bacon in a small drizzle of oil in a frying pan (skillet) until golden brown and crisp. Roughly chop the reserved chestnuts and add them to the bacon along with the thyme leaves. Stir together then set aside.

To make the béchamel, add the butter to a large pan and place over a medium heat. Once melted, add the flour and mix together. Stir over the heat for 2 minutes to cook out the raw flour taste. Slowly add the infused milk and cream mixture a little at a time, whisking between each addition to ensure there are no lumps. Once all the liquid has been incorporated, add a little grated (ground) nutmeg followed by the Cheddar, half the mozzarella and the mustard. Season well with salt and pepper and bring to a simmer.

Continued overleaf...   Ready in 1 hour+

200g (7oz) macaroni
2 slices of sourdough,
   crusts removed, finely
   grated or blitzed into
   breadcrumbs
1 tablespoon dried thyme
salt and pepper

Keep stirring: as the béchamel starts to simmer, it will thicken. Once it is the consistency of thick double (heavy) cream, turn off the heat and set aside.

Add the macaroni to the pan of boiling water and cook until al dente, using the timing on the packet instructions as your guide.

Meanwhile, add the breadcrumbs to a bowl along with the remaining mozzarella and dried thyme. Season with salt and pepper and mix well.

Drain the macaroni and stir it into the béchamel. Add the bacon and chestnut mixture and mix well until combined. Pour into an ovenproof dish. Sprinkle over the breadcrumb mixture then put in the centre of the oven for 20–25 minutes or until bubbling and golden brown on top.

Index

Acknowledgements

First, thank you to each and every person who has followed, read and cooked a recipe from The Monday Pasta Club so far. Without you I would never have got to this position: being able to write this cookbook and fulfil one of my lifelong dreams. The support and following I gained from The Monday Pasta Club gave me the confidence to pursue this dream and create this wonderful cookbook. For that I am eternally grateful.

Thank you to Judith, my publisher at Kyle Books for approaching me with the idea for this book. Without you and the belief you had in me, this book could never of happened. Also thanks to Isabel, my editor who has made writing such an enjoyable experience from start to finish. And from Ola and Martyna to Troy, Esther, Anna and Nicky – the whole team who worked on the shoot and brought my recipes to life in such a wonderful way, thank you all.

Finally, I need to say the biggest thank you to the amazing people I have around me. To all the family and friends I have in my life, thank you for your support and the appreciation you have for my love of cooking. And of course my partner, for being chief pasta taster and the best right-hand man I could ask for. I'm certain being surrounded by such wonderful people has played a key part in the journey that lead me to writing this book.

First published in Great Britain in 2024 by Kyle Books, an imprint of Octopus Publishing Group Limited, Carmelite House, 50 Victoria Embankment, London, EC4Y 0DZ

An Hachette UK Company
www.hachette.co.uk

ISBN: 978 1 80419 198 9

Distributed in the US by Hachette Book Group, 1290 Avenue of the Americas, 4th and 5th Floors, New York, NY 10104

Distributed in Canada by Canadian Manda Group, 664 Annette St., Toronto, Ontario, Canada M6S 2C8

Publisher: Joanna Copestick
Publishing Director: Judith Hannam
Editor: Isabel Jessop
Art Director: Nicky Collings
Designer: Claire Rochford
Photographer: Ola O. Smit
Food Stylists: Troy Willis, Esther Clark
Prop Stylist: Anna Wilkins
Production: Allison Gonsalves

A Cataloguing in Publication record for this title is available from the British Library.

Printed and bound in China.